I0581918

CLAW MACHINE

an anthology of speculative and dark fiction

CLAW MACHINE: THE ANTHOLOGY

Copyright © 2024 by Elizabeth Mitchell.

"Ocean Wonder!Lands" by Simone Cooper
"In This and Every Universe" by Valerie Geary
"Lucky Dragon" by Marianne Xenos
"Alternate" by Angelique O'Rourke
"Never on a Monday" by Curtis C. Chen
"Horizons" by Sarah Walker
"Cursed Things" by J.B. Kish
"How to be a Player" by Angela Yuriko Smith
"Create-a-Chimera" by Beth Cook
"Win Big at the Body Shop" by Laura K. Burge
"The Makeover" by Summer Olsson
"Purchase Required" by Wes Mitchell
"Pilot Program" by Mark Teppo
"reFresh" by Pia Baur
"Bad News" by Elle Mitchell
"The Witches of the Neon Carousel" by Erik Grove
"Narrowly, Narrowly Caught" by Katherine Quevedo

All rights reserved.

Published in the United States by Little Key Press.

Claw Machine is a work of fiction. Names, characters, businesses, places, and events are either the product of the author's imagination or are used fictitiously. Any resemblance to actual persons, living or dead, businesses, companies, or events is entirely coincidental.

No part of this book may be reproduced in any manner without written permission, except in the case of brief quotations included in articles and reviews. For information, please contact the publisher.

First Edition

Cover by Elizabeth Mitchell
Cover font: DayPosterBlack and Gotham Light
Cover photograph: Elizabeth Mitchell

contents

CLAW MACHINE

an anthology of speculative and dark fiction

For those who love nostalgia,
who love the strange, the dark,
who are drawn to bright lights and neon colors,
who live for arcades and un-winnable games,
who play for plushies they don't need or actually want,
who always open a prize egg with excitement,
who can't help but spend just another quarter, just one more dollar.

For that one more game.

a note from the editor

Some of the following stories are dark and include violence or murder, but they are rarely graphic in nature. None have sexual assault or show animal deaths.

Each story is bound to elicit an emotional response, though. One may stir something deep in your stomach—a feeling so deeply relatable yet hard to name. Another may be a reality so close to home it causes an ache in your bones. Maybe you'll have hope for a different future or fear of who we could be if left unchecked. Or the glimmer of possibility that there is *other* out there will bring you solace and a moment of peace amongst the noise.

Magic and wishful thinking, worst case scenarios, and claw machines galore fill the pages you're about to read. But most of all, you'll find humanity in this anthology. And I do so hope you enjoy it!

—Elle Mitchell

introduction

Will Errickson

by Will Errickson

First, a confession: when I was a child, arcades and amusement parks and fairgrounds were a source of anxiety for me, rather than pleasure. There were all sorts of reasons for that reaction. I knew that most of the games, of whatever kind, were rigged against the player (thanks for that life info, Dad!). There was the pressure of wasting your quarters on a game above your skill level that you'd play for, oh, 30 seconds or so. If your parental unit dropped you off at the arcade while they shopped or ran errands, you had a set time limit, and of course it was then, when you were due to be picked up, that you suddenly became the *Ms. Pac Man* master, and would have to be dragged away just as you approached the High Score! Oh no…

However, what I really recall bringing on my arcade anxiety were the older kids—the ones who always seemed to be lurking around the dim yet neon-lit aisles, congregated around the more difficult games that older teenagers liked. The bullies in their Black Sabbath, Blue Öyster Cult, and Molly Hatchet bootleg tour shirts, rife with spooky occult sigils and flames and swords and all. If you weren't careful, if you didn't make yourself small enough to scurry past them, they might harass you or take your quarters from you, maybe even physically shove you around while girls, mysterious young women, snickered at your hapless lot. No thanks!

Those times in which the stars aligned, when the arcade was bereft of those older kids, when the good games were free to any kid with a quarter, man, that was livin'. I came of age during the great era of the early video game wave, *Space Invaders* and *Pac Man* and *Donkey Kong* and *Defender* and *Centipede* and *Frogger*, and there was a real feeling of freedom when those anxieties lifted off and you stepped up to a game filled with confidence and wonder.

But the claw machine was different. Its promise of choice—more of an illusion—is what made the claw machine so appealing to children and young teens, people who weren't often given the independence of free choice too often in their daily lives of school and chores and boring/scary grownups. Rather than dropping in a coin and accepting whatever plastic bauble the grocery store vending machine decided to plop into their hands, a claw machine allowed the player to at least *attempt* to grab an object of personal choice. Maybe a stuffed Garfield, a plastic dragon, or a tiny Rubik's Cube keychain, a wicked temporary tattoo, or something maybe your older cousin could fashion into a bong. Kids need, at times, to feel in control, that their lives belong to them, and the claw machine could let them feel like that for a moment.

Like any good anthology of speculative fiction, the stories collected here have great range, but all are in service to that great claw machine we remember from childhood. This variety of styles, from little dollops of frivolity to headier, more complex world-building, allows the reader to ponder anew how the claw machine, relegated to the dim recesses of our past, can reveal itself in fresh guises and tell us secrets about ourselves.

There is no way to predict where any story is going to go: some highlight the nostalgic quality of the game, back to a period of awkwardness or hope. Sometimes the claw machine appears as itself, in all its tacky fairground glory; other times, it appears as more of an analogue for the complexities of our mind's memories and identity. Friends bond over the contraption, fantastical creatures are reborn from them, high school reunions are centered around them. Another will slowly descend into a maelstrom of horror. Others offer a vision of the human body as malleable and replaceable, or perhaps a revelation of life that comes all too late. Like the myriad of prizes the claw machine use to lure us into its clutches, there is a little something here for readers of all tastes.

It did not escape my notice that virtually all the stories note one truly important fact about claw machines, and that is that they are rigged, designed to part people from their money and their time. Any successful maneuvering of said claw is more chance and luck than skill or determination. I don't think you can ask for a better life metaphor than that!

ocean wonder!lands

Simone Cooper

By Simone Cooper

Emmaline wrung blue water out of her sponge, the remains of some kid's magic marker "enhancements" to the pirate mural at the back of Ocean Wonder!Lands. As manager, she should have assigned someone from the morning shift to do it, Willa or Rudy, but she liked a little detail work. It got her to the quieter back half of the arcade, which suited her after her breakfast of arguing with her daughter. There would be plenty of bathroom-stall muck outs and multicolor-candy barf cleanups for them to deal with later.

Besides, Em felt a little possessive of the mural and its swash-buckling captain. Over twenty years, she'd been seeing him, summer in and summer out, and she still had her child-self's fondness for him and his crew and the mermaid princesses they wooed. The good pirate captain had been repainted twice already this season, and Em, who also did the books for the arcade one evening a week, understood the owners couldn't afford another re-do until next year.

She looked over her work. The captain's trouser area was now too clean, maybe, the kind of clean that had probably drawn the attention of the Penis Picasso in the first place. It would be better if she did the whole wall, but with the repairman for the overly generous claw machine coming in an hour, she wouldn't be able to do it herself, not the careful way she wanted. The captain's feather-plumed hat had lost its gilding, and a lot of the finer details were fading, this time around. Em patted his painted arm. "Sorry, Cap'n. I've got to leave you to the mercies of my crew."

When Emmaline was a child, Ocean Wonder!Lands Arcade had seemed wonderful in fact and not just in name. Family vaca-tions had been a treat, and child-Emmaline, always so withdrawn during the school year, could make a new best friend for two weeks every summer—promise you'll write! She and this companion could change a dollar from collecting cans into a couple of Skee-Ball games or a two-gun round of Zombie Blast or an ice cream bar to share from the freezer.

The mermaids and pirates filled their dreams with fantastic adventures. They would spend hours staring into the lit glass cases of the highest-ticket treasures, blown-glass sailing ships and Swarovski crystal animals and stuffed parrots with real feathers, planning what they'd pick if their wishes came true. Wonder!Lands was full of magic: clanking, shining, siren-wailing, sticky-fingered, ice-cold and sweet-on-tongues popsicle blue.

Wonder!Lands was also the last place Em had been before her mother died and took Em's childhood with her. Em's father disappeared into a bottle. Clinging to the makeshift raft of her prior grades, Em drifted, rudderless, through graduation and a grant-funded start at Oregon State University. Every time someone said how wonderful it was Em had gotten so far, you know, *under the circumstances*, the raft shattered a little more.

Em quit college after her first year, tired and angry and newly a mother, and somehow, she and her baby girl had washed up at Wonder!Lands. She didn't really know why, or else, maybe, her whole past added up to why. When she'd pulled up in her rattle-trap Volvo and thrown herself on the mercy of the arcade's owners, Mr. and Mrs. Kwan, she'd found herself employed. They'd rented Em the small apartment above their home. They even enjoyed having baby Leah around. That was something. Everything.

The impulse had been stupid, people told her. Even if the owners paid more than minimum, "tourist arcade manager" wasn't exactly the title valedictorians dreamed of. College Dropout and Single Mother hadn't been in Em's crystal ball, either, but here she was. Her old dreams, when she let herself remember them, tasted of soda-caffeinated evenings while her eyes ached from reading and studying and staring at computer screens. There would come that old home smell, the Mom smell: skin lotion and the dust of office files and pipe smoke from one of her mom's law partners. There would come the tea, warm and sweetened, and her mom's voice asking about assignments and reading lists and helping Em frame essays for her high-school AP classes. All those good things were poison, now.

The first few years Em had worked at Wonder!Lands, if he got drunk enough, her dad would call to pour a different poison in her ear. "You're smarter than that place deserves, Emmaline," he'd slur out, no matter it was 3 a.m., no matter she hadn't seen him since the funeral, no matter he spent his time drinking his Disability check away. "That job's beneath you." Come back, was what he meant. Come and take care of me. It took Em three years to learn she could send those calls straight to voicemail, two more to get a new phone and a new number.

In that time, she also learned that Wonder!Lands, for all its lack of wonder, was not poison. It was comfort and responsibility. The owners, ever more elderly, needed her, and they loved Leah more than anything.

Leah. Oh, Leah. She was almost eleven, which apparently was "basically a teenager." She currently hated Em with "the passion of the sun"—a direct quote—and "didn't ask to be born"—also a direct quote. Leah's father, Grant, lived in Corvallis, where he and Em had met. He was still—still!—a graduate student double-majoring in failure to pay child support and cannabis. Grant was fun, Leah had told her. Grant still took her to movies. Grant let her color her hair. Let her! As if Em wouldn't if they could afford it. "You are the enemy of fun." Em had been hearing that refrain for two months, since Leah's return from the week's stay Grant had so grudgingly agreed to back in June.

Even as Em finished the morning work, met with the repair man, ordered the snacks for the shop, she was steeling herself for a call to Grant that afternoon. School would start in two weeks. Leah needed new clothes, her physical for P.E., and shoes for the soccer team. Since Leah's visit, Grant had been traveling for research, and the payments had somehow gotten lost in the mail. Somehow. Predictably. The call was a hated, semi-annual tradition, and Leah's newly renewed membership in the Grant fan club hadn't made the prospect any better.

Finally, during her afternoon break, Em rang Grant's number.

Grant picked up. They started their old dance. Calm request, check. Itemized list of needs, check. Receipts—she had them, yes, here; yes, I can email them—check. Grant seemed bored with the conversation. On his end, a video game beeped out a tune in the background, competing with the pings and whoops of the games on hers. Em's carefully controlled enumerations devolved into argument, and her face flushed hot when she realized she was shouting. Her therapist wouldn't be happy. She took a breath. Before she could get to the upstairs office for privacy, Grant dropped his favorite refrain, sullen and tired. "One mistake, and you want to ruin my life."

"Your life?!" In her head, Em went through her well-worn list. She'd print out those expense accounts, again; she'd contact the lawyer, again. That was usually enough to pry something out of Grant. Sometimes his wealthy parents would send her his back payments, always with a stiff note saying, "this is the last goddamned time" and sometimes calling her a variety of names based on "money grubbing whore."

Then he said, "You really are the enemy of fun."

Oh.

Fuck him. Fuck this. "You … fucking … manchild." Em's pulse thudded in her ears, her neck. She had never killed anything on purpose, not even a spider. Couldn't. Wouldn't. But she felt in that moment how it might be, her hands clenched around some gun, some knife, some goddamned table lamp, elbows shocked by the action, head fizzing with visceral electricity.

That's not who I am. That's not who I am.

But still it stole her breath, and whether it was hating him or loving Leah that ached most, she didn't know.

Maybe Grant sensed it. When he mumbled, "Fuck you, Em," he sounded scared. "Don't call me again."

Back downstairs, Em jittered through the last of the day like she was coming down from adrenaline.

The arcade was slow, even for a Tuesday, and she chased the younger employees through the end-of-day chores to let them leave early.

Leah called to ask if she could stay with Judy, and Em said yes before asking who Judy was.

Finally, the sun sank low and red on the horizon, a squat ball of fire channeled, blinding, by the windows lining the street. It was only a few minutes to closing. Em cut the lights, and someone said, "Oh! Hey!"

A little girl's voice, it sounded like. "Sorry!" Em called back, automatically, and put the lights back on.

"Thank you! We're almost … done …."

Tinny music came, like an ice-cream truck running through a funhouse tunnel. Em recognized it right away, one of the repaired claw machines, one of the newer ones filled with brand name stuffed animals and plastic eggs with vouchers and earrings and what looked like a set of car keys. It cost five dollars just to play.

"It's okay. I jumped the gun." Em hoped her guess of it being a kid was right. She felt wrung out, and she didn't want to deal with some entitled tourist who would drag out the seconds to closing. "If you get a prize, bring your egg up here, and I'll cash you out." There wouldn't be a prize, of course. The claw machine was programmed, its grip strength set. Only the timing of when the claw descended was controlled by the player, so even if they aimed it precisely, it wouldn't pick up even the lightest prize until the machine had banked enough money. The big prizes in the plastic eggs were weighted, too, and couldn't be picked up at all unless the owner set the machine to do it. The service guy had repaired it just that morning, to make sure.

Em hated knowing that about the machines. It was the sort of knowledge that ran counter to whatever magic the arcade had left. But, she supposed, the claw machines had always been that way, even when she was little, and she'd still managed to love it, back then.

There was a whoop, joyous, and improbable. Definitely a girl's voice. "I got it! I got it!"

The lights on top of the machine went off, spinning gold and blue and silver.

"She got it!" Another girl. "Miss, come look!"

Em felt warmer. That last, ugly image of Grant loosened its grip. "What is it?" she called as she walked, threading her way down the row of machines. "Let's see."

She rounded the corner.

Two girls about eight years old, obviously sisters, maybe twins, were hugging and jumping and trying to squeal all at once. They were filthy, in the way of kids who filled their days walking the beach in their street clothes: sand-covered shoes; big loops of hair pulled half out of pony tails; dark, salt-smelling streaks swiped across their pants and pink t-shirts.

Em remembered what that sort of day felt like, and she smiled. "Okay, okay, what is it? And then you have to go. It's getting late."

"Look, we got it. We tried all day."

How long was all day? How much had that cost? Em wondered how she hadn't noticed them. Of course, she hadn't been her most observant self since the call.

One of the girls held out a glitter-painted egg.

Em took the egg from the girl's hand. So thin, that hand, attached to a scrawny arm. Em looked closer. Both girls were thin. Starving thin. One of them had a big bruise on the side of her leg. Em tried not to frown. Instead, she lifted the egg up so she could squint through the clear side. In the flashing light, she could see it was empty.

Oh, no. "Oh, sweethearts, I'm sorry. This one is empty."

"It is now," the bruised one said. Her tone was very serious. "We used it already."

"You did?"

The nods that came back were even more serious. "We saw the wish in there, so when we won it, we used it right away."

"You saw it?" Em didn't want to ask. She felt stuck, frozen, suddenly afraid.

"Our brother told us about it," said the first one.

"He died." said the second.

"He's an angel!" The first girl was crying, suddenly, and flung her arms around Em's hips.

At the same time, Em's work cell rang, a forwarded call from the office phone, some local number. "Okay, you two. Come sit down while I take this call. Then we can call your parents. I bet they're wondering where you are."

"They're not, though," the crying girl whispered through hiccups. "Not no more. It's okay, but they're not."

"Yeah," said the other one. "We'll be okay now."

Blinking, Em answered the phone, her voice flat and automatic. "Ocean Wonder!Lands, can I help you?"

Through the glass of the front window, the bar lights of a police car also flashed, stuttering along with the machine's whoops as the car zoomed past. Another and another went by, heading east toward Necanicum Creek or the freeway.

"This is Mica Lowes. I'm a friend of the Collinses. Are the girls there? Two blondes, long hair. They're ten and eleven. I think they were wearing pink this morning."

"Two …?" But they only looked eight. Skinny. Dirty. Older than they should be. Em turned to the girls, the phone muted. "Do you two know someone named Mica?"

"Yeah, yes." They both smiled, the older one beaming through tears. "I told you it would be okay."

"What did you wish for?" Em asked. It suddenly seemed very important to know.

But the girls didn't answer. At the same time, the woman on the phone said, "There's been an accident."

After a while, Em smelled burning.

Two hours later, the girls were taken off in the back seat of a DHS vehicle. A very nice-seeming woman had come to collect them, to take them to an aunt's house down in Ashland. Long drive.

The woman thanked Em over and over for staying with the

girls while they waited. Em had given them cocoa, and some stuffed animals from the prize cupboard, and hot dogs and potato chips.

"How'd you know they were here, though?" Em asked.

"One of the parents' … roommates gave the girls money this morning."

"Mica?"

"Mica. They'd told her they were going to the arcade."

"This morning?"

The woman smiled tightly. "Yeah. I know. It's … well, I'm just glad we had that to go on, and there's someplace to take them."

When they'd gone, Em turned off the lights and sat in the semi-dark. The machines chuckled and blinked to themselves. She thought about calling Leah. She thought about Leah, about Grant and the rich, sneering parents he'd learned so much from. Had he been at their house during the call, just back from his summer trip? Were they all together, sharing their poison? She thought he'd mentioned something about intending to go there.

On the wall by where she sat, the mural mermaids and pirates played. Why the pirates were good guys in this scenario, adult Em didn't know. Child Emmaline had never questioned it. Why were the mermaids all princesses and queens? Why did children all come back to bed, tucked in and all forgiven at the end of every story? Magic, maybe. Lies or wishes.

On the other side of that magic, she knew, something else lurked, curdling milk and licking sharp fangs. If this were a world of wishes, if there were fairy godmothers to make a child's wish come true, then there were also ogres to grab them, false grandmothers to trick them into their pots. Killers. Derangers. Caperers and Gibberers.

It was almost midnight, probably too late to call, but not too late for voicemail. Em entered Leah's number. To her surprise, Leah picked up.

"Mom? Is something wrong?" She sounded sleepy and worried at the same time.

"Nothing. Just wanted to say goodnight."

"Okay. There was a big fire in town. Did you see it from work?"

"I did. I just, I love you, Leah. I love you out to sea and back." Em winced. That was what she and Leah used to say, playing pretend mermaids and pirates when Leah was littler. Leah thought it was pretty gross, now.

"The sea and back, Mom. Love you. G'night." Leah hung up.

Em hugged the silent phone to her chest. What if this were a world of wishes? If, even only once in a year, once in a lifetime, for good or for ill, a wish came true?

She sat a long time more.

Then she took out a five-dollar bill, ran it over her thigh to flatten it for the machine, and went to find out.

in this and every universe

Valerie Geary

In This and Every Universe

By Valerie Geary

If Maya could choose a universe in which to exist, it sure as hell wouldn't be this one.

Every Thursday night, her husband insists they go to the dive bar down the road for a beer and burger. Tonight, instead of the Grizzlies vs. Bobcats basketball game playing on the television in the corner, the bartender tunes in to the State of The Union Address. The man who calls himself President huffs and puffs, red-faced, asserting that women need to leave the economy and politics to their husbands, return to their picket-fence homes and contribute to society by making babies and baking pies. "The birth rate is declining." He pounds his fist on the edge of a podium. "And what good is a woman if she's not sacrificing everything for the future of our great nation?"

"You hear that, babe?" Her husband pours another pint from the pitcher to drown himself in. "The president just ordered you to make me a sandwich."

Her chair slides back from the table with a loud screech, but her husband doesn't even flinch. His gaze is fixed on the television in the corner, on the man who promises to return the country to its once-former glory when money trickled down and they could say and do whatever the hell they wanted and not have to worry that one day their wives would get sick of it all, pack up and leave.

The bathroom floor is sticky with something Maya tries not to think about. The overhead light strobes and sizzles. Through the window above the sink, on the other side of wire mesh, the sun dips behind dusty fields and the whole world turns blood orange.

This can't be all there is, Maya thinks, as she washes her hands.

A man on television calling her worthless. A half-drunk pitcher of cheap beer and another on the way. Soggy fries and an overcooked slab of meat. A bathroom that reeks of yesterday's piss. An emptiness in her heart where love used to be. A window too small to escape through.

She didn't notice the claw machine on her way into the bathroom. The way it's pushed into the dark alcove makes it all but disappear. She stops in front of it now, drawn by the colorful plush toys piled in a haphazard heap. Their button eyes and stitched on smiles offer more of her reflection than the bathroom mirror did.

It's vintage and only costs a quarter to play. Cheap entertainment is a rare find these days, considering inflation. Maya shoves her hand into her pocket, palming two coins leftover from her afternoon at the laundromat.

Maybe it's the desire for something small and soft and real to hold on to. Maybe she's only delaying the inevitable return to a husband she couldn't leave even if she wanted to—the man on the television made it impossible to get a divorce unless you can prove your husband cheated or is otherwise violent toward you, and Greg is neither a cheater nor a beater. It doesn't matter that there are other ways a husband can break a wife and fade her to nothing.

Maya pushes a quarter into the slot and grabs the joystick.

"These things are rigged, you know." Greg's hoppy breath against the back of her neck makes her flinch and push the button at the wrong time.

The claw goes down, sputters and rises back up, then drops a second time, grabs a yellow plushy, and Maya is flush with anticipation and the feeling that Greg is wrong, Greg is finally wrong. As the claw comes up, the metal talons open and the toy drops back into the pile.

"What did I tell ya? Bunch of crooks. But there's always one sucker gullible enough to keep trying." Greg laughs and shakes his head. Then he presses a twenty-dollar bill into her hands. "Order us another pitcher, would ya? I gotta take a piss."

With the men's room door pushed open, he scowls over his shoulder. "Don't even think about wasting any more of my

        In This and Every Universe

money on this racket. If you want a stuffed animal, I'll buy you a freaking stuffed animal."

The door slams closed, but it's not enough of a barrier to stifle the sound of Greg's stream, or the way he whistles as if he's the main character in his, and everyone else's, movie.

Maya stuffs the twenty-dollar bill into her pocket and takes out another quarter, her last one. She rubs the coin between her fingers and stares at a fuzzy stuffed bear that reminds her of the one she brought home the first time she found out she was pregnant. Before a crib, before diapers, before bottles or a changing table or anything practical, she bought a stuffed bear that she slept with every night so that it would smell like her. She thought the baby would like that.

Greg comes out of the bathroom again. "You're still trying? It's a lost cause, babe."

Like so much of this life.

She slips her last quarter back into her pocket and follows Greg back to the bar.

It doesn't take him long to drain another pitcher. He offers her a pint, but she pretends she's not thirsty. The red-faced man on the television has paused for a commercial break. A new erectile dysfunction medication claims his male viewers can rise again and be ready to take charge when it counts.

Greg slams the empty pint glass down on the table and wipes his hand across his mouth. "One more piss before we go."

Maya blinks, confused. He just came back from the bathroom. But no, it's been an hour since, and she has no clear memory of anything during that time. She dipped some soggy fries into a pooling puddle of ketchup. Greg talked about work. But then, that could have all happened last Thursday. So many of her minutes blend together now, so many of her days made up of the same.

While her husband ducks into the bathroom, Maya again palms her last quarter in front of the claw machine. The bear stares out at her from behind the plexiglass. During the first trimester, she had nightmares.

She would wake panicked, sweat-drenched, heart racing, certain her dreams were real. She would squeeze her baby's stuffed bear as tight as she could, rub the plushy fur against her cheek until she fell asleep again.

She thought being married would be like that—comfort against the darkness.

Maya moves the quarter toward the slot, but before she can drop it in, the emergency exit door near the bathrooms swings open, and a woman barges in, dragging a vending machine bigger than her through the narrow entrance. She's using a dolly and wearing a back brace. Maya rushes to her side to help.

"Nah, sweetheart," the woman says in a rolling rumble of a voice that reminds Maya of a purring cat. "I've been doing this a long time, and while I appreciate the gesture, it's less of a liability for me to do it alone."

Maya nests herself against one side of the claw machine to watch the woman set up the new vending machine. She grunts and huffs as she wrestles the bubble-shaped contraption into an empty corner next to the boxy, and much larger, claw machine. When the woman finally gets the new machine positioned where she wants it, she smacks the plexiglass side with gusto, and the hundreds of plastic balls inside, no bigger than limes, jostle and then settle again. Whatever's inside them sparkles and glints.

The woman pulls a red handkerchief from her pocket, and as she wipes her hands, she turns to Maya and tips her head at the claw machine. "You ain't gonna find what you need in there. It's been broken for a while now."

From the same pocket where she pulled the handkerchief, she now pulls a large roll of yellow tape and wraps it several times around the outside of the claw machine.

Bold black letters repeat the same three words: Out of Order, Out of Order, Out of Order.

Not a lost cause then, and not a gullible sucker—just a broken set of gears or sprockets or widgets. Maya has no idea what the inner guts of a claw machine look like, but she imagines them as

     In This and Every Universe

metallic teeth covered in grease and dust, grinding to a halt, after years of neglect.

She wonders if there's a way to get inside, a key that might open some secret back door so she can grab the stuffed bear and bring it home.

The claw machine is broken and already stole one of her quarters, so it only seems fair. And anyway, who's going to miss a bear like that? A bear so small and unassuming.

She doesn't know what happened to the one she bought for her first baby. After Greg brought her home from the hospital, she looked for it for days, hoping it would help ease the hollow ache, but she never found it. When Greg found her on the nursery floor, curled into a ball, sobbing over the misplaced toy, he told her not to worry—everything was replaceable.

But the woman leaves before Maya can ask about the key. She turns away from the bear, sidles up to the new, smaller vending machine. It takes quarters, like the claw machine, but unlike the claw machine, you win something every time.

Any second, Greg will burst from the men's room, tugging on his zipper and expelling a loud belch.

A hard crank of the handle, a *clack, clack, clunk*. Maya jabs her fingers into the dispenser and scoops out one of the small plastic capsules.

The sticker across the glass of the vending machine is a mess of stars and comets and planets in mid-spiral. A smiling cartoon child holds one of the capsules in the palm of her hand, out of which arches a brilliant, shining rainbow. **Galaxies: Carry the Universe in Your Pocket.**

Maya lifts her new toy to the flickering bare bulb hanging from the ceiling. The goop inside is dark blue and shimmering. She cracks the lid on her pocket universe. The bright scent of jasmine and fresh cut grass wafts from inside. She inhales, and the floor tilts ever so slightly off its axis.

She reaches for something to hold on to, finds the cold glass of the claw machine, and presses her hand against it.

The bar noise dims around her, replaced by a crackling static, the hiss of a thousand different voices. She doesn't understand it, the pull she feels, the way her stomach drops like she's falling into something, tumbling headfirst.

"You ready, babe?" Greg smacks her ass, and she's so surprised, she bobbles the plastic capsule, almost dropping it. Almost. She clamps her fingers around it, snapping the lid tight again.

The feeling of vertigo dissipates, but her head still feels buzzy, and maybe she shouldn't have had that second glass of beer after all. She blinks at Greg, forgetting for a second who he is, this man she's supposed to love with every fiber of her being.

"Are you sure you're okay to drive?" she asks.

Her husband's grin is sloppy. "We both know I drive better drunk than you do sober."

Windows down, radio blaring—the street lights flash by faster than she'd like, like shooting stars through the dark, but she says nothing. Greg doesn't like it when she nags.

Maya holds the plastic capsule tightly, as if it might save her. As they near the bridge, she wonders if other universes do exist. Out there somewhere—and it's nice to think about—could be a universe where she doesn't spend every waking minute pretending.

Tires screech, burning rubber, as the car swings hard to the right, then to the left. The overcorrection sends them into a tailspin that yanks Maya out of her seat. The seatbelt catches her waist, cinches. Then she's tugging on it, desperate to break free. She bashes her shoulder against the door until it groans and pops open. She tumbles from the car, ears ringing. Gasoline fumes choke the air.

Greg calls her name, but she ignores him and stumbles away from the broken glass and bent metal, away from the hissing steam that looks like smoke.

The gravel shoulder becomes a narrow concrete sidewalk that

　　In This and Every Universe

leads up and over a bridge. In the middle, she stops and presses her hands to the steel railing. Below, dark water rushes toward an invisible horizon. The moon dances silver in the eddies and swirls. And in the distance, she hears sirens. Sirens, and a woman shouting, "You have to get out of the car! I see flames! Can you walk?"

A single snowflake falls on Maya's nose. Funny, because it's the middle of March and it rarely snows this late. She brushes off the flake. Not snow, but a fleck of ash.

"Was anyone else in the car with you?" The woman shouts, her voice so small and drifting, carried down the river over rocks, carried away and away to the sea.

Maya doesn't hear Greg's answer. And she doesn't turn to look at the chaotic scene she left behind. She stares down at the muddy black churn and thinks: *This can't be all there is.*

The plastic is smooth against her fingers, and cool, despite having been pressed between her hands since leaving the bar. The lid gives a satisfying pop as the night fills with the scent of jasmine and fresh cut grass.

"Ma'am?"

A deep voice roars through time and space, an earthquake rumble that causes Maya to blink and take a step back. A hand clamps around her arm, holding her steady. "Ma'am, are you hurt?"

Dizziness upends rational thought. Again, she is in the car spinning and spinning, only this time there is nothing to crash into and when it finally stops, she is on the bridge again. The bridge at night, with the Clark Fork flowing beneath her, and Greg is at her side asking if she's all right. His breath smells of mint, not beer, and his hair looks different—trimmed long, but swept back.

He says, "No one's hurt. The tow truck is on its way. Come sit down, Mai. You look like you're about to faint."

Greg hasn't called her by that nickname in over a decade.

That Greg was her Greg and also not the man she knows at all. The way he touched her was different. He stroked her cheek and brushed her hair back with such gentleness as he checked for injuries. There was something different, too, about the fluttering sensation in her chest when he drew near. She isn't afraid of him in that other universe. In that universe, they are still very much in love.

"Ma'am?" The voice again, waking her from such a pleasant dream.

She doesn't want to, but they are making her, dragging her through the narrow slit in time and space, forcing her to return.

Maya looks down at her empty hands, as panic sets in. "Where is it?"

"Ma'am?"

"I was holding—" But how does she describe an entire lifetime, a universe that looks nearly identical to this one except she is happy?

"There was a toy," she says. "A little plastic ball with this blue glitter goop. It's only this big?" She holds her finger and thumb an inch apart.

The EMT looks at her like she's crazy.

She jerks free of him and spins around, looking everywhere around her feet for the capsule with the green lid.

"Ma'am, if you'll just come with me." His hand ensnares her elbow again, guiding her toward a waiting stretcher. He's trying to be gentle, but there's an impatience to his grip, irritation at her unwillingness to cooperate. "We're gonna get you to the hospital and get you checked out."

"I'm fine." She struggles against him a moment more before finally giving in.

As she slides onto the stretcher, her eyes continue scanning the ground for a fleck of bright green, a glint, a sparkle, a flash of what she didn't know she was even missing.

"I'm not hurt. I just need that toy. It's important. I need it. If you find it—"

"Your husband's already on his way," the EMT interrupts, as if he hasn't heard a single word she's said.

Maybe he hasn't. Maybe when Maya opens her mouth only sighs come out. She doesn't quite feel real right now anyway. Her skin is stretched too tight over her bones. Her head throbs. And there is a pressure in her chest, a sharp tug, as if her heart is attached by a thread to that other universe and the rest of her is forced to be here, stuck in heavy cement boots, unable to escape a world that reeks of motor oil where no one listens and it hurts to breathe.

The EMT snaps an oxygen mask over Maya's mouth and nose. She lays her head on the stretcher and closes her eyes, feeling every jostle and bump and small stone as he rolls her off the bridge and away from the dancing moon.

She dreams about the other universe, and when she wakes, for a long moment, she feels herself expanding again. It's the strangest sensation: a tingling all over her body, the desire to leap to her feet and run into a grassy meadow spinning and spinning with her hair tossed back as the sun falls golden over her bare limbs. Every wildflower petal crushed underfoot releases a sweet fragrance of endless possibility. There are, in this life, infinite paths to take, and infinite chances, and infinite ways to be happy.

She smiles at her husband, who's asleep in a chair by the window.

Greg proposed to her under a waterfall. The force of violent rapids was so loud, she almost missed it. *I want to spend the rest of my life with you. You make me the happiest man alive. There is nothing else I need in this world as long as I have you.*

God, they were young, and filled with so much hope.

They got married under the shadow of a snow-capped mountain with a raven officiating. That's how she tells it anyway. Greg rolls his eyes and says, *That damn bird wouldn't shut the hell up. If I'd had my rifle with me, I'd have popped him a good one.*

The raven landed in a tree near the actual ordained minister and bobbed its head and fluttered its wings, and Maya can't help but think the bird was an omen.

At the time, she assumed good luck because ravens were smart and she was a newlywed. But later, she would visit a tarot card reader who would draw a Death card with a raven perched on a skull, and the woman would mutter about transformation and taking a new path. *Not true death,* the woman said, *but a death of your old self, an awakening to the possibility of something new.*

She would tell Greg about it after, and Greg would warn her about calling on the Devil like that, opening gateways to other worlds without knowing what's on the other side. He would remind her that in some states the use of tarot cards is punishable by up to a year in prison, but then reassure her that obviously he loved her and would never turn her in for something so small. Two weeks later, they lost their first baby.

She stopped telling him things. Six months after that, she lost their second.

She stopped thinking about the possibility of something new. He stopped reaching for her in the middle of the night.

She buried her old self so deep it was a kind of death, and both of them pretended to be happy.

On that bridge tonight, the moon pale and diminished above her but sparkling alive against the fast-flowing river beneath, she felt that long-forgotten part of herself coming to life again.

Greg grunts and shifts in the chair. He stretches and rubs his neck, rolls his shoulders, scratches his crotch, finally realizes she's awake, and says, "Thank God."

He's not thanking God she's alive, that he won't have to exist in this world without her, that he didn't kill her with his drunken speeding. He's thanking God because the hospital food is terrible and he can't eat another dry piece of chicken and overnight stays are expensive and who knows how much the insurance will cover and she didn't tell the cops he'd been drinking, right?

They're in the rental car, halfway home and stopped at a light, when Maya realizes the sweatpants she's wearing are ones she stopped wearing years ago because they are too tight around the waist and worn thin in all the wrong places. She should have thrown them out, but they are the ones she wore to her very first ultrasound, so of course they are the ones Greg picked for her to wear home. She starts to speak, but as if they've been here before, lived this moment a hundred times already, he says, "Those are the only ones I could find."

"Where are my other things?" she asks.

"What things?"

"My purse. My clothes. Whatever I came into the hospital with?"

"We can get you new things."

"They didn't give you my things?"

"Were they supposed to?"

"You could have asked."

If she doesn't calm down, he's going to tell her that she's being shrill, that her voice is giving him a headache, and could she just stop nagging him for once in her life. But she can't calm down this time. Her hand hurts. When she looks down at it, she expects to see a cut, a bruise, some remnant from the accident, but there is only her hand—her empty, aching hand.

"I don't see what the big deal is," Greg says with a mild shrug. "It's just some grubby clothes."

"And my wallet. And my ID. And my credit cards." If it has anything to do with his money, he'll care. He'll turn the world upside down to find even one of his hard-earned dollars.

"Oh, no yeah, I got all that." He jerks his thumb toward the backseat where a plastic bag sags in the spot where they would have put their child, if they'd ever had one.

Maya drags the bag into her lap and fumbles open the plastic.

"Jesus, babe, slow down. It's all there."

But it's not all here.

"There was a toy," she says.

"What?"

"A little plastic ball, about this big." She shows him with her fingers.

He frowns at her before turning his eyes back on the road. "What the hell are you talking about? Plastic balls."

"At the bar, there was this machine—"

"That stupid claw machine?" His voice is louder than it needs to be, upset over something that has nothing to do with him. "I told you not to waste my money on that trash heap piece of shit."

"I didn't."

"My money, your money. It all comes from the same place, you know."

There it is again, the twist of the knife that she's not working. It doesn't matter that she can't, that no one would hire her if she tried. She does her fair share of work inside the home, more than her fair share, but it doesn't count. Work without a paycheck is nothing but a hobby. A home without a child is nothing but a place to sleep and shower.

"Never mind. It doesn't matter." She slumps against the seat and hugs the plastic bag against her stomach.

Maybe if she holds tight enough, she'll be able to hold herself together.

It happens quickly and without her permission, the tears streaming down her cheeks, and even though her sobs are silent, swallowed down before they reach his ears, Greg still rolls his eyes and tightens his grip on the steering wheel.

"What are you crying for? Jesus Christ, Maya. It's just a stupid toy."

A stupid toy and her entire life.

Later at home, when she's changed into new sweatpants that smell like cotton breeze and fit like a hug, and Greg's had three beers and the basketball game cuts to commercial, she brings him a fourth and, perched on the arm of his recliner, asks, "Do you ever wonder if we exist like this in another universe?"

"Like this?" He swigs his beer, then swings his eyes around the room as if seeing things for the first time. Then he squeezes the side of her hip and says, "The accident really knocked you around, didn't it? In another universe, we'd be rich, and I'd be married to your sister."

His laughter rolls over her, and she knows it's a joke, but that's the problem—in this universe, and who knows how many others, her life is a joke to him.

She lifts herself off the chair, but he grabs her and pulls her down again, this time into his lap. A little beer sloshes out of the bottle onto her arm.

"Don't be mad, babe. Don't be mad. You know I love you. In this and every universe." He clamps his arms around her, holding her down.

The man is on the television above the bar again. Screaming, again. It's just the way he talks. In this and every universe, but in some universes, not everyone has to listen. This time he's saying something about immigrants, about how walls don't work unless men are given the authority to shoot. *Take the Berlin Wall, for example, now that's a wall that got it right.*

Maya's leg bounces under the table. She can't stop glancing toward the dark alcove where the bathrooms are. She finishes the last sip of her first beer. Her husband is on his third and the pitcher's almost empty. They both screech back their chairs at the same time. Greg laughs and says, "You read my mind."

Maya says, "I have to use the ladies' room."

Which makes Greg frown and glance at his pint glass like they're in on it together. "Well, be a dear and grab a pitcher on the way back, yeah?"

She sees the claw machine first. It's lit up and the tape is gone and the plush toys inside are all stitched replicas of the man on the television. Tiny balled fists, tiny blue suit and red tie, that same arrogant smile stitched on to a peachy-rose face, his red hair swept back in a ridiculous pompadour that doesn't fool anyone. Bald little dictator in this and every universe.

The Galaxy machine is gone. Maya rubs her eyes, hoping it is only her concussion making things disappear, that the machine dispensing sparkling pocket universes will re-materialize and she can spend a quarter and, this time, never return. But the Galaxy machine has been replaced by a different toy vending machine, something called a Slap Happy that appears to be full of rainbow-colored hands made of sticky polymer, hands that slap and stick on many different surfaces. She doesn't know what the point of them is, but it's not what she needs.

Maya hurries to the bar and leans over it to get the bartender's attention. The man takes his time helping three other people before he finally gets to her, so by the time he says, "What can I get for you?" Maya is frantic.

"The galaxy machine!"

His brows pinch together. "I don't know what that is. A mixed drink? What's it got in it? I might be able to make it."

"By the restrooms. There was a vending machine that sold little pocket universes."

The corners of his mouth twitch into a smirk. "That sounds cool."

"It was here last time we came in? Last week? Last Thursday? I think it's blue? It had stars and planets all over the outside of it? Little plastic capsules inside?"

The bartender leans both hands onto the bar and cranes his neck to look toward the dark alcove. "I don't think we've had anything like that."

"You did. I used one of my quarters to buy—"

"I don't give refunds for vending machines." He turns to help another customer.

"Wait! There was a woman. She brought it in. Short but strong. Steel-toed boots. Red handkerchief. If you could just give me her phone number or tell me what vending machine company she works for? Please. I—" But Maya stops herself because how does she explain to someone who's only ever been in one universe, the sheer terror of no longer being able to slide into another.

"Please," she repeats.

"I don't know any woman like that. Our vending machine guy is Bruce. He comes on Wednesdays. Come back next week and ask him about the galaxy machine. Now, do you want something to drink or what?"

When Maya gets back to the table, Greg grins at her like a kid at Christmas. He's hiding his hands behind his back and chewing on his lower lip the way he does when he's working up the courage to talk.

She refills his pint glass from the fresh and foaming pitcher, but leaves hers empty.

"Maya." He rarely says her name, and the sound of it sends a shiver through the base of her spine. She feels again the tug of another universe, the other place that's lost to her now. She doesn't want to call it better, because she doesn't know. She was only there for a minute, maybe two—long enough for her to crave more, but not long enough for her to experience what had changed—and she's smart enough to understand that better for her is not better for everyone.

"Maya." Greg's annoyed now. "Are you even listening to me?"

She forces a smile and wraps both hands around her empty pint glass. Ever since the accident, she's been doing this—holding on to inanimate objects like anchors.

"Don't say I never do anything for you."

It's clear from the tone of his voice and the snarl of his lips, that between the time she brought the pitcher back to the table and now, he's lost patience with her.

She's yet another disappointment on top of so many that came before, a lifetime of disappointments, and it's no wonder they're both so unhappy.

Then she sees it.

The hideous little doll from the claw machine.

Greg must have tossed it on the table between them at some point, and she didn't notice in time to force the proper enthusiastic response. It's tipped to one side, sagging and sad and unable to hold up the weight of its overstuffed head.

"You were so obsessed with that stupid claw machine last time, I thought I'd do something nice for you," Greg says, refilling his pint glass.

The doll's beady eyes stare at her unblinking, casting judgment. Even though the mouth is stitched shut, she hears his voice raging about the weaker sex needing to do their fair share to keep the household running, and getting The Poors to pay for roads since they sleep there, and isn't it about time for men to fulfill their evolutionary obligations and build a new era of greatness?

Before she realizes she's moving, she's in the bathroom, gripping the edge of the sink. Overhead, the light strobes and sizzles. Outside the small window, the sun slips beneath fallow fields and the whole world washes out gray. *This can't be all there is.*

Now, she knows it's not. But it doesn't matter, because she is here, and here is all she is.

Maya splashes water on her face and smooths her ponytail. Greg will come looking for her soon, not because he's worried, but because he can't stand being alone.

As she wads up the paper towel to throw away, her toe connects with something on the floor near the trash can. Something that skitters and hits the wall with a small clunk. Maya bends to pick it up. For a moment, she freezes. Her hand hovers over the plastic capsule with the green lid, then she snatches it up and locks herself inside an empty stall.

Clutching the capsule close to her chest, she waits.

In the parking lot, a car starts up and drives away, bass music thumping, rattling her teeth. The neon bar sign flicks on outside and the harsh, red light buzzes through the bathroom window, and turns the shadows to blood. Still, no one comes.

Her fingers unfurl. In her palm rests someone else's universe. Unlike the one Maya lost, which was midnight blue with a dusting of glitter, the goop inside this one is a bubblegum pink, and the glitter bits are large, catching the light like a disco ball.

She doesn't know what the rules are when it comes to pocket universes.

She could slip into someone else's universe, a place where she was never born, where her existence matters to no one. Or maybe all the pocket universes lead to the same place with the fresh cut

　　　In This and Every Universe

grass and jasmine wind, and it will feel as familiar to her as home. She cannot know until she cracks the green lid and peers inside.

Someone starts thumping on the bathroom door. Maya flinches and curls her fingers tightly around the plastic capsule, as Greg shouts at her, still banging his fist. "Maya? You in there? What's taking so long? I want to get home before the game starts."

"Be right out." She barely recognizes her own voice, meek and capitulating and everything she never dreamed she'd become.

The thumping stops.

There's more, and Maya has lived inside it.

Step outside this bar, sneak away from Greg, past the fallow fields, beyond the distant horizon and farther still—there are versions of her, places where Maya is, if not happy again, real. She rubs her thumb over the smooth green lid until she finds the sharp edge.

lucky dragon

Marianne Xenos

By Marianne Xenos

A nighttime breeze drifted through the back door of Strabo's Beachside Cafe. After midnight, the air freshened, bringing the smell of ocean, seaweed, and aging wood. Tonight, the air was laced with ganja and tobacco as staff from nearby venues lingered in the parking lot. Lu flared her nostrils, curious about the smoke habits of humans, but kept her claws still. Both her hidden claw and the one hanging down over her horde. Manny Petrakis, Strabo's short-order cook, arrived to clean her plexiglass, holding a rag in one hand, a spray bottle in the other, and a cigarette tucked behind his ear. She wondered if he would go outside to smoke soon.

Strabo's was a hole-in-the-wall eatery holding only ten tables. Lu's lair, an antique claw machine about the size of a phone booth, stood at the back between two vintage pinball games. On the claw machine's sign, a red dragon spread bat-like wings over a horde of eggs.

Manny finished polishing Lu's nest, the plastic case where she brooded like a hen, and had been brooding for twenty years. He tucked the rag into his belt and made the sign of the cross. Then he touched the tips of his fingers, calloused and tanned like oak, against the plexiglass casing. He leaned closer and whispered, "Lu, I need to ask your help. I told you about my daughter already, but sometimes—I just stumble. I don't know how to be a father."

The red light of Lu's dragon sign reflected in a mirror across the room. Years ago, somebody, probably Strabo himself, had taped a handwritten notice—*Quarters Only!*—over the name "Lucky Dragon." Now only "Lu" remained. Those who knew her, who believed in her, called her "Lu." Those who didn't were simply gambling, and she let them make their own luck.

"The world changes so fast," Manny continued. "I thought I

could be a good provider like my father. Back in the day, that was supposed to be enough. Now, I'm struggling."

In the kitchen, Alba Morales, Strabo's general manager, sang along with the radio as she tallied the tips and receipts. Most of the staff talked to Lu at quiet moments, but never acknowledged those talks to one another, except for calling her by name. If Alba came out of the kitchen, Manny would pretend to start polishing again.

"All I ask..." Manny bowed his head, and Lu's hidden claw, the one tucked against her chest, twitched. "All I ask," he repeated, "is that I keep my heart open."

This is why they come to me, to ask themselves a question, Lu thought.

Nothing in Lu's horde of eggs held an open heart, only heart-shaped charms, a plush valentine, and buried towards the back, a purple bear with a pink chest. Lu touched Manny's thoughts, where she often heard the language of his childhood. She guessed his wish was poetic and not anatomical.

Manny took four quarters and put them in the slot. He once told Lu that in human church he would light a candle and leave an offering for the saints. Here, he offered coins to a captive dragon. Putting his hand lightly on the joystick, he let Lu control the mechanism.

Lu engaged her motor and sifted through the pile of plastic eggs and translucent capsules, past the trinkets and toys to a prize she'd created last week, one night after closing time as she'd brooded about Manny and his daughter.

That night Manny had confessed to Lu that his adult daughter was gay. And not only gay, she'd proposed marriage to her girlfriend—they even talked about opening a business together. And even more, she had asked Manny if he would walk her down the aisle.

"First I wondered, what would my father say? And my uncles?"

Lu had twitched her visible claw and let her engine engage in a low rumble.

                    Lucky Dragon

Manny said, "No need to growl! You're right, and I'm an idiot. Why do I care what those old guys think? I want her to be happy, to be loved, but still... I stumbled. I hesitated, and she felt me hesitate."

Then he talked for a long time about things Lu didn't understand, about books she'd never read, and he quoted a line by his favorite Greek author. Something about fire, an ax, and a heart—things she assumed had something to do with human love.

Tonight, finally, Lu found the prize she'd made, grabbed it with her claw and dropped it in the bin. Manny opened the clear plastic egg, and a paper scroll crinkled in his hands, looking ancient and weathered, even though Lu had birthed it last week. Taking reading glasses out of his shirt pocket, Manny chuckled and held the scroll up for her to see. The scroll had three emojis: fire, an ax, and a heart.

He said, "Years ago, I read this quote in Greek, and then later in English. Now I get to read it in emoji." He paraphrased from memory, "If I were a fire, I would burn. A woodsman, I would chop... or something like that. But the third part says: since I am a heart, I love." He rolled up the scroll and put it back in its capsule. "Someday you'll be writing your own poetry, my friend, whatever language you choose. Even emoji." Smiling and leaning against the booth, he settled into his thoughts, which wandered back and forth between languages.

Lu studied the cigarette tucked behind Manny's ear, wondering what it would be like to draw smoke, to breathe smoke. She wished she could touch the plexiglass, to reach her claw and connect with her friend's fingers. Instead, she pulled her hidden claw under her chest and rumbled her motor.

Manny looked up with a frown. "Just a heads up. Old Strabo is thinking about selling the place. He said he can't keep up with the work, and his family wants him to retire. Not that he ever lifts a finger around here. But don't worry." He tapped the plexiglass. "We'll figure something out."

He gave the booth a final wipe and went back to the kitchen.

Lu's motor rumbled more quickly now.

We'll figure something out? Alba handled the money, because Manny couldn't be trusted, being prone to both impulse and generosity. Lu gave him poetry because it was the only thing he wouldn't lose.

Manny and Alba talked in the kitchen. Lu enjoyed their voices. They spoke differently together than they did in their heads. Manny spoke one language, Alba spoke another, and together they spoke a third language. Lu was learning all three.

Water splashed against metal as Manny worked, probably scrubbing the big stainless-steel sink, and Alba called good night to him as she left the kitchen with her coat and two bags. She stopped at Lu's booth and stared for a moment at the horde of treasure. The staff shared tip money, and Alba always had quarters in her pockets, but rarely used them at the claw machine. Lu knew Alba needed the money to feed her kids. Usually, she just stopped to say hello.

This time, she took four quarters from her purse and slotted them in. Before touching the joystick, she whispered, "We're in trouble, Lu. Old Strabo, that bastard, is selling the place. What are we going to do? We're like a family—and that includes you. You're our beloved *Santa Lulita*." Alba chuckled to herself, but quickly put her hand over her mouth. The deep red of her nails matched her lipstick. Taking her hand away, she whispered, "Tonight, give me something for direction. For hope."

Lu engaged her motor, and Alba put her fingertips on the joystick, which moved under Lu's direction. She dug down through her treasures, wondering what would give her friend hope? She had created an experiment, one she wouldn't give to Manny, but one which she could trust with Alba, the guardian of the tips and receipts.

Manny shut the lights in the kitchen and checked the locks on the front door. Alba waited for him in front of the claw machine, which they called by name but had never discussed out loud.

     Lucky Dragon

"Alba, what's wrong?"

"Lu gave me something. I asked her for a direction, and look." She held out a hundred-dollar bill. Like the poem, it had typos, emojis, and mistakes. Lu knew it wasn't perfect, but had hoped they would understand her meaning. "Has Strabo ever noticed that he never stocks the machine, but we still have the best prizes on the boardwalk?"

Manny shrugged. "I don't think he notices much."

"He can never find out. Nobody can find out."

Alba turned and put her hand on the booth, leaning forward so her forehead touched. Lu wondered if Manny would care that the plexiglass was smudged again. "We need our jobs, but we also need to save Lu." She kissed her fingertips and touched the booth, leaving a smear of red lipstick on the plexiglass. "But counter-feiting money is not the answer, Lulita. We need a different solution."

Manny nodded and tapped his fingers on the plexi before moving away. "Let's talk outside for a minute. I need a cigarette."

They left the back door open, and Lu smelled tobacco as she listened to the mix of their voices, each differently accented. Manny's lower and slower, and Alba's rose like a bird once or twice. Then Manny's cell phone rang, and he spoke in the language of his memories, probably to his daughter. Finally, they locked the back door and everything became quiet.

Not entirely quiet. The refrigerator hummed in the kitchen. Lu's own motor raced—she'd made a mistake with the money and felt warm with emotion—but the refrigerator's hum calmed her. She stretched the hidden parts of her body, flexed all four of her claws, curled her tail, and shifted her nascent wings.

Certain her friends were gone for the night, she flipped the hinged panel on top of the booth and pulled herself up, glancing at the mirror across the room. She admired her silver wings in the reflection, still a work in progress, glowing red in the light of the sign. Her scales clattered like chimes as she climbed down the side of the booth and scurried to the kitchen.

The staff kept a box of dented utensils for recycling, mostly battered cutlery and kitchen tools. Lu tossed a mixture of spoons, spatulas, creamers and butter knives into the stainless-steel sink, then burrowed into the jumble of metal and groomed herself. With a tongue as rough as an emery board, she cleaned herself from tip to tail and sharpened the new talons growing under her original claws. As she groomed, she absorbed the steel, using the material for scales on her torso and wings. And with a spark of will, she constructed new pathways in her brain, because a dragon was more than just wings and claws. A dragon knows fire and flight, but also language and heart. Tomorrow, perhaps, she would write a poem about it and give it to her friend.

The cool metal of the sink reminded Lu of her siblings. She'd been born in chaos. Her mother was fire, and her father minerals torn from the earth. After the heat and the pressure, and the harsh sculpting of her original claw, she lived with her siblings, all nameless and tucked tight in a cardboard box. Metal to metal, they held each other in the dark. They'd been so young, just single claws soon to be separated. Did the others evolve into the promise of their machines?

Lu must have fallen asleep, because she woke with a start as the back door opened. Familiar voices shouted in an unfamiliar way, yelling about Lu, about theft and kidnapping. She jolted upright in the sink, knocking a spatula to the floor with a crash. Manny, Alba, and Manny's daughter, followed by the daughter's fiancé, rushed into the kitchen. They flicked on the fluorescent lights, and Lu lay exposed on a bed of utensils with a gnawed soup spoon in her claw.

Everybody shrieked.

Lu jumped out of the sink. Her scales crashed as she hit the floor and scrambled between their legs, rushing to hide her unfinished body. She climbed up her booth, tucked herself inside, and pulled down the lid.

Her motor rumbled uncontrollably, but she let one claw descend, hovering over her trove. Eyes closed, she willed herself to be still, chewing on the sharp talons of her hidden claw, and tried to quiet her motor—tried to pretend nothing had happened.

Manny tapped on the plexiglass.

Lu opened her eyes. Her friends stood in front of the booth wearing name tags. Manny and Alba had their everyday tags from work. Liya and her fiancé wore handwritten notes scrawled on an order pad and pinned to their jackets. The fiancé's name was Becca, which Lu knew but had forgotten. She's seen her once before, early in the summer. Becca had light brown skin, darker than Alba's.

She looked up and saw her own name on the dragon sign, appearing backwards in the mirror. *My name is Lu*, she thought. *All beings have names.* The name tags helped Lu steady herself, and she read them to herself three times. Then, as her motor began to quiet, she listened to Becca's mind, since she knew her the least. Becca carried music in her head along with a language Lu had never heard. Liya often thought in pictures, Alba in numbers, and Manny in endless words. Lu enjoyed Becca's mind and the snippets of a new language.

Manny said, "It's okay, Lu. You're with friends. What can we do to help?"

Lu spread open her claw, not knowing what to say. Nobody had ever offered to help her before.

Liya moved to the front and took four quarters out of the pocket of her jeans. She held them in her hand and said, "We've been up all night talking about stories, especially about genies and wishes and golden geese. There's a story about a goose who laid golden eggs. And a bad man, a very bad man, who valued gold more than friendship or magic or geese. We don't want you to be our goose, Lu, because it never turns out well."

"Especially not for the goose," said Becca. Lu liked her outloud voice as much as her mind.

Liya slotted her quarters into the machine. "And, not to mix my metaphors, but I have a genie wish for you. Nobody ever wishes for the genie to be free, but they should. So, tell us how to help you. What is the wish that will make you free?" Liya rested her fingers on the joystick.

Lu's motor engaged, and she reached deep into her trove.

Nothing she found suited the wish, so she twirled her claw and birthed a new egg. An egg made of gold-colored plastic with a surprise inside. As the golden egg plunked into the bin, Manny laughed, and Lu preened her hidden wings. Manny always got her jokes.

Liya opened the golden egg and found five perfect diamonds inside. Lu knew they were perfect, unlike the hundred-dollar bill. Alba had disapproved of her attempts to make money, but jewels were like Lu herself, made from minerals and pressure and time.

Liya looked uncertain. "Papa, is this even legal? And what is she saying?"

Manny shrugged. "Lu is a poet, more than a literalist. Look, she gives us the golden egg to show she understands your story. But there are five jewels, and there are now five of us. She wants us to work together. She is asking to be our partner."

The clatter of keys came from the front door of Strabo's, followed by the jingle of the welcome bell over the door. Liya closed the golden egg and hid it in her pocket.

"What's all this?" Strabo asked as he walked in. He was a big guy who seemed to occupy half the space in the small restaurant. As he moved towards the claw machine, Lu detected an unpleasant odor, like something gone wrong, and she flared her nostrils. Perhaps he was sick, or perhaps it was the smell of a man who killed innocent geese.

"Just a quick staff meeting, Mr. Strabo," Manny said. "My daughter and her fiancé are helping out for the day."

Strabo frowned at Becca, but didn't comment on the scrawled name tags or the word "fiancé." As Manny had said, Strabo didn't notice much. He made a surprise visit about once a month, delivered a few mandates, and collected his profits.

He walked to the front of Lu's booth. "I think we have a buyer for this old thing. Some collector in Boston likes weird stuff like this."

Lu's motor began to growl, but Manny kicked the base of the booth with a soft thump. *Don't be a goose!* Manny thought in her mind. She caught the meaning and smiled to herself.

"She's... it's... usually more quiet than this. I'll check the motor later."

"Let's see how it's working. Does anybody have quarters?"

Alba took four quarters from her purse, and Lu felt like growling again. That money was for Alba's kids! But she waited for him to slot the quarters. Strabo wasn't a believer, and she didn't like his smell, so she considered giving him a poop emoji, or a whoopie cushion. Or just let him gamble his quarters. But these were Alba's quarters, so she touched his thoughts lightly and saw his wish blinking like a star at the front of his mind. She saw a child, his great-granddaughter, dressed all in pink and purple. She also saw a hurt in his body, a sickness. Pain so bad it stole the breath from his lungs. Pictures flickered in his mind. He fretted about moving but fretted more about being alone. Lu heard his thoughts mixed with the language of his childhood, the same language as Manny's. Strabo wished he could give the girl—her name was Melissa—a gift from his famous claw machine.

Famous? Lu resisted the urge to preen her wings. Strabo never said nice things out loud, but in his mind, he called her famous.

The old man took the joystick, and without much effort, Lu led him to an oversized egg hidden near the back. She maneuvered the egg to the bin, working to make sure he didn't drop it.

"I did it!" Strabo said, opening the big blue egg to find a purple bear with a small red heart embroidered in the middle of its pink chest. "People say our machine has the best prizes on the board-walk," he said, giving a rare compliment. He examined the bear, his face so soft and open he looked like a stranger. "We'll get a good price from the buyer."

Everybody looked at each other, except for Strabo, who looked only at the bear.

Alba cleared her throat and put on her best customer service smile. The smile she used when she bargained with suppliers and irate customers. She said, "Or maybe you could include the claw machine in the price of the venue? Could we talk in the kitchen, sir? We might have a proposal for you."

After they were out of earshot, Manny whispered, "Let's give her a while to warm him up, then we all go in."

"But Papa," Liya said. "Even with the diamonds, if the diamonds are real," she looked towards Lu's claw with an embarrassed shrug. "Sorry, Lu, I don't mean any offense—"

Lu didn't feel at all offended, so she waggled her claw.

"But even if they're real and even if we can sell them—"

"I'm sure Alba knows a guy. She has cousins...."

"What I'm saying, Papa, is that things will be tight. Becca is selling her house, and I have mom's insurance money, but things might be rough for a while. Maybe we should put off the wedding."

Manny and Becca looked at each other. They both seemed surprised and unhappy about Liya's suggestion. Nobody spoke for a moment, and Lu wondered if she should begin hatching more diamonds. Finally, Manny shook out a cigarette from the pack in his pocket and tucked it behind his ear.

"How's this instead? You get married on the beach and have the reception here. Like a village wedding in the old country. We'll cook for days, and then we'll dance. And Lu can watch from her nest."

Liya hugged her father, and he kissed her cheek, and Manny reached to shake Becca's hand. They shook, but Becca laughed and pulled him into a hug. Manny hugged awkwardly at first, then kissed her on the cheek as well. Lu laughed quietly. Manny stumbled but always caught himself. Like a dance.

Manny tapped the plexiglass. "I need a quick smoke before we talk to Strabo. Let's go out back for a minute."

The smell of tobacco carried through the back door, along with the scent of flowering shrubs and sun-warmed asphalt. Lu listened as they talked about menus and cake, and the threads of song in Becca's head sang bright.

"I know!" Becca said. "Let's rename this place."

They threw out names: Lu's Beachside Cafe, Casa Lulita, Lucky Dragon, and Lu's Place.

"Let's see what Alba thinks," Manny said. "And we need to give Lu a vote."

Grooming her talons and shifting her tail, Lu daydreamed about copper clad saucepans and wondered if they would add color to her scales. Drifting on smoke, she let her motor purr low and slow.

alternate

Angelique O'Rourke

BY ANGELIQUE O'ROURKE

County fairgrounds are almost universally depressing. That sounds kind of elitist, but it's also true. I'm not really sure why Hailey and I agreed to come here together in the first place. It was one of those moments where the rogue impulse to send someone you haven't spoken to in years a 'happy birthday!' text spirals into a 'we should hang out!' exchange that becomes a runaway train. And even though I highly suspected neither of us actually wants to be, here we are.

"Major nostalgia factor," she says, spying the purple and orange stripes of the big top tent rising above the chain link fence as we walk up from the parking lot.

"For sure," I agree.

For whatever reason, people our age, Millennials, are obsessed with nostalgia. I suppose it's because for a lot of us, while we were growing up, even if we personally didn't have happy childhoods, there was a general sense of hope for the future before the housing crash, recession, and sort of overall downward spiral that followed. Collective hope just never rebounded. There's never really been a reason for it to. So in our leisure time, immersing ourselves in the things that felt good before circa 2008 and adulthood, back when it had seemed like maybe we would have a chance—well, it takes the edge off of the present.

Anyway, we are two childhood friends now in our thirties attending a county fair together. The vibes, though, are off from the jump. We get to the ticket booth, and behind the iPad is Bobby Patterson, from one year above us in high school. His collared fair employee shirt, also striped in purple and orange, has a name tag near the upper right shoulder with a little balloon icon next to the word 'Bob'.

"Oh my gosh, Bobby!" Hailey says, with a level of familiarity that is really outsized to the situation, given that he'd only been our acquaintance. "How are you? It's been forever!"

Bob—still handsome but now in a more mature, rough around the edges, blue collar way—looked up from his phone. His sardonic smile, ever at the ready, spread slowly across his face. "Well, Hailey and Kelsey, as I live and breathe. I've been great, as evidenced by working the door at a fairground. How about yourselves?"

I genuinely laugh, pleasantly surprised, remembering that he's always had that droll, self-deprecating sense of humor.

"Oh, I'm also crushing it," I begin. "Just started my tenure back in town, sleeping in the living room of my mom's one bedroom apartment to help out while she gets chemotherapy. Expecting my Pulitzer nom any day now, though."

He holds my gaze for just a little longer than is necessary as he chuckles. Hailey laughs lightly as well, but it's the groupthink laughter of a person on the outskirts of a conversation she doesn't understand.

She hands Bob a one hundred dollar bill and asks for two day passes and a bunch of individual tickets for rides, food, and beer. I don't move my hand to reach for my wallet, and she doesn't even glance in my direction to indicate she thought I would.

Bob waves the money away and puts the day pass bracelets on our wrists.

He rolls off a stack of those pull-apart little orange raffle type paper tickets and hands them to her. "Don't worry about it," he says.

Hailey sets the bill on the counter by the tablet and says, "Just keep it then, for old time's sake. Text me when you're off work. We can meet you back here and have some drinks." She writes her number on one of the nearby sticky notes.

Bob raises his eyebrows a little in confusion, but replies, "Okay, sounds good. See you guys later tonight then. I'm off around 8."

As we walk away from the ticket booth, I ask her why she did that. I mean, I've deduced that a hundred dollars is border-line meaningless to her and she can see Bob could really use it, but why are we suddenly hanging out and getting drinks with him?

                    Alternate

"Um, because I've always kind of had a crush on him and he definitely can still get it?" she laughs.

I don't remember that at all from high school and wonder if she'd never told me for some reason. It seems too in the weeds to ask, so I just agree honestly that Bobby can definitely still get it.

It's a crisp autumn evening, and we're both wearing boots that crunch the gravel into the dust under our feet, adding to the cacophony all around us.

"So, what do you want to do first?" Hailey asks, gamely making conversation. She's really trying.

It makes me feel like someone is pulling on a cord that's been lassoed around my heart and stomach. I scan our surroundings. Games, food carts, rickety rides that strike me as taking your life in your hands if you got on one, and under the biggest top tent, a small circus that did a few performances a night.

"Um, shooting the cans down? My hand eye coordination is still for shit, but maybe you can win me a prize."

A few hours go by. We do stupid shit like you do at a fair, and between the beer and the cotton candy, it's getting easier to interact like we used to. I look at her face and remember when she got a terrible pixie cut sophomore year, and am suddenly swept with the urge to hug her (which I suppress). Why hadn't we seen each other in so long?

We take a moment to sit on a wooden bench and finish the last of our drinks. The sun just dips under the horizon, the air is lavender and electric in the last fleeting light. A breeze that's colder than I expected moves through my hair. Across from us is a booth that, at first, looks completely empty, until I see what it contains in one abandoned corner.

"Hey," I suggest, "let's do the claw machine."

Hailey turns to me with slightly glassy green eyes that make me consider if she is a bit of a lightweight—we've only had two beers, and light domestic shit at that, but she's down, so we make our way over. As soon as I step past the poles keeping the booth up (all of the booths were basically miniature versions of the purple and orange big top), I have a peculiar feeling, like a mixture of dread and deja vu. Uncannily, I worry we shouldn't be here and also know that we are going to stay anyway.

"Isn't it kind of weird that no one else is over here?" Hailey asks in a tone of voice that makes me think she might be having the same feeling.

"Maybe no one else can see it," I reply, like a nutcase.

She doesn't say anything back.

We walk to the front of the claw machine. It is lit from within, and the booth itself has a string of LED lights around the top. Somehow, being brightly lit is making everything weirder. In a moment of horror, I considered if something was slipped in the beers. But I watched the girl fill them from a tap and hand them directly to me. Then, we hadn't set them anywhere. We just walked around holding them. And I didn't actually feel inebriated at all, just unsettled.

Hailey is staring intently into the glass of the claw machine. She reaches forward and puts in two paper tickets. The joystick is black with a red button on top and maneuvers in the herky-jerky way you expect from a machine that is sort of deliberately trying to fail. Designed to do poorly at its sole purpose, I think.

Same, girl.

I hear myself laugh out loud. Hailey whips her head to the side to look over at me. "What is it? I can't be that bad at this." The defensiveness and almost wounding in her voice takes me completely aback. What the fuck? Why would she assume I was laughing at her?

"I wasn't even paying attention. I just had a funny thought. The claw machine is basically set up to fail, right? So I just found myself thinking, 'same', and it made me actually lol."

Her defensiveness visibly evaporates and is replaced by… something worse than pity, really, because this is pity that has convinced itself it is empathy, or even friendship. She took my joke way the fuck too seriously.

"You don't really think you're going to fail, do you?" Incredibly, she looks almost on the verge of tears. It is wild to go from holding yourself back from hugging someone to holding yourself back from slapping them in the span of an hour or so.

"Do I think I'm *going* to fail? No. I am aware of the fact that, by every conventional societal measure, I already have. I don't think of myself as a failure based on my own values, but if I used our 16 year old mindsets to measure my mid-thirties self, I'd have walked into fucking traffic years ago. I've had to unlearn a thousand things to get to the level of peace I have with where things are for me right now. It's not helpful to be delusional about the past or imagine some deeply unlikely future. The reality of the now is all we really have. So I'm just present, doing the best I can, enjoying myself and my life for what it actually is." My little monologue started out caustic, a heated reaction to her condescension, but as I spoke, the truth of what I was expressing calmed me down, so by the time I finish, my voice is even and matter of fact.

"Okay, I get that," she begins, and my teeth are immediately set on edge.

"You know, I don't actually think that you do. I get that you're trying to be nice, but you can't really relate to me in this way."

"Sometimes I want to start all over again," she offers. "A new job, new city, just hit the reset button."

"Well, the good news is that you can sell one of the homes you inherited and go do that," I say, not interested in pulling punches.

She puts her arms to her sides and opens her palms in a sort of shrugging gesture. "Yeah, I guess I have options." She says wistfully.

Acid rises in the back of my throat at the navel-gazing oblivion of what she's just said. There's always been this between us. Her romanticizing poverty like it's a proxy for meaning, not a lived experience. Never understanding that I, and countless others, have had to live, actually, literally live each day, each breath, in the world of her cosplay. That our families lived there, that we may well never find a way out. She goes home whenever she wants, to options. I *live* without them, with the rest of the plebs. Gallingly, the bar is so low that most would give her abundant credit for trying to understand at all.

I study the glare of the lights on the glass of the claw machine. This entire time, she's been standing there with one hand still on the lever, and I've been standing near the other side of the tent, a small dirt expanse in the middle.

"Do you blame me for what happened?"

In the sepia glow, I look across the empty space into her eyes. They are wide, shiny, and somehow slightly bigger in her face than they were just a few moments before, giving her face a cartoonish, manic quality.

I blink, pulling myself back from the uncanny valley. Several beats of silence stretch between us.

She already knows I do—to some degree—but we both know that I really can't, anymore than one can blame fate, or luck.

"No." Half a lie. "I know that logically you're not actually at fault. You can't tell the future any better than I can, but on an emotional level, I can't help that I still associate you with it all." Closer to the truth. I heave a leaden sigh.

Of its own accord, the claw in the machine moves over the piles of... what is that in the case? I realize somehow the entire time we've been standing here, I never actually clocked it. Staring into it now, I still can't make it out.

"What is that? Can you tell what's in the claw machine?"

Hailey is transfixed, the glow reflecting in her eyes almost like the tapetum lucidum of a cat. "No." she breathes. "I know we're looking right at it, but—"

The claw opens, and something falls into the slot at the bottom of the machine.

Hesitantly, she flips the little door in to look. "Oh what the fuck," she whispers, more a statement than a question.

Her phone dings. It's 8 o'clock.

  Alternate

"They build from you and off of you, and you learn too late that was all creative energy you should've spent on yourself. Every nails-on-a-chalkboard interminable dinner barely tolerating a boyfriend's enmeshed family, every moment listening to him complain, every second you ever spent, ever somehow, incredibly, inexplicably allowed yourself to spend, in your one precious life on earth, being treated like the dishonorable daughter-in-law archetype of yore by people you wouldn't trade lives with if you had a gun to your head, who parented the sinking ships you willingly boarded—that you'd take all of it back in a single heartbeat, without a second thought, and pour it into creating the life you dreamed of, where it should have been all along." My palm is sweating onto the handle of the claw machine; I release it. I wasn't expecting to say any of that, but another beer in and the subject of relationships came up and it all just came tumbling out. Like my hand was wrapped around a rod made out of truth serum, or something.

Well, now Bobby knows I'm a hot mess.

Holding a beer, he runs his free hand over his face. "Yeah. Yeah, men can be... like that." There's a heaviness under his words. I'm surprised.

"You said that like you know it from my perspective."

He sighs. "Well, I am a man. I'm also bi."

"Ah," I reply. "So you kind of do know."

"Minus the first hand misogyny, yeah. Men can ask so much that they drain your lifeblood. Women can hold you to secret expectations and say you broke their heart when you didn't do what they never asked for. With nonbinary people, it's dealer's choice, in my experience. And in general, bringing home the bi boyfriend has resulted in many an excruciating event with a partner's parents."

"So, overall, a bit of 'life's a bitch and then you die' energy?"

"Actually, I'd take any of the other stuff over being drained like that, honestly. Conflicts and bad communication are surmountable, but someone who, like you said, builds off of you, out of your reserves of attention, your love and energy, just bleeds you dry like that? They don't really think of you as a person. When they see you enjoying yourself from across a room, they don't appreciate who you are or feel happy for you; they look for reasons to shut you down, to turn your focus back to them—and them alone. In a weird way, it's like you're totally interchangeable with any other person who would fill those needs. You could be anyone. The only move is to get out."

"Oof, Bobby, I feel that in my fucking bones."

"You know what's so weird? Nobody's called me Bobby since high school."

"Do you mind it? I can call you Bob," I offer.

He laughs. "Actually, now that you guys have been saying Bobby, Bob sounds weird."

"Okay, we'll stick with Bobby."

Hailey pops her head around the pole of the tent, back from the bathroom. "We're sticking with Bobby, huh? Glad to hear it." She smiles at him flirtatiously. "It was super odd just now. I went right to where this tent was before, but it was gone. I couldn't find it anywhere. I looped around, and suddenly it was back."

"Yeah, people get lost in the fair a lot," Bobby replies.

Hailey looks perplexed still, as if there was something she is trying to convey that didn't come across.

"Hey," Bobby suddenly asks, "did anybody ever get anything out of the claw machine?"

"Uh yeah, Hailey did. But I never asked what it actually was. We had to come meet you."

"Oh that's wild," Bobby says. "No one has been able to get anything out of it since the fair opened; it's been broken."

"Well, it worked earlier. What did you get, Hailey?"

Hailey looks sheepish, and wears a similar expression to the previous moment, like she wants to share something but doesn't quite know how.

"It's, um, this is going to sound weird, but it's, um, a chance to start the day over again and have a different outcome."

There's silence for a second as Bobby and I glance at each other.

What's so strange is that I know I should be thinking Hailey is either wasted or has lost it, but instead, I just… believe her? I just know what she's saying is true. From the look on Bobby's face, he feels the same way.

"Sweet," he says. "Are you going to use it?"

Hailey sighs in relief. "I was going to ask you guys if you minded, actually. It feels shady to restart our narrative of the past few hours without you knowing."

"I think I'm up for it," I say.

"Same," echoes Bobby.

I'm not really sure why Hailey and I agreed to come here together in the first place, I think, as the claw picks up something from the pile of—what is that?—and drops it in the shoot.

Hesitantly, she flips the little door in to look.

"Oh what the fuck," she whispers, more a statement than a question.

Her phone dings. It's 8 o'clock.

"You go," she says, closing her fingers around whatever she pulled from the claw machine.

"What? Like, meet up with Bobby without you?" I'm nonplussed.

Suddenly, with a determined visage, she reaches forward and takes both of my hands in hers, pressing whatever she was holding into my palm. A warmth builds in my hands, slowly moves up through my arms towards my heart. Hailey is looking at me intently, her hazel green eyes still slightly too big and feline, and it strikes me that *she* is moving the warmth, and she's sort of wordlessly sending it through me. It should be frightening, but it isn't. The opposite. The feeling of warmth touches the center of my chest, and it's as if I can see inside her mind. Images in my head of us as girls together, going to concerts, eating ice cream, getting ready for prom. My face, my hair flying around me as we dance. Young adults struggling, helping each other, hurting each other, growing apart.

I see myself from her point of view—literally. Times when I made her laugh, when she heard me sing. Times she held me when I cried. Time itself, I can tell, is being distorted- I'm being filled in on years, decades of experiences in a mere fraction of that. All the while, in the tent, our held hands remain. Hands that hadn't touched in years. What happens to physical closeness as we age? Does everyone stop touching over time? It's difficult to imagine now, laying on a bed with her, resting my head on her chest, her arms around me so tightly while I sobbed with heartbreak, but it happened, and it brought me such solace. It still does, even in memory. Even in the midst of her memories. I feel the love she felt for me, the way *she* felt it.

We haven't spoken during this, just stood there holding hands, her eyes gently glowing in that supernatural but somehow unthreatening, almost comforting, way, and mine streaming with silent tears. The feeling and images slowly ebb, and she brings the back of my right hand to press against her cheek briefly before letting go.

"Okay?" she asks.

"Okay." I nod. "Go meet Bobby at the gate. I'm heading home. I'm glad we said a proper goodbye."

Though we're no longer in silent communication, I know that this will be the last time we see each other for many years. Maybe forever. Bittersweetly, we did the best that we could.

It's her day's different ending.

"Oof, Bobby, I feel that in my fucking bones," I say.

We're standing in the claw machine tent, chatting over beer. I started to give the machine a try, but have been distracted by our conversation about relationships.

"You know what's so weird? Nobody's called me Bobby since high school."

          Alternate

"Do you mind it? I can call you Bob."

He laughs, holding my gaze for a beat longer than necessary again. "No," he says in a low voice. "I like it." His eyebrows raise in a sudden thought. "Hey—did anybody ever get anything out of the claw machine? It's been broken this whole time."

"Um, yeah, Hailey did."

Bobby looks interested. "What did she get? I can't ever tell what's in it."

The answer comes to me right away, and I know it to be true, even though it sounds nonsensical and I'm not sure how I know it.

"She got a chance to start the day over and have a different ending, and then she got a way to share a loving goodbye." My voice chokes a little on the end of the sentence, and Bobby reaches for my hand.

Next to us, on its own accord again, the claw machine fires up and drops something into the slot. We smile at each other.

"Come on," Bobby says. "Let's see what we got."

never on a monday

Curtis C. Chen (陳致宇)

By Curtis C. Chen (陳致宇)

Cady knew she wasn't going to like the new girl as soon as they met. It was a Tuesday, and New Girl was wearing an Aimee Mann t-shirt sporting the slogan "Voices Carry." *So* on the nose.

Not only that, but New Girl had the audacity to actually walk up to Cady at the start of lunch period, put out her hand like she was in a fucking business meeting, and introduce herself without even making eye contact first. What the shit?

"Hi! I'm Eva. I'm new here." New Girl was actually smiling. With *teeth*. How dare!

"No shit," Cady muttered, still avoiding eye contact.

New Girl's smile barely dimmed. "'No shit' to me being new here, or my name being Eva? Do I look like an Eva? I've never thought of that name as having a *look* before, but—"

"Ohmygodstoptalking." Cady turned and fixed New Girl with the same deadly glare that had withered many a freshman over the last two years of high school. Cady had been looking forward to a mostly harassment-free senior year, now that she'd found a place and locked in her respected-loner status. Didn't New Girl know the rules? "Why. Are you. Talking. To me?"

New Girl shrugged, still clearly oblivious to everything. Was this bitch from another planet or something?

"I saw you sitting all alone here under the tree and just thought you might like some company. Also, like I said, I'm new here. It's actually my first day, and I'm trying to meet people..."

Cady actively zoned out while New Girl droned on. True, Cady was sitting all by herself under the big oak tree in front of the school, but that was because she preferred being by herself, and nobody else had the cojones to wander that far out to the edge of school property during lunchtime. Principal Sethmillen had expelled students for less, but he knew Cady's mom would litigate his ass raw if he tried anything like that with Mrs. Kao's precious honors student.

"...so much for being Catholic, right?" New Girl's laugh—perhaps better described as a *cackle*—brought Cady back to the annoying here and now. "Anyway. I didn't catch your name."

"I didn't throw it," Cady responded reflexively, then clenched her jaw while kicking herself mentally. *Rookie mistake! Joking around implies that you want to continue the conversation! What the fuck, Cady!*

"You want me to guess?" New Girl said. "I'm good at guessing. What'll you give me if I guess right?"

Maybe this would be a quick and easy way to shut her down. "Nothing. I don't want you to guess."

"You're no fun. But you can't stop me. I'm going to guess anyway." New Girl lifted a finger to tap her lips—black nail polish, so millennial—and then pointed the finger at Cady. Rude. "I'm going to guess that your name is... Cady."

Cady's heart slammed against her ribcage. "What?"

"Yeah. Cady. Spelled C-A-D-Y. And not like Lindsay Lohan's character in *Mean Girls*, but like the astronaut Dr. Coleman." New Girl's smile suddenly seemed sinister. "Did I get it right?"

Okay. Cool trick, bro. You got me. Cady put a hand behind her, against the tree, and pushed herself up until her full-height five-ten frame towered over New Girl's dinky five-four at most. "You been spying on me, bitch?"

"No, Cady." New Girl wasn't blinking. Shit, had she blinked *at all* during this whole conversation? Wouldn't Cady have noticed that? "I don't want anything from you. But you might want something from me, later."

And then she turned and walked away before Cady could think of a clever retort.

On Wednesday, New Girl—Eva—was wearing an Addams Family t-shirt. Cady accosted her in the morning, next to the flagpole on the way into school.

"You." Cady grabbed Eva's left shoulder as she passed, halting her in her tracks. "I want to talk to you."

Eva smiled, without teeth this time, but that just made it feel more threatening. Because Cady already knew the teeth were there. "Sure, Cady. Lead the way."

Cady shoved Eva ahead of her toward the big oak tree. When they got there, Eva turned and leaned back against the tree, both hands hidden behind her waist. She was standing in the shade, but her eyes still seemed to glow.

"Will this take long?" Eva asked, her voice low and... purring? Cady shook her head, trying to shake off that adjective, but Eva apparently took it as a response. "Good. I don't want to be late to class on my second day. Still trying to make a good impression and—"

"I know all about you, Evangeline Rednats," Cady said, getting right in Eva's face and making sure she worked a little spit into her speech. Her sources had dug up some nice dirt on New Girl, and of course she also had a super weird last name. Childhood trauma much? "Sad-sack little witch wannabe whose daddy had to move her out of San Diego after a historic mission got torched during a field trip. No witnesses, but daddy dearest knows what's up, doesn't he?"

"Oh, that's impressive!" Eva actually *giggled*. What a loser. "You like games, Cady? I like playing games."

Why did Cady suddenly feel so warm? Why were Eva's eyes so big and dark? Why was she standing so close?

Eva's fingertips touched the side of Cady's face. "I would really like to play some games with you."

What the actual *fuck*. Cady put her hand against the tree, rough bark scraping her palm, and pushed hard, shoving herself backward, away from Eva, away from her face, that scent—what was that scent? Perfume, obviously, but—

"Stay the fuck away from me." Cady jabbed a finger toward Eva from a safe distance.

Eva grinned, baring her teeth, and suddenly there was no distance between them at all. "You don't want that, Cady."

"You don't know what I want, you fucking weirdo."

Eva shrugged. "Okay. But do *you* know what you want?"

Cady turned and walked away.

Mrs. Kao left town early Thursday morning to attend a conference on the East Coast. Cady drove herself to school, and at lunchtime, she found herself sitting behind the wheel of the Subaru in the parking lot. She didn't normally leave campus for lunch, but she had gotten a pass from the office this morning. Why waste the opportunity to get away for a little while?

While checking the map on her phone for a fast lunch place that wasn't horrible fast food, the passenger door opened, and Cady knew who it was even before she smelled Eva's weird perfume.

"Get out of my car," Cady said, staring forward.

Eva buckled her seat belt. "No."

Cady turned to look at Eva. Today she was wearing a black t-shirt with a white stylized bird logo that Cady didn't recognize. The bottom of the shirt was cut off, showing Eva's pale belly. She had a silver ring pierced through the lower part of her navel. And she was wearing tight blue jeans. Very tight blue jeans.

Cady focused on the bird logo. "What is that shirt?"

"It's a band. Thursday?"

"The band's name is Thursday? Literally just *Thursday*?"

"Yeah."

Cady shook her head. "So fucking lame."

"Hey, watch the ableist language." Eva poked Cady's shoulder with one finger, and Cady felt pressure and heat radiating through her whole body from that spot, making her feel uncomfortable in a way she wasn't familiar with. Not unpleasant, exactly, but... like she suddenly realized there was something missing. Something that she really wanted.

"I'm going off campus for lunch," Cady said, her mouth

suddenly dry. She swirled her tongue around to get some saliva going, then swallowed. Better. "Do you have a pass?"

Eva held up a slip of yellow paper. "I go where you go."

Slick Mick's wasn't technically a restaurant—it was a bowling alley with an arcade and a bar and nominal food service—but their menu offered a variety of deep-fried things and made them quickly, and it was only a five-minute drive away from the high school. Cady and Eva both ordered the chicken tenders combo, which came with fries and a soda (free drink refills) and sat across from each other with their fizzing icy cups while waiting for the food.

"So." Eva leaned forward, resting her elbows on the table. "You want to know about the mission fire?"

"No." Cady gulped down the Dr. Pepper and Orange Fanta she'd mixed together. It tasted like too much, too many flavors all together, but that was what she wanted. She didn't want to know. "Are you going to tell me anyway?"

Eva shook her head slowly, then sipped her own drink, and Cady forced herself to very much *not* intently study the way Eva's lips puckered around the straw. "I won't tell you anything that you don't want to know, Cady."

Their food arrived, and they ate in silence except for the noise of the arcade machines against the back wall. Cady focused on those boxy cabinets, which she'd never paid much attention to before. Some kind of old spaceship game. Some newer zombie shooting game. And one of those sucker-bet claw machines, filled with cheap trinkets that you could never actually get out because the mechanism was clearly rigged. Cady had fallen for it when she was younger—she figured every kid had to learn that the hard way—and she resented the fact that these scam-o-trons were still so ubiquitous.

"You like claw machines?" Eva asked, leaning forward again.

Cady shook her head. "Fucking bullshit. You can never actually win anything."

"Oh, I've gotten plenty of prizes out of claw machines!" Eva reached across the table and grabbed Cady's hand. Cady felt light-headed. "Come on. I'll show you how it's done."

Cady let Eva drag her over to the arcade section, then rested her forehead against the cool glass side of the claw machine while Eva got some tokens from the automated change maker. New Girl's jeans were *indecently* tight around that ass. And when she turned to look over her shoulder at Cady, her smile was—still sinister, wasn't it? It had to be sinister. It couldn't be anything good. This couldn't be happening like Cady thought it was.

She could hardly believe it when Eva pulled something out of the claw machine on her first try. New Girl finessed the joystick with the steely-eyed laser focus of a drone pilot targeting insurgents, and before she pressed the big red button to lower the claw, she lifted two fingers and ran them across her tongue.

"For luck," she said when she saw Cady watching, and Cady realized she was breathing hard. And she stopped that shit, because why would she be breathing hard right now it didn't make any sense.

Eva pushed her wet fingers down on the button, the claw dropped, and when it lifted up again, the mechanism whirring loudly, its three spindly talons were firmly closed around a Hello Kitty coin purse.

Cady pressed her cheek against the cold, sharp metal at one edge of the claw machine's glass enclosure, willing herself to not feel so warm. Had she eaten some bad chicken? It would serve her right, getting food poisoning at a fucking bowling alley. What was she even doing here?

Eva fished the purse out of the claw machine slot, standing up so fast that her breasts jiggled under her stupid bird t-shirt. Jesus Humperdinck Christ, was she even wearing a bra? That's not something Cady should be noticing. Stop it! Just stop it!

"Okay, useful, but weird design choice." Eva opened the zipper, which was at the top of Hello Kitty's disembodied head, and pulled out the crumpled paper stuffing from inside. "'Milady! I have beheaded Hello Kitty that we may now use her taxidermized skull to store our treasures!' And people wonder why kids are fucked up."

Cady watched the crumpled paper flutter to the floor. It looked like—not newspaper, but it wasn't blank, either. She bent down to pick it up. There was definitely some kind of marking on it. Cady uncrumpled the paper, flattening it against the side of the claw machine glass, expecting to see some kind of lot number or slogan from the printing company or maybe an ad for more Sanrio crap.

The rough, beige-colored paper was blank except for some thick black letters and one number:

CADY4EVA

Cady felt like the back of her neck was on fire. She turned to look at Eva, who was just standing there, holding the Hello Kitty purse with both hands in front of her exposed belly, smiling at Cady.

"Oops," Eva said. "How did that happen?"

Cady threw the paper on the floor—or tried to, it didn't fly very well, just kind of flopped around and settled—and stepped over to Eva, stopping before she got too close, she didn't want to smell too much of that perfume again, that strange scent, those bottomless eyes—

"Who the fuck are you? Why are you stalking me?"

"Whoa, Nelly," Eva said, remaining motionless except for those wet lips and those big eyes. "Stalking? That's a real strong accusation there, Cady. That's like a legal term and shit. Are you sure you want to accuse me of such a serious offense? When all I've done is win a prize for you?"

"I don't want a stupid fucking cat-head purse."

"Well, what *do* you want, Cady?" Eva stepped forward, her knuckles touching Cady's jeans just below the waistline, pressing into her in a place that nobody but Cady had ever touched before. "What do you *really* want out of this one and only life you've been given?"

Cady blinked and stumbled backward, her elbows clanging against the claw machine. "Get away from me. I definitely don't want any part of whatever insane religious evangelical cult you're pushing."

"That's not what I'm offering, Cady." Eva walked forward again, before Cady could collect herself enough to slide away to the side, and put her hands against the glass on either side of Cady's face. "Here. I'm gifting these remaining tokens to you. I'll walk back to school. You try out this machine for yourself, then drive back when you're done. Plenty of time left before lunch period ends."

She pressed the purse into Cady's hand, tokens clinking inside, and turned and walked away. Her jeans were probably still very tight, but Cady wasn't looking anymore—she was astounded that she finally recognized the unusual smell lingering around her head. She expected perfume to be somewhat floral, but no.

It was waffles. Fucking *waffles*. Who the fuck wore waffle-scented perfume? Where the fuck did Eva even get it? Did *Great British Bake Off* have a merch store hawking this shit? Why would anyone want to smell like a breakfast pastry?

It was just so aggressively *weird*.

Cady couldn't get the scent out of her head for the rest of the day.

Eva wasn't at school on Friday. Cady asked around, but apparently New Girl hadn't bothered to attempt interacting with any students other than Cady that week. It seemed like Eva had barely made an impression. Like maybe Cady had imagined her or something.

But Cady knew she hadn't. She hadn't imagined those stupid t-shirts. Those big dark eyes. The way Eva's fingers had felt when they touched Cady's face, the way her body had—

And the smell of waffles. Fucking *waffles*, for fuck's sake. So fucking weird, and stupid, and *foolish* and *risible* and *contemptible*

      Never on a Monday

and as many other pejoratives as she could think of during all her morning classes. Thanks for the synonyms, Kumon. Super helpful in real life.

Cady drove back to Slick Mick's at lunchtime. She hadn't spent any of the tokens in the Hello Kitty purse yesterday; it had taken her nearly ten minutes to calm down after Eva walked out of the arcade on Thursday, hiding in the bathroom and staring at herself in the cracked mirror above the dented metal sink and telling her ugly reflection that she was an idiotic teenager for feeling any of those feelings, why was she so broken and hormonal and animal-istic. Why couldn't she just be the obedient honors student who was shipping out to Princeton next year, why couldn't she forget all of these other moronic adolescent distractions, didn't she want to make her mother happy, didn't she want to make the spirit of her dead father and all his countless ancestors proud of her?

Yeah, sure, Cady wanted all of that. She had to say out loud that's what she wanted. That's what she was supposed to want.

But maybe she also wanted to be happy. Maybe, just once in a while, to be happy with herself.

If only she could know who she actually was.

Cady had to admit that she hadn't really paid much attention to the claw machine itself the previous day. She'd been consumed by watching Eva, watching how she moved, what she did, trying to see into New Girl's soul and figure out who this person was that had bewitched Cady so thoroughly with just a few words. Because Cady wasn't a person who got horny just from *looking*. She was demi, "an individual who does not experience primary sexual attraction." She knew that. She'd known that since last year, when Aaron Liu had showed off his summer-camp-acquired abs and most of the girls and some of the boys in AP English had swooned and Cady had felt absolutely nothing. She needed some kind of mental connection; she wasn't turned on by purely phys-ical or even sensory stuff.

Except... Cady had never smelled anything quite like Eva's perfume before. Never in her life. It wasn't actually the scent of real waffles, it was a heightened, jacked-up chemical version of whatever was in the actual food, cruelly designed to assault your senses and make you *think* of waffles. It wasn't real. It was all a trick.

This was all Eva's fault, obviously. Cady couldn't be blamed for not being prepared to react properly to some rando who was horny for her for unknown creeper reasons. Cady had repelled a few crushes early on in her high school career, losers looking to rise in the social ranks once they realized she was going places, and the underclassmen knew to steer clear these days.

But New Girl didn't know the rules. Or she just didn't care.

What game was Eva playing?

The interior of the claw machine was filled with a variety of different prizes, all roughly the same size and shape as the Hello Kitty coin purse. There were some spherical Angry Birds plushies, some Pokémon branded palm-sized beach balls—obvious lures, you were supposed to think they were light and easy to lift, but they'd turn out to be too slippery for the claw to hold onto—and merch from several other animes that Cady didn't immediately recognize. There was too much of that stuff for her to keep up with these days.

She had been into Hello Kitty, of course, when she was younger. What little Asian girl wasn't? That wouldn't have been a difficult cold read for Eva. And the writing on the paper—simple sleight of hand, Eva could have done that while Cady was distracted by New Girl's stupid tight jeans. It wasn't much to write, she could have hidden a Sharpie... somewhere on her person...

And then Cady saw it, half-hidden behind an orange My Little Pony plushie with wings. It didn't even make sense. Why would someone design and make something like this, for any purpose? But there it was, a real physical object inside the claw machine: a brick-like plushie made to look like one of those rectangular green street signs with a flat fin-like bit on top and a white border and white block lettering. Only the back part of it was visible above the ass end of the MLP, three letters: **AVE**.

E-V-A backwards.

          Never on a Monday

There were four tokens left in the Hello Kitty coin purse. The first two were burners; Cady could tell that she'd have to move that stupid pony out of the way if she were to have any chance of extracting that street sign plushie.

When her second clawing shifted the pony forward, she saw more of the lettering on the sign: ...**DER AVE**.

It hit her as she was putting in the third token. Eva's last name was Rednats. Reverse those letters and you'd have D-E-R at the end.

Cady's palms started sweating when the machine activated again, lights and sounds trying to distract her from her task. But other things were more distracting right now.

Then she remembered Eva's signature move.

Cady lifted two trembling fingers to her mouth, extended her tongue, and licked her fingertips. *For luck.* Her skin tasted salty, and she did her best to not think about the last few things she'd touched just now.

She maneuvered the claw into position and pressed those two wet fingers down on the big red button.

The claw dropped.

The talons clacked open around the street sign plushie.

The claw lifted, whirring loudly.

The street sign plushie came up with it, out of the mass of cheap manufactured junk, into the open air where Cady could see all the letters stitched into it: **STANDER AVE**.

"Eva Rednats" spelled backwards, exactly.

Cady felt dizzy. She started putting out a hand to steady herself against the claw machine, then realized *No! I don't want to knock the thing out of the claw!* and shifted her weight away. She released both hands and stumbled backward into the nearest table, clutched it with both hands, and held on tight, hoping she wasn't going to throw up.

It felt like an eternity before the claw whirred over to the dispensing ramp, swaying shakily the whole way, then opened, and finally released the street sign plushie to gravity.

It hit the ramp with a soft thud and tumbled down to the open slot at the bottom of the machine.

Cady fell to her knees, scrambled forward, and grabbed the street sign plushie out of the machine with both hands. She sat on the floor and turned the plushie over once, twice, three times, checking to see if the lettering was the same on both sides.

It was. **STANDER AVE**.

"Where the fuck is Stander Avenue?" Cady muttered.

The map on her phone said that the nearest Stander Avenue was three freeway exits away. Cady briefly debated waiting until after school to investigate, but then decided fuck it. She was a senior. She'd already gotten into college. What the fuck was Principal Sethmillen going to do—write a strongly worded letter to the Dean of Princeton that would get Cady un-admitted?

Sure, she might catch hell from her mother next week for ditching, but it was a Friday fucking afternoon. Cady had never even missed a day of school for being sick, not since she was ten years old. Cady had snuck out to go see *Rocky Horror* with her friends in sixth grade and Mrs. Kao still hadn't found out. Cady could handle her mom.

Stander Avenue was a cul-de-sac in a subdivision with nearly identical houses for several blocks around. Cady would totally have gotten lost if her phone map hadn't shown her the way. When she reached the dead end, there was one house that stood out from all the rest.

Every single McMansion on the way in had been painted some innocuous shade of off-white or light gray, with an occasional splash of muted accent color on a door here and there. But the house in the dead center of the cul-de-sac was made to be seen, with bright orange-red walls and brilliant white trim and a sky-blue front door.

Cady pulled into the driveway—once again, *fuck it*—and sat there for a moment after turning the car off, staring at the mural covering the entire garage door. It used the same orange-red and sky-blue and white color palette as the rest of the house, but here were some crude but recognizable images: a black-lined red disk of a sun bordered in triangular rays, centered inside a blue sky with blotchy white clouds, and the sky was seen through a heart-shaped window in the middle of a field of orange-red, surrounded by other abstract shapes drawn in thick, wobbly black lines.

It all seemed very familiar, as if it were meant to evoke some specific artwork, but Cady had no idea what that might be. She wasn't into modern art shit.

She wasn't sure she had ever felt her heart beat as fast as it did while she walked up to the front door. Not even when she had run away from that awful first date with Brendan Kim, when he tried to feel her up in the car *on the way to the restaurant*. That guy was a fucking asshole.

The only time Cady could remember herself ever coming close to being this tachycardic was when she had gotten her admissions email from Princeton, for those endless minutes of waiting while her mother figured out how to record a video on her phone so they could preserve the moment forever. It was the same fear, the same uncertainty, of not knowing whether it was going to be very good news or very bad news, just knowing that it was going to be extreme one way or the other. And fearing that it was going to be the worst day of her life so far. And not knowing what that actually meant.

Cady put her hand flat on the front door. It was metal, cool to the touch. Cool like the glass of the claw machine. Cool like the icy soda that she'd been drinking, sitting across from Eva yesterday.

What did she want?

Cady made a fist and rapped the sky-blue front door with her bare knuckles, then stepped backward, suddenly afraid she might have the wrong house. But then she didn't move. She couldn't move.

After a moment, the door swung open, and the very first thing

Cady noticed wasn't Eva's t-shirt—today it was a black-and-white screen print of some kind of emo boy—it was the overwhelming scent of waffles, flowing out from inside the house. Warm dough, caramelized sugar, sweet maple syrup. Plus a hint of something bitter and smoky, maybe coffee?

Cady couldn't see inside the colorful house. It was a sunny day, and the light was behind her, and Eva was framed in the dark open doorway.

"You found me," Eva said, beaming.

Cady pointed at Eva's shirt. "Who the fuck is that?"

"Robert Smith. The Cure?"

Of course. On the fucking nose again. And of course, that was what the house reminded her of.

"Your parents big fans?" Cady gestured back toward the garage. "That's the album cover, isn't it? *Friday I'm in Love?*"

Eva chuckled, teeth glowing, and now they looked like a row of promises. "You wanna come in? We're making pancakes."

Cady had a million questions, but what she said was, "I thought they were waffles."

Eva shook her head. "Nope. Pancakes."

Cady stepped forward onto the porch again. "Whatever. And yeah, I do want some."

Eva stretched out her hand. "You can have whatever you want, Cady."

Cady took Eva's hand and believed it.

horizons

Sarah Walker

"What's that?" Amir pointed.

"Where?" I asked.

"There." He jammed his finger towards a bank of defunct video games and broken coin operated massage chairs. Behind where the shadows met, construction workers had what looked like the world's worst arcade.

I didn't see anything. Just darkness and shadowed machines, the tiled floor, and an empty mall.

"Where?" I repeated.

Amir grunted in frustration. I liked Amir. As my supervisor, he'd been one of my better bosses. From Syria he'd started his security by living through a war. He'd been injured by a bomb and as a result walked with a limp, his left leg permanently damaged. He moved in his slightly off kilter manner towards the storage area.

"Don't you see that? In that claw machine, over there!"

"Amir, I still don't see what..." I scratched at the cast I'd been fitted with after breaking my right ulna a week ago. Goddamned, the thing itched.

Amir, annoyed, walked back to me, grabbed my hand, and physically pulled me through the maze of broken machines.

"Look! There!"

What the hell? Inside the glass, a wallet sat perfectly in the center of the claw machine's now empty prize tank.

"Isn't that the one your wife got you?" he asked, voice low.

Goddamn it, Amir!

"Ha-ha, very funny." I rolled my eyes in irritation.

This security job had been unbelievably boring, and pranks were one of the only ways we could pass the hours. For eight hours each night, we walked up and down the soon to be demolished mall.

A Sisyphean task, we were supposed to look for vagrants,

criminals, and thieves when all the empty shopping malls had inside were dead dreams, plastic wrappers, and dust.

Joking had been the only way to try to break the doldrums the first few weeks, but of late Amir was doing it all the time now and the pranks were getting tedious as it became more obvious the job wasn't going to pick up.

I searched his face for his normal 'ah you got me' look that usually accompanied these sorts of workplace shenanigans, but there was no joyful Puckish glint in his eye this time.

Instead, he looked confused, maybe even a little worried.

He put his hands up and shook his head, raising his eyebrows for emphasis.

"I didn't do it, I swear."

"Seriously?"

He shook his head. "Seriously."

"Okay… whatever. But can I at least have your key to get it out?"

Amir shook his head.

"What do you 'no'?"

"Because I don't have a key."

I raised my eyebrows in surprise. "Really?"

Amir nodded. "Yup. Why would I have one? Does Smolski give you keys to all these machines? Because he sure as fuck didn't do that for me."

I frowned. He was right. As construction security, we only had keys to all the big doors to the empty mall, but the individual shops, games, and kiosks, those we did not.

A few seconds passed.

Somewhere in the bowels of the place, something shifted.

It was a small noise, but maybe that's why my arms broke out in gooseflesh.

"You hear that?" I listened, but the noise didn't repeat. Amir wasn't even paying attention, though. Instead, he was running his hand down the glass in front of the claw machine, staring at my wallet.

"Amir, come on. You really didn't put it in there?"

Amir shook his head and smacked the glass. "No! How'd I put it in there without keys, Einstein?"

"Okay! Jesus. Let's just get it out."

It was much harder to get out of the claw machine than we'd anticipated, and I was beginning to think I'd have to leave it until I came back later for tomorrow's 10 o'clock shift and could get the key from whoever had one. But finally, Amir managed to pull it through a small slot on the front with a bent wire. This was where a prize was dropped if you could pick it up with the claw, though I knew no one ever won the damned things.

"Here it is," he said, as he carefully took the wallet from the wire and pulled it into his hand.

He violently threw it at me, hitting me in the face. It fell to the floor near my feet.

"Dude! Fuck, man," I grumbled, rubbing my cheekbone where it'd smacked me.

Amir had a shocked look on his face.

After a moment, he spoke. "Uh… sorry."

"It's alright," I waved it off and reached down to pick up the wallet, when I too involuntarily jerked my hand back.

"What?" Amir asked, dark eyes excited and black in the ambient low light of the closed mall.

I didn't want to say. "I don't know."

"What do you mean 'you don't know?'" Amir asked.

"I…. I don't know how to explain," I finally said, embarrassed.

"Try words," Amir said, annoyed.

"Well. It was. I don't know. It was just… well, it was cold."

Amir raised his eyebrows and opened his hands for emphasis. "Yes! I felt that too. See?"

"Too cold."

"Yes!"

Emboldened by Amir's agreement, I continued. "Like it's been put in ice."

I reached out a second time, touched it, picked it up, because now, it felt like it *should*.

If you were to ask me what that meant, how a wallet is *supposed* to feel, I wouldn't be able to say.

But whatever was wrong with it was gone. At least that's what I initially thought.

Despite that, I suddenly wanted to just throw it away.

Badly.

It felt dirty somehow now, though it looked perfectly fine.

This was obviously stupid. Monogrammed on the inside, a gift from my wife, she would be very hurt if I lost it.

I looked at the place where the players would try to drop their prizes. Who had put it in there?

I didn't think more than of the wallet and how it'd felt at first. I wish I had. But perhaps it wouldn't have made much of a difference.

I apologized. "Sorry."

"For what?"

"For thinking you were pulling a prank. You gotta admit you do that a lot."

He nodded and shrugged. "I get it."

We were both silent for a moment.

"Okay, so you didn't do it. Who the hell coulda' put it in there?"

"That's my fuckin' point, Alan. I don't know. Unless it was Smolski."

We both knew that was impossible. We'd seen him leave in his truck hours before. The closed mall had one un-barricaded entrance, and we knew it was locked. A motion detecting light would trip as soon as the door was opened. And the man had never pulled a prank before.

"Well, I guess it doesn't matter. Let's get going. We need to finish the last round before the shift ends."

I slid the wallet into my back pocket, where it bulged uncomfortably. I shivered unconsciously as I thought about it touching me through my pants. I kept thinking of the leather, how it'd not just been cold, but how it had felt *changed.*

But I said nothing to Amir. I just kept quiet and tried to position myself to minimize contact with the wallet.

The motion detecting light came on.

Smolski had arrived at the main door of the mall with the daytime crew to begin to tear the old place down once they'd moved out the last merchandise and equipment.

I looked at my watch.

6 am.

"Thank God!" Amir said, and I grunted an assent.

I just wanted to leave. Beer sounded good. I think even then I was afraid, sensing something preternatural, sensing its gravity there—invisible, but as present as either of us, drawing us in.

"Wanna get a beer?"

Amir nodded.

We both thought that would be the end of it.

But it was just the first time.

Two days later, we were at the claw machine again.

"You seeing this, right?" Amir whispered.

I nodded. "Yup."

A wig lay in the center of the glass box. Brown and slightly curled, visibly molded in some parts, but still obvious what it was.

"What the fuck! I don't want to touch it."

"Neither do I. Just leave it. Let's check the cameras again."

Finding nothing odd on any of the CCTV cameras, just like the times before, we circled back to the machine.

With some relief, I saw that the wig was gone—at least for a time.

Back in the break room, eating our respective lunches, we tried to make small talk to avoid talking about the weirdness. I had theories, but could I manage the probable ridicule of my coworker?

"When is Smolski coming back?" Amir asked around a mouthful of PB and J.

The black coffee I was sipping was too hot, so I put it back down to answer his question. "I think the day after tomorrow."

Amir nodded and took a swig of some energy drink. I could barely manage the coffee with my nerves.

"I checked the tapes again," he said.

"Did you see anyone?"

Amir shook his head emphatically. "No, I didn't."

I titled my head. "Seriously? This is just...."

Amir nodded. "Well, it's true. I can't see for shit on these crappy cameras. So, I was thinking I could try angling them towards the machine better."

"Yes, let's try that. Maybe it won't happen again."

"You know, it's almost like those things are just appearing in the damn thing."

I said nothing back.

A day later, the wig returned.

In the break room, I pushed the button on the big stainless steel 1970s coffeemaker, but nothing came out. I picked it up and felt the weight of the liquid sloshing inside but also something with a solid mass shifting.

"What's wrong?" Amir asked as he stood up from the break room table.

"It's plugged in, but..."

"Here." Amir grabbed it, set it down, and opened the main tank where the coffee was stored.

A full minute passed before he spoke, and when I saw what blocked the valve, neither of us spoke.

When the silence stretched into a few minutes, I realized Amir was angry.

"So that was disturbing."

"Are you doing this, Alan?" he asked, eying me suspiciously.

"No! What? Jesus, why would I…"
Amir gave me a dark look.
"To what? Get back at you?"
Amir nodded.
"Look… I keep thinking this is your joke, man. "
"Well, someone is doing it." He slapped the drenched hair-piece into the sink.
"Or something," I whispered so low he didn't hear.

Friday found us back near the damned thing. We were standing too far away to actually see the claw machine, as if by some unspoken agreement. It would be better to stand here like cowards instead of seeing something else inside.

Some security guards.

My face got hot when I realized this.

I needed to act. It wasn't like the machine was…

What? Possessed? Haunted?

That thought really annoyed me, which gave me the motivation to look.

"I'm going."

I walked forward, but Amir grabbed my shoulder. I looked back at him.

"What?"

He looked at me, eyes hidden by the shadow of his security guard hat. I had a sudden overwhelming sense of déjà vu.

Amir said, "I'll come too."

I nodded.

He stopped me again. "This is real, right?"

I nodded. "It's happening somehow, Amir."

"There's weird stuff in the world, man."

"What, ghosts?"

"No, blackholes—miniature ones—or other dimensions that could make stuff like this happen."

I stared at him. This was getting ridiculous. I was determined to stop this shit.

"Stop it." I said.

Amir looked embarrassed and turned away. A moment later, he was all business, realizing I wasn't interested in his theories. I just wanted to get in and out as fast as we could.

"Come on."

Of course there was something in the machine again.

"You see that..." Amir said softly.

"Yeah," I said in a whisper.

A possum we both recognized by its missing ear and shortened tail—a regular scavenger at the dumpster nearby. Standing off kilter, it looked out of the glass paneling with beady black eyes. At first, I didn't notice, but soon, I saw the possum had changed. It was the legs. Was it laying on another possum?

It moved, and I jumped back in surprise. It wasn't another possum. The thing had too many legs.

Six of them.

We didn't know what to do. Maybe if we could get it out, we could direct it to an exit?

That plan was better than no plan.

We made a rudimentary net, but when we came back, we discovered that the machine was empty. And then saw to our horror, the possum was loose.

Somehow, it'd escaped the claw machine. And it was unbelievably fast.

The bizarreness of the situation was overshadowed by the desire we both had to get the damned thing away from us.

We chased it around until we thought to try opening the door.

It seemed to understand and ran out into a cool autumn night. I felt shivers up my back as I watched it scurry, moving as fast as a man in full flight.

Maybe that would be the end of it.

But of course, it wasn't.

Yes, even then, its gravity was too intense for us to escape.

The next shift was the end of the work week, and I was counting the seconds until I could leave. All night, by unspoken consent, we'd avoided the area where the machine sat, and as a result, the shift had gone by so far without incident.

But that didn't improve my mood in the least.

When I'd gotten home the night before, I'd been trying to find a change for a tip for the delivery guy when I noticed that the wallet was different. I hadn't much wanted to keep it, but I didn't have a choice, and I didn't have a good reason to throw it away so my wife would understand.

But then I noticed something it had taken days for me to notice.

My monogrammed initials on the inside of the handmade leather: *DAA*

My name is Alan Andrew Davis.

The initials were reversed.

I couldn't believe it. I touched the slightly raised dark blue sewn letters one by one, trying to reason it out.

Had it been like that all along, and I just didn't notice?

A gift from my wife or not, I took it, put it in a shoebox, duct taped the outside shut, and shoved it deep into the crawlspace at the other end of the apartment.

Hopefully, my wife would never find it, and it would be as far away from me as I could get it without actually throwing it away.

I managed to make it through the shift without seeing anything else appear in the machine.

"Maybe it won't happen anymore," I said to Amir as we left for the weekend.

"It hasn't stopped."

I looked at him incredulously.

"What do you mean 'it hasn't stopped'? Did something appear in the damned thing again, and you didn't tell me?"

Amir shook his head. "No. I just think whatever was making those things appear can now make them appear outside of the machine. "

I thought about the possum.

I wanted a drink.

"Beer?" I asked Amir.

"Yup."

The weekend went by quickly, but not without its own weirdness.

On Saturday, as I walked through the local park, I saw the six-legged possum. A burning feeling of reality spinning away hit me full on, and I almost vomited. I turned away, hands on my knees, shaking like in withdrawal, only managing to regain my composure after a minute. My arm was aching a little from the pressure, making the skin under my cast itch again.

It was gone when I looked back.

I walked to the nearest bar. And I drank.

By Monday night, I didn't want to go back to work. But no work, no money. No money, no rent. No rent, no house, and ending up on the street.

I sat in my car outside the mall in a gathering dark thinking—knowing—I was stalling.

It was already 10:10 pm.

And I was ten minutes late. 10-10-10.

Are 'threes' of things bad luck or good? I wondered.

I could not live like this.

That did it. I would start looking for a new job as soon as I got home. Whatever was going on here, I didn't care. I just wanted things to be normal again.

Maybe they will be. No explanation for the appearances. Maybe they'll just go away in the same unexplained way?

Just hold out a little longer and then quit, I advised myself. I got out of the car and locked the door. Amir's truck was parked closer to the entrance, on time as usual.

I entered the mall and headed to the break room to clock in.

I knew I was easily 15 minutes late, so I apologized as I walked in. "Sorry I'm late, Am—" I stopped talking when I saw my coworker was not here.

Why it bothered me, I wasn't sure. He often wasn't there when I arrived, off checking something or taking care of paperwork. But tonight, when he didn't appear, I got a feeling of foreboding.

I looked for him at first without really looking, slowly walking up and down the aisles expecting him to appear. But when I found no Amir and saw only unlit storefronts, mannequins piled in the corner, and dust everywhere, a sense of urgency began to grow in me.

The real fear was coming from the thought of looking for Amir by the claw machine. So I searched everywhere I could, but eventually, I ran out of non-claw machine places.

Now I stood near the storage area. With dread, I began to walk in that direction, footsteps clicking much too loudly.

I came round the corner and saw the machine. Or rather, didn't.

I sucked in a sharp breath. The main part of the tank where the prizes would go looked like it had been smeared with a black pen. Nearby, the air seemed to be moving, almost bending, reminding me of how the air just above hot asphalt shimmers in a city's daylight August heat.

I kept trying to aim my flashlight at it, but no matter how I angled it, I couldn't seem to actually get the flashlight to show the whole machine. The light kept bending away from it.

"What the fuck…" I whispered, and everything went dark.

I woke up on the floor. I could hear footsteps. I looked and saw Amir was here and rushing to my aid from some other area in the mall.

"Dude! You alright?" he asked as he arrived. There was concern in his voice as he squatted down.

"What happened?"

I opened my mouth, but then shut it when I realized I didn't want to say what had happened.

Something had changed with Amir.

Yes, he looked like Amir. I'd worked with the man for so many years, I knew him better than my own family, in some ways. It's not like I wouldn't have remembered he had a bald spot in the center of his brown head. But now, he did.

I rubbed my eyes.

"I said, 'what happened?'" Amir reiterated. "Are you hurt? I need to know if I need to make a report or not."

I managed to sit up. "Oh, no, no. Not at all. "

"You wanna stand?"

"I think so…" I took his offered hand and stood shakily.

"You've got a little—" He reached to brush my shoulder off.

I recoiled away involuntarily, but not before he noticed.

Amir's face grew red.

"Yeah, I know. I can't find my hairpiece," he said.

For some reason, horror began spidering up my back. It shocked me that I was not aware the man wore a hairpiece. It seemed an odd thing for him to never mention, for me to never have noticed.

I tried to think back. My thoughts were blurry. Hadn't there been a hairpiece…

The coffee pot!

How could I have missed it? Did he have a second hairpiece? I was certain he'd had hair when we fished it out.

Had this all just been a practical joke, after all?

I couldn't think straight. I remembered the beam of the flashlight bending away, the air moving.

"If you're okay, let's get back to it." He motioned me to follow.

"Come on. We've got a ton of stuff to check before the end of the shift."

I turned and looked at the claw machine.

It was watching—waiting for some secret signal or change in the environment to become whatever it had become again.

Amir had turned away. He began walking faster than usual, probably trying to get the work done and go home sooner than later.

My head spinning, I sped after him. I also didn't want to be here. I wouldn't come back to this job ever again.

I started pleading with God to spare me more insanity at the mall. I'd sleep on my mom's couch. I'd pick up cans and turn them in. I'd walk people's dogs.

I was so caught up in desperation that I didn't notice his limp had also changed.

Amir was now limping on his right leg.

Then my left arm itched, and I looked down.

I felt a scream rise to my throat.

cursed things

J.B. Kish

First, Chad Adler sold himself. At two-minutes old, he charmed a birthing suit full of nurses with a kind of cooing smile that no one his age ought to be capable of. Each commented on how talented the child was, how special, how he was most certainly one to watch, yes. Chad was only warming up. As a toddler, he studied the art of selling among adults as if it were a mobile of stars: our dollars for your groceries. My handshake for your trust. You give me this, I give you that. No matter where he went, people were always selling something. He wanted to better understand.

In Kindergarten, Chad attempted his first sale. He gave his lunch to another child in exchange for the girl's Barbie doll—it worked! Chad tried again the next day for a pop-up copy of *Three Little Pigs*. It worked a second time. In fact, it worked so often that Chad's mother finally called the administration to ask why their pre-school found it acceptable to give children toys at lunch instead of food.

Chad didn't want the toys. He simply marveled at the process of taking them away from others. He placed each in a row on his bedroom floor and puzzled over how they once belonged to someone else. Now he could do whatever he wanted with them.

At the age of nine, Chad made six-hundred dollars selling concentrate lemonade on the corner of his street. At fourteen, he doubled that in magazine subscriptions, and at eighteen years old, Chad set a local record for most Christmas trees sold on Christmas.

Not for Christmas.

On Christmas.

Forty trees bound for the landfill, redirected into the living rooms of men and women who—upon second thought—agreed with the young salesman's logic. (Something about second chances and holding the holiday magic close. No one could really remember a week later when the tree sat on their curb).

Chad began to wonder if there was anything he couldn't sell. The idea took root like a gnarled, red finger pushed deep into his brain, poking at his matter. So, the day after high school graduation, Chad strolled into a used car dealership and sold himself all over again.

"I'm not hiring salesmen," said a bulldog-shaped man with a 'Manager' name tag.

"Give me until five o'clock to show you what I can do."

"No."

"Four o'clock."

"Out."

"The worst vehicle on your lot," Chad finally said. "Sold by four o'clock or you'll never see me again."

That raised the manager's eyebrow; he glanced at the clock. He'd already bought what Chad was selling, the man just didn't know it yet.

At exactly five PM that afternoon, Chad walked off the lot with his new hire paperwork and two-hundred dollars in commission from the sale of a 1989 Chevy Corsica with 150,000 miles and no back window.

The thing about selling was that any asshole could do it. Chad just had a knack for it.

—No, that wasn't exactly right. *Knack* didn't quite excuse Chad's singular interest in the activity. It was closer to a craving. Chad woke up each morning with a painful and wringing desire to approach someone he'd never met before. He had to convince them life could be better; they had to know Chad possessed the thing that could make it so. He often struggled to walk down the street because the pang in his gut was so powerful that he grew lightheaded, and it wouldn't stop until he sold something. He yearned to make deals that favored his station. Ones that advanced him forward in life, if even in a menial way. Really, he had to sell something so that the hunger couldn't take hold of him.

It wasn't long before he was car salesmen of the month, but it was even less time before the shine of that achievement wore off.

Not for the first time, Chad found himself unsatiated. Magazines and lemonade had paid his allowance easily enough, but Chad hoped his sales commissions at the dealership would bring in the kind of money that finally calmed the feeling in his stomach. But it didn't. Chad needed to sell something more valuable if he was going to scratch this itch.

Chad quit his job and started buying defaulted storage units. He got the idea from a popular show on television. The pressure was ingenious. He only had a couple moments to scan the contents of each unit, so he had to be quick-witted. He quietly loved driving up the bids, forcing others to push themselves to the brink of their savings before finally out bidding them by a few dollars. Or maybe he'd let them take it last second and then watch as the life drained from their eyes, knowing that they'd never see a return on that investment.

Each unit promised the opportunity to find something uniquely valuable. Spotting that rare baseball card was an adrenalin rush, but selling it for six figures was an ecstasy unlike anything he'd experienced. Records, stamps, sports memorabilia: these things swam through his mind as he slept each night.

Sadly, the rush was fleeting. The craving only deepened. No matter the dollar amount, Chad's drive was only satisfied a few days before an inexplicable sorrow set in. What would it take, he wondered, to finally be happy? How much money must he make on a sale?

He found temporary relief in blind auctions, when facilities need to move storage units quickly, and so people bid without knowing what was inside. It was an extra layer of challenge that provided a bump of dopamine. The scarcity in these units put him in the position of finding new ways to sell junk for more than it was worth. It was novel, but ultimately boring.

Then came the blind auction down in Baker City, when everything changed. Chad spent most of the day sulking in the background, not bidding on anything. It was nearly the end of the day before he finally raised his hand for a unit, and he got into a bidding war with a woman who clearly needed this more than he.

He was so depressed that he barely enjoyed the look on her face as she realized it was a losing battle. After *once, twice,* the unit was *Sold to Chad Adler, the gentleman in the black hoodie!*

The crowd moved on, but Chad didn't follow. He waited until no one remained and removed the clipped bolt from the lock. With a grunt, he pulled the door up and felt the storage unit take in a lungful of air.

It took a moment for his eyes to adjust. Chad stepped into the dark. The unit was empty, save for a towering, rectangular object in the middle of the space. It was nearly six feet tall and covered in a starched-white tarp, which he ripped off with a flourish. When his eyes finally understood what they were looking at— what they'd just purchased—Chad pulled in his chin and barked with laughter. It was a 90s era claw machine, still harboring a few stuffed animals by the look of it. Chad had never sold anything like this before in his life, and he delighted in the fact that he had no immediate connections to anyone who might consider taking it off his hands. This was exactly the kind of distraction he needed. A novel challenge. A temporary boost while he figured out what to sell next.

Chad stood outside his garage, impatiently waiting for a collector named Amir. Amir was fifteen minutes late. When he finally arrived, the man was younger than Chad expected, with a slow walk and plain addiction to his phone. Chad opened the garage door and looped a smile over each ear. He'd turned the machine on already; *'The Claw!'* shone out in bright, bold letters across the front of the cabinet, beckoning them inside with faint, hollow laughter from its speakers. A rusted, metallic claw dangled over a pit of stuffed animals menacingly.

There was a feeling in Chad's stomach like he too was being clawed at, but he pushed it aside while listing out the various features of the machine. Amir nodded his head, despite not looking up from his text messages.

   Cursed Things

"So," Chad finally said. "What do you think?"

"Huh? Oh, it's nice." Amir sounded like he was a child describing his least favorite sibling. *She's nice, I guess.*

Chad's pulse thrummed along his carotid like a piano wire. "You'll take it?"

Eventually, Amir lowered his phone. He leisurely walked around the machine. He crouched over and poked the small metal flap where players can claim a prize. "No. I'm not in the market for something like this."

Chad set his jaw. It took everything he had to maintain a wide, toothy smile. "That's funny. When we emailed, you said this was exactly the kind of machine you were looking for. I even sent detailed photos."

"Sure." Amir was texting again. "Now that I'm here, it's just not doing it for me."

Chad wanted to strangle the boy.

It had been three months. Three devastating months of this exact conversation, no matter where Chad took the machine. One buyer after another declined his sale, and each 'no, *thank you*' felt like a pike being driven through his chest. Chad could sell anything in the world; he knew he was destined to move big, impossible things: airline jets, skyscrapers, presidencies. Chad could sell anything to anyone. But for some inexplicable reason, he couldn't sell *this*.

An oversized children's toy. An assembly of scrap metal and rudimentary mechanisms. Chad had made more money selling lemonade as a child. The longer this machine sat in the garage, the more he grew to hate it. In fact, he loathed it. He told himself it wasn't him. It was the machine's fault. The very sight of it seemed to turn people obtuse.

As Amir got in his car and left, the claw machine's laughter seemed to turn on Chad. He couldn't help but think it was enjoying this.

A horrible, metallic *clunk* lurched Chad from his spot on the floor. Two massive doors opened, splashing sunlight on his face for the first time in hours.

"We're here," said a large man with thick forearms. He pulled a loading ramp from the back of his semi-truck, then turned and said, "I'm stepping inside for a coffee. When I get back, I'd like you to be gone."

Shielding his eyes from the sun, Chad nodded weakly. "Can you help me with this?"

The truck driver smirked through his nose and walked off. Funny. He was happy to take the last of Chad's money back in Portland—he was driving out to the coast anyway—but now that they'd arrived, the trucker wanted nothing to do with his new stowaway. Chad painfully crawled to his knees and began unstrapping the large, dirty claw machine from its anchor points. With each click of the ratchet, he could feel the machine pulsing outward toward him, as if exhaling a lungful of air along Chad's face. The claw dangled inside the glass box; Chad could feel it reaching for him.

Despite how thin he'd grown, Chad managed to get the machine down the ramp without tipping over. A family of three watched from a gas pump as he pushed the machine across the parking lot with a hand truck. He didn't mind them staring. He'd gotten a lot of stares those last six months.

First were his parents, who stared when they found him sleeping on a plain mattress in the garage. Next, his landlord, who evicted him for not being able to pay rent. She stared with alarm as Chad angrily pulled the machine down the street on its metallic edge, making a sound like a child screaming. Most recently, a pair of healthcare clinicians stared as they approached Chad on the street. He was panhandling outside a grocery store next to the claw machine, which was sodden with rainwater and growing mold along the glass's interior.

They wanted to treat Chad for addiction but couldn't decide from what. The signs were plain. Singular obsession. Inability to keep a job. Emaciated. Everyone thought the claw machine was a

     Cursed Things

symptom. A quirk. Poor mental health. What they couldn't see was how it had worn Chad down over time. How it's rusted, little claw seemed to cast a shadow at night that followed him. How it pulled at his ankles when he slept. They didn't understand that Chad wanted nothing more than to be rid of the box forever. He stopped trying to sell it months ago because no one would take it —not even for free. Worse, it wasn't just the claw machine either; he couldn't sell *anything* anymore: baseball cards, memorabilia. He had no income because the machine had cursed him. His only gift in life deactivated by its quizzical nature.

He tried abandoning it. Chad left it behind a city dumpster and rode the bus across town, but when he woke up under a bridge the next day, the fucking thing was looming down over him! So, he must have to destroy it, he thought. But every time Chad raised a pipe to its glass, a shadow seemed to take hold of his wrist, shaking him loose of the notion.

It was the claw. It wouldn't let Chad go, and he was beginning to think it would kill him if it had to.

A week prior, when camping next to an abandoned lot, Chad woke to the sound of two men trying to steal the machine from him. Locals that probably thought they could sell it to a pawn shop. Chad laid there, shaking with excitement as they quietly tipped it onto a hand truck. He was about to whisper, "thank you," when the cabinet suddenly slammed down with preternatural force, landing on one man's boot. The machine crushed the man's foot like a piston. It didn't stop, even as the man's shoe began to split, as blood spurt from its cracking leather. The man screamed as his toes were ripped free from his foot, and the echo of his moans followed him into the night.

This is why Chad was so suspicious of this trip to the Oregon coast. When he woke the next morning, the man's blood still puddled beneath the machine, he didn't expect to find a raven staring down at him. It perched, unmoving, until Chad noticed the letter lying flat on his chest.

He unfolded it, and it read:

He was baffled. An implication simmered just beneath the words that shook something inside Chad. A dormant pang spurred to life at the prospect of a possible sale—not only did someone want the machine, but they knew of its true nature, and they still wanted it? This could be an opportunity to feed the thing inside him at long last. His drive to sell had gone disturbingly quiet, and Chad was afraid he'd lost something core to who he was, or who he was meant to be.

So there Chad was, walking the streets of Seaside, collecting stares, looking for someone who left no name. The salty air filled his lungs and rejuvenated him, despite the growing concern that he'd been played. Where exactly was he supposed to go now? There was no address on the note.

Around sunset, he was gifted a sandwich by a man with a pitying gaze, so Chad dragged the claw machine to a bluff that overlooked the ocean, where he ate the sandwich quietly. About a mile down the shore, he could see a boardwalk dotted with shops and ice cream parlors and happy children running about. People were selling there. He lost himself in the daydream of a simpler life. Perhaps he could have owned a tiny bookstore where he could sell big, important ideas to people. That was a wonderful thought.

An unexpected shadow fell upon his face and knocked him from the dream. Chad opened one eye and was met by a gaunt fellow with a thin smile. He had pale eyes, long blond hair, and a familiar raven sat on his shoulder.

"You got my message," the man said, admiring the claw machine. He took a seat next to Chad on the bench.

Chad was very nearly surprised, but decided he didn't have the energy. "You like things like this?"

"Oh, I very much like things like this." The man's hand mindlessly caressed his own knee, pinching at the fabric of his black trousers, like he was grasping at a prize inside the box.

Chad licked his lips and set down the half-eaten sandwich. He cleared his throat. He even wiped a palm down over his hair. "She's a real knockout. Wouldn't take much to clean her up. A collector's dream."

"I can tell."

"I've grown pretty fond of it," Chad said.

"Oh?"

"I may be willing to part with her." Chad's heart pounded in his throat. It was perhaps his worst pitch yet, but he'd lost all sense of himself these last few months. "For the right price."

The man's hand stopped pinching.

He turned to Chad and smiled with an open mouth. The back of his throat was nowhere to be found. It stretched into his neck and was so dark that one may as well be staring into the night sky, pin-pricked with light from stars that were long since dead.

"I've been collecting for a long time," said the old man. "I have a knack for tracking down cursed things."

Chad didn't know how to respond, and so he didn't.

"I own a shop," the man continued. "Curios and the like. This machine could be a fine addition."

Chad exhaled in relief. "It would be."

"So, you would consider selling it today?"

"I would," Chad admitted. "You'll find my price more than reasonable. I guarantee it."

The man tilted his head like a mother watching her baby. Suddenly, his hand appeared on Chad's cheek, caressing it with— *hungry fingers*, Chad thought, his chest tightening.

"I can tell you're a very good salesman," the gaunt man said. "For something like this, I'm not sure we can agree on a dollar amount."

Chad's heart broke. He nervously swallowed a dry lump in his throat. "I'm willing to go very, very low."

"You shouldn't be," the old man said. "An object such as this is worth quite a lot."

"I'll take anything for it. Please."

"If it's money you seek, I can certainly give you that." The man removed a roll of one-hundred-dollar bills from his breast pocket. Chad's eyes widened.

"But how long," the man asked, "Until that feeling inside you would have to be fed once more? What would a hundred dollars buy you? A week?"

Chad was scared. He had no idea how this man knew the things he did. "Maybe two?" he whispered.

The old man nodded. "And then we'd be right back where we started."

"I don't know how to stop it," Chad said. "It just wants more."

"Well then, have you considered feeding it something *more?*" The old man held up the roll of cash. "Something other than this?"

The question didn't land on Chad as much as it made him feel suddenly lighter. Like a dirty secret finally spoken out loud. Yes, he had sometimes considered exactly that.

"There are other payments to be collected in this life, Chad Adler. Payments that only the most skilled of salesmen could collect."

The man withdrew his hand and pointed toward the boardwalk. "I have a shop just there, in the middle. Tucked behind the used bookstore."

Chad turned, squinted in that direction.

"I've only kept one employee, but I'm afraid he's grown very old. His time will come any day now. So, you see, I'm in the market for a good salesman."

Chad turned back.

"Someone like yourself."

"I'm sorry," Chad said, almost chuckling. "Even if I wanted to…" His eyes drifted to the claw machine. "It won't let me."

The old man nodded. "I understand," he said. "And what if I

told you I could rid you of this machine forever. Give you back your gift. Would you consider working for me then?"

"You could do that?" Chad asked, his words nearly lodging in his throat.

The man smiled that cosmos-like smile once more.

Chad looked at the machine with nearly questioning eyes. He half expected it to weigh in. Curiously, it was the first time since owning the object that the grip of its shadow felt indifferent. Chad looked at the boardwalk, then back to the machine. Under normal circumstances, this was a terrible sale. Curses aside, it was certainly worth *some* amount of money. But Chad knew the old man was right. There wasn't a true dollar amount in this world. No amount of money would ever calm the thing inside of him, and hadn't he always known that on some level?

"Yes," he said, grabbing the gaunt man's hungry fingers and shaking them vigorously. "Please."

The old man sucked air through his teeth as if it were the first breath he'd taken this entire conversation. His fingers wrapped around Chad's palm, like a snake strangling its prey. Like teeth sinking into flesh. Like a claw that's grabbed its prize.

\#

The little brass bell above the entrance rang, drawing Chad's eyes up from his book. The door creaked opened and a pair of teenagers practically fell into the store, laughing as they caught their balance. The door slammed shut behind, cutting their flirtation short.

"Whoa," the boy said, his eyes adjusting to the dark. "This place is… freaking awesome."

The girl tucked a loose strand of hair behind her ear and adjusted her coveralls. "Weird," she said. "I've never seen it before."

"It has that affect," Chad said, announcing his presence.

The kids jumped at the sound of his voice. They turned and spotted him behind the register. The girl smiled politely and waved, while the boy took to the shelves, picking up things that he really ought not to touch.

"Freaky," he laughed, crouching down to examine a monkey's paw inside a glass cloche.

"Happy 4th of July," the girl said.

Chad smiled. Was it Summer already? It was a marvel how easily he lost track of time. That must have made it—what was it —his eighteenth year working the shop? How time flies when you are having fun. As it turned out, finding that claw machine was the best thing that ever happened to him. Had he not lost everything, he would have never met the owner of the store. He would have never been given his new gifts or found the one job that finally quieted the craving inside him. The old man couldn't have been more right. Money was never what Chad needed to be happy. He longed for something much, much more valuable.

"Have you been in business long?"

"Since nineteen-twenty," Chad answered.

"It's so weird," the girl said. "I've never seen this place, and I've spent every summer here since I was five." She studied him inquisitively.

"Well, I've found that sometimes, things in this world don't want to be discovered." Chad gently closed his book. "Until they do."

A look passed over the girl's face that he recognized immediately. *Stranger danger.* Instinct. This place was wrong, but she couldn't say why.

"Come on, Rory," she called. "We'll miss the fireworks."

"Just a second," the boy responded. He picked up a square puzzle box from the back shelf and held it under a lightbulb. "No way," he said, spotting something else inside a glass cabinet. He carelessly tossed the box aside and pointed at a wind-up toy monkey locked behind the glass. "I've always wanted one of those." The monkey had a wide, toothy smile and two cymbals in each hand. "And look at that," he said, pointing at a VHS tape with no label. "You don't see those anymore."

"C'mon," the girl said, appearing at his elbow. "This place is weird."

"Holy crap, Jenn. A Polybius. I thought these were made up."

Rory raced to the old video game and pulled a quarter from his pocket. He pressed a button, but the screen wouldn't turn on.

"I don't think it works," the girl whispered.

"Oh, it works," Chad announced. "But that's not what you're here for."

Rory's smirked and turned. "How do you know what we're here for?"

At that, Chad smiled. He waved them over to the counter, and leaned down, withdrawing a long wooden box. It was old bog wood, engraved with symbols that even he didn't understand. The teenagers watched attentively as Chad lifted the lid and revealed what was inside. Jennifer's eyes grew wide and her breath hitched. Her hand instinctively reached toward the box, but she stopped. "May I?"

"Please do," Chad said, pushing the box toward her.

Inside, there were four vintage fountain pens of various size and shape. Jennifer's fingertips brushed over each as if they were made of glass. They came to rest on an ebonite Pemberly from the 1920s. Not particularly special or expensive looking, but Chad knew firsthand that looks can be deceiving.

"Nice choice," he said. "A beautiful pen… especially for the aspiring writer."

Jennifer's eyes darted upward. Her gaze was thick with skepticism, but her intrigue betrayed her.

"Cool, babe." Rory put his arm around her shoulder. "You should get that for your class."

Jennifer smiled cooly. "No, I don't think so."

Chad snatched the pen from her and placed it back in the box. The girl jumped a little. "For the best," he said. "Especially after what happened to the last owner."

Jennifer narrowed her eyes. "The last owner?"

Chad pulled his lips tight. "Vivian Henshaw"

"Vivian —" Jennifer slapped a palm over her mouth. "You're telling me that pen belonged to Vivian Henshaw?"

"The one and only."

"Who's that?" asked Rory.

Jennifer sighed and elbowed her boyfriend. "I've told you a million times; she's my favorite author."

"Oh. You mean the one who…" He drew a line across his neck with a finger.

Jennifer placed both hands on the counter and leaned down toward the pen. "She wrote six bestsellers in less than two years. Do you know what I'd give for something like that?"

A soft, disarming smile grew across Chad's face, and the feeling in his stomach crouched like a predator lying in wait. In fact, he knew *exactly* what Jennifer would give for something like that.

how to be a player

Angela Yuriko Smith

How to be a Player

By Angela Yuriko Smith

Brina almost turned back. The alley reeked of stale cigarette smoke and incense. The pungent scent curled up inside her nose and made a home there in her brain. Another odor lingered beneath it—sour, reminiscent of old regret, something dead. The combination made her stomach lurch. A battered neon sign flickered from a window ledge, half the letters burned out so it just read "pen" in a lower case, fly-specked mystery typeface. It crossed her mind that maybe part of the sign had also been rejected. She clutched her purse white-knuckled, thinking she may have made a mistake.

But wouldn't it just be the latest in a long litany of failure? This was the combined voice of her sisters—three polished overachievers with degrees dripping off their resumes. They were the ruling fates in her life, the triumvirate of worldly success: engineering, law, medicine. Their houses were neat and tidy, decorated with tastefully framed diplomas and purpose.

And here she was, the fourth and youngest daughter who had never finished anything of merit. A middle-aged mother to a handful of awkward adults and a stack of half-finished manuscripts all still waiting to find love. She used to tell herself that motherhood and art meant more than awards and honors, but the last few rejection letters told another story. Her life amounted to nothing.

Then I guess I have nothing to lose, she thought.

She opened the warped wooden door and stepped into a narrow hall lit by blinking fluorescents. Charcoal symbols ran along the walls—spirals, Egyptian eyes, and other occult looking shapes shifted in the strobing shadows. Brina inhaled a lungful of stale air. The stink of old cigarettes was even stronger but the smell of rancid flesh, thankfully, remained in the alley.

"Am I really doing this?" she whispered to the empty hallway.

"Of course, or you wouldn't be here."

Unnoticed, a gaunt man sat waiting at the other end of the hallway partially hidden by the stairwell. He wore a threadbare robe belted over stained, baggy jeans, but his silver hair was thick and fell past his shoulders in waves. Brina tried to fix on an age based on his hunched and frail form until he stood up. He seemed to leave his old age in the shabby armchair.

"Shall we?" He gestured to the open door next to him, almost gallantly.

Brina's eyebrows shot up. This is not what she had expected. "Your ad… claims a revolutionary spiritual treatment. Is it… safe?" Her voice sounded small in her own ears. She was the baby of the family, the so-called dreamer—everyone said so.

"Does it matter?" he asked. "Apparently you have nothing to lose." He smiled and beckoned her to follow him into a cramped parlor. Stunned, she followed.

The walls were lined with faded tapestries depicting mandalas, colors muted with age. More of the occult type symbols were drawn in permanent marker around the borders and on the dingy walls. Brina's pulse quickened. The loveseat against the wall looked like it had seen better days, held together by coffee stains and torn fabric cushions.

"Sit." he directed, pointing to it. "You won't be standing."

Brina obeyed, her nerves pinging danger cues to her racing heart.

The old man set a cigar box on the side table, producing a dirty glass pipe and a baggy of something granular. "DMT," he explained, holding it up to her. "It will illuminate the line between what you know and what you fear. The Electric Maitreya waits. She'll reveal the illusions you've nurtured and give you the answers you seek."

Brina's breath constricted in her chest. She thought this was going to be more like a tarot reading. She'd heard of DMT—some call it the spirit or god molecule. She'd read a story about a husband and wife that experienced it through ayahuasca in Brazil. They had spoken with deities and it changed the trajectory of their lives from mundane to divine. She wanted that.

 How to be a Player

She'd also heard the horror stories: reality fracturing, monstrous entities that cling to your thoughts... demons. But wasn't she already there? Her entire life was one slow slide into oblivion, like a sad exhale. If she left, she would wake up tomorrow, exactly the same, overshadowed, talentless, and pointless. *If this is what it takes to live....*

"Okay," she managed.

"Okay," he answered. "Have you ever smoked with one of these before?" He held up the pipe.

Brina shook her head. "I got high in high school once or twice. We made a pipe from a beer can."

He laughed. "Then you will be fine. It only lasts about five minutes. That is all you will need."

"I can handle five minutes."

He sparked a butane torch, lighting the contents of the pipe. A harsh, synthetic stench hit Brina's nose, accompanied by bitter heat. She coughed, felt tears prick her eyes, but she inhaled and held it, ignoring the burn in her lungs.

The first wave hit like a nuclear shock. Her ears rang with an odd pressure, as though she'd plummeted to the bottom of the sea. In the corners of her vision, the parlor walls wavered, the tapestries undulating as if turned to liquid. Reality receded in a wave, leaving behind a one dimensional representation of the reality she was used to. Her bones melted, and she sagged into the upholstery. Somewhere in the room, she could hear a heart monitor beeping, slowing, and then one long, continuous beep.

I've died, she thought. *And I'm okay with that.* She closed her eyes, expecting nothing.

Instead, she found herself defying the laws of gravity as she flew down a dark tunnel made of geometric blocks that looked to be composed of space. Rather than being black, they were empty, fit together in complex geometric patterns that rotated. Between the crevices where they connected shone technicolor light. It was like flying through a kaleidoscope. Her ears were filled with the rush of wind and shattering and something akin to music that she recognized as always being there, and yet she had never heard it before.

And then she burst forth from the tunnel to enter a sudden silence. Her body was gone, and she was limitless, and true. This was reality, and she realized everything that had gone before was the dream. Her sisters, the bills, the rejections and unfulfilled dreams were now as significant as a child's worries. None of it mattered anymore, but all of it mattered.

When nothing is sacred, everything is.

The thought came to her from everywhere, a universal language not bound to the simplified 24 symbols she had considered holy. The celestial language was limitless, as was she. Her understanding expanded to connect with the universe. It reconnected, she realized, and she was overcome with love.

In this void, she turned, or was turned, and found herself in a colossal box. Neon colors—impossible hues she had no names for—created the box with simple lines, solely for her reference.

Before her was the face of a deity, filling space and time with a divine presence, again, created from impossibly hued neon edges. It was as if the vast dark were shielding her so she could get a glimpse of the reality that lay beyond the dark. The fabric of existence was shifting to give her a peek, taking this form. A figure of prismatic light, shifting and flickering with stained-glass galaxies compressed into cosmic essence, existing in unhearable music.

Electric Maitreya…

The intention shimmered from this deity, a divine wave of silent joy. The message traveled to and through Brina.

See…

And Brina did see. Before her, in the center of the box, was a vessel of some type. A bowl, a pot, also a representation created in lines of light, it was featureless. Above it hung a massive iron pincer.

I'm in a claw machine…

Brina found she could turn her attention and she did, trying to see what lay beyond the box, seeking the edges of this reality,

　　　　　How to be a Player

looking for a seam where she could go beyond to the brilliance that waited.

Electric Maitreya returned Brina's focus to the unassuming pot on the pedestal beneath the claw.

See...

They were one. She was Electric Maitreya and Electric Maitreya was her. They had always been this but she had forgotten while dreaming in what she had mistaken for reality. Her life had just been a fever dream and this thing, this simplest of things, was the most important. Of all the eternity of possibility and limitless purpose, here lay Brina's.

Still, Brina looked away, distracted by the vastness and impossibility surrounding her. She became her questions, a fabric of unrest that flew in all directions from her own essence, untethering in this ether as she had untethered in her dream of existence, a hesitant spirit who had let the illusion seal her lips against the abundance meant for her.

For a final time, Electric Maitreya returned Brina's focus to the unassuming pot on the pedestal beneath the claw. Brina had limited time and would be returning.

See...

Brina focused. It was a puzzle, a story, a metaphor. If she could understand it she would know everything. It wasn't the secret to everything, just *her* secret... but to Brina, the only one that mattered was Electric Maitreya, who coalesced into light, which was knowledge and understanding.

A claw machine, a mundane cosmic clue, and Brina was inside with a simple pot. She expected the secret to everything to have more flourish, some complexity, something to shatter her existence into the ethereal. She was inside this game with nothing but a pot.

Not just a pot. An ink pot.

The answer flooded her on a molecular level. Her atoms collided into sympathetic fusion that blasted her consciousness with an instantaneous gnostic attunement. Brina was inside the game, waiting for the claw to descend and take the prize.

She had not been a player at her game. She had chosen to remain inside, hoping to be selected as well... her and her purpose fading into dormancy as she waited to be chosen. Nobody would play this game for her. She was the only player.

I see...

With that, her illusory former existence caught at her being, like hooks, and pulled her backwards into the kaleidoscopic tunnel, but Brina had no need to resist. Reality wasn't going anywhere, and her time in the dream was her time to grow. Her sisters no longer threatened her. She no longer felt fear over rent and rumors of war. She had remembered who she was, who they all were. Her purpose was to remind everyone with her words, as clumsy as they might be with only 24 letters of an alphabet to work with. Nothing mattered, and because of this, everything mattered.

Brina opened her eyes to see the parlor taking shape around her. The dingy walls came into focus. The particles that made the illusion of *couch* gathered beneath her, faithfully supporting her because she believed they would. Everything existed because she believed it would. For a second she let her eyes unfocus, and she could see multiple realities layered, coexisting. The parlor's dim light flickered, and she became aware that the old man was watching her a few feet away looking pleased with himself, almost smug.

"You see now," he said, grinning.

Brina swallowed back tears, overcome with unanchored gratitude and joy. There was no source for this, no reason to be overcome with such love. There didn't need to be a reason. "I see..." She broke off, chest tight. "I see who I am... who we are."

The old man nodded. "Yes. When nothing is sacred, everything is."

Brina was too stunned to be surprised at his words. Legs trembling, she pushed herself upright, feeling empty, but also full of light. Her purse lay on the floor, an ordinary prop in a suddenly extraordinary world. She marveled at how insignificant it now seemed.

     How to be a Player

She took a shaky breath, straining her ears to catch a snippet of music she knew echoed throughout creation. There was nothing but the faint hum of the fluorescent light, and yet, that was part of it. Every sob, every dog bark, every flutter of breath harmonized into the music of the spheres for those who would listen.

She drifted out of the parlor as if in a trance, her mind alive with vivid afterimages of the fractal geometry, the whispering darkness, the radiant Electric Maitreya. Brina herself felt radiant, electric and charged.

Outside, night had fallen, thick with city smog and washed out neon. Rain-slick pavement reflected the overhead lights in mesmerizing patterns, runic shapes peeking from other layers. Her existence was just a translucent layer upon endless layers. Brina stood there, letting cold drizzle seep into her hair.

When nothing matters, everything does. If everything matters, then everything I do matters. Therefore, I can do anything.

Slowly, Brina closed her eyes and exhaled, letting the tension drain from her body. No more waiting for someone to choose her so she could play her game. She would choose herself. She was both the dream and the dreamer, the player and the prize... and she had unlimited lives.

create-a-chimera

Beth Cook

<u>**CREATE-A-CHIMERA**</u>

BY BETH COOK

At ChimerIt, we bring your dreams to life! Thanks to recent advancements in genetic engineering and 3D printing, ChimerIt's patented LifeCode™ technology is revolutionizing not just what nature can create, but what nature itself means.

My eyes adjust to the framed posters along the back wall. Images of a pug-icorn on the lap of an older woman in a turquoise skirt suit. A bride riding in on a white elephant with enormous butterfly wings. A dragon-winged tiger strutting through a stadium at half time alongside its costumed human counterpart. Big game hunters posing with a freshly killed shark-headed polar bear. Troops of ant-headed gorillas with laser-canon arms.

I had felt the soundless screams vibrate downward through us, all the spare parts in the Create-a-Chimera claw machine in the basement of ChimerIt Laboratories. The heads on top could see the Claw descending.

Round after round, we heard the distant cheers on the other side of the glass. The Claw had descended, cold steel piercing down into the spaces between us, scraping past cryo-frozen fur and feathers. Pincers had squeezed and lifted, choosing a random clump of parts—goat tail, dog legs, cow face. Over and over.

Tonight is the annual Culling, when the tech bros at their Christmas party upstairs get coked up, stay late, descend to the basement, and slide their company cards to pay for several new chimera.

Gladiators for one night, pieced together with lasers and bio-gel, who never asked for life and must immediately fight to the death.

After last year's Culling, I was no longer so deeply buried among the other spare parts. Disconnected legs that still remembered how to run and crouch but remained frozen. Wings that knew how to fly and nothing else. And the occasional head—like me.

I'd gone from hearing distant muffled sounds to hearing Kevin's voice clearly for the first time. He introduced himself, sounding like he gave this little speech every year. He said it's rare to have a real conversation companion again. Mostly, he just tries to communicate, *It's over. The scary thing is over. You're safe for now.* to severed heads with ancestors that invented fear

Tonight, my view is no longer blocked by a dung beetle's thorax (legs and wings removed). The light from the top of the machine was blinding at first. Unable to blink, I rode waves of colorful pain behind my eyes as Kevin's voice came through clearer than ever, reedy and sweet. As my eyes began to adjust, the first thing I saw was the back wall of posters. It helped me to have something to focus on, to wonder about. But the clearer they got, the less I wanted to look.

One nice thing about being prey, though, is our ability to look in many directions at once, even with cryo-frozen eyes. So now I seek out Kevin, trying to store the posters away in my mind, as irrelevant as a tree in the landscape—will hurt if you run into it, but will not try to kill you. *Let's focus on finding that nice sound.*

I see his silhouette sharpen and his dimensions deepen as he comes into focus. He looks just as he described himself—front half of a mouse with tiny antlers and bumblebee wings, back half of a frog with a spotted puppy's tail, each piece shrunken or grown into proportion to end up with a creature about the size of a guinea pig. He said he was designed as the Create-a-Chimera machine's mascot, now living a life of mostly leisure—and occasionally shepherding us through the Horrors—in his custom cottagecore terrarium. He also said that the front of the machine has a cartoon image of him, but none of us can see it from inside.

When I first told him I used to be part of a unicorn, he was surprised.

There are many unicorn heads in the ChimerIt labs, but only

some get to keep their horns as full unicorn heads (ultra rare component). They mostly just get their horns removed (rare component) and get reused as horse heads (medium common component). Only the "defective" or "unmarketable" scraps (ultra common component) get sent here.

And while a chartreuse unicorn may blend right in with the rest of the rainbow, a chartreuse nullicorn is just a sickly green horse.

"I was created as a lie," Kevin says one day. "Maximum adorable. 'Look at what a cute critter you could create by playing this machine!' And then you have to watch the night janitor's daughter stare in horror and then burst into tears when she ends up with five torsos and nothing else stitched together. And you have to try and explain to all the spare parts added to the machine, over and over again, what fate awaits them at the end of all this." Kevin looks away. "At one point, I stopped telling them the truth. Pretended I was as clueless as they were. Then I just stopped speaking to them altogether."

As gently as I can, I ask, "Why?" I try to make it a door and not a magnifying glass.

"I thought... I *told* myself it was because I had no responsibility to them. It wasn't my fault they were in there, so why did I have to clean up someone else's mess? But I think I was just hoping that it would make everything easier to bear. I just couldn't keep trying anymore, it was too hard."

Something in the legs and lungs I no longer have remember slowing down from a long, long run to pause, sniff the wind, take shelter, and sleep. And in the next moment I also know that every part of the mouse, deer, bumblebee, frog, and puppy that made up Kevin carries that memory, too—figuring out when to keep running and when to rest.

"Did it help?" I ask.

Kevin adjusts his mismatched pairs of legs back and forth a

few times before getting comfortable again. "Sometimes it helped, now and then, to just silently scream along with them. If I heard their questions and knew the answer was horrifying, I could convince myself that it was better for them not to know. But if I heard a question that I knew the answer to and the answer was good and hopeful… then I found that I couldn't hold myself back from answering. And I started telling them about how after I was put together, all my parts started learning from each other. Sharing memories of leaping through meadows and splashing in puddles for the fun of it. Gorging on sun-ripened blackberries. Splashing in cool waters. Taking naps in flowers. Snuggling in a safe nest with my family. And even if none of me can figure out how to get those things where I am now, all of me remembers how to want them. And that's gotta mean something, right?"

I first see Violeta, the night janitor's daughter, several days after the Culling. She rushes right up to press her nose against the glass of the claw machine until it touches the lenses of her glasses. Something in the angles of light and lens meet in such a way as to show her eyes with perfect clarity—brown velvet lit up like Broadway curtains.

An instant later, the angles shift, and in her glasses I see myself, a lemon-lime eyesore of a horse's head, reflected among the various other parts that surround me—a panda's back legs, an elephant's tail, an orange caterpillar torso without its dozens of little dancing of legs.

Violeta looks up, and now the mirrors of her glasses show me the cartoon depiction of Kevin at the top of the machine. He looks absurdly cute-ified with shining oversized eyes. And yet, something in the unhinged amounts of love and hope was accurately, uniquely Kevin. All of me, somewhere, remembered how to laugh with affectionate, teasing delight.

Every weekday evening, Violeta arrives with her father into the basement staff break area, stopping to gaze into the claw

            Create-a-Chimera

machine for a moment or just pass by with a wave. Her father changes into his work scrubs in the bathroom as she buys a bag of peanut M&M's from the vending machine and settles in to start her homework. He kisses the top of her head and clocks in for his shift.

Kevin explains, "Violeta's father once told her that the reason why she can see new bits revealed in the claw machine when they come back from Christmas break is because the people working here use the claw machine to make pets as Christmas gifts for needy children."

"They do?" I ask in wonder, having only been told about the death-battle side of things.

"Nope," says Kevin. "Those are specially designed months in advance as the annual CreatIt Critter™, given out to kids in hospitals with much publicity. 'Fully hypoallergenic models available' they advertise."

"Does he… does Violeta's father know that's not what happens to us? Does he really believe it, or is he lying to her?"

Kevin rubs his little pink fists into his eyes for a moment. "If I had to guess by the exhausted, dissociated terror behind his eyes when he told her, I'd say he knows. He's been here long enough that he doesn't have to work holiday shifts anymore, so I don't think he personally has to clean up those Christmas blood pits. But people talk. He knows about it, at least. He knows how he can make some extra money under the table if he wants to—'And don't we all need it around the holidays?'"

After a long silence, he turns back to me.

"Anyway, the point I was trying to make is that Violeta has been looking into the machine more often lately, ever since she could see you right there at the top. She hasn't looked into the machine every day since she was six, which was… gosh, five years ago now. She started noticing how her father would get a little quieter and sadder when he had to try to explain how money works each year as she's gotten a little older and could understand a little more. Going from him just hushing, 'I know, I'm sorry', to a wailing toddler, to her noticing on her own and *choosing* to stop asking him about it because having to tell her they couldn't afford it made him sad." Kevin's nostrils flare.

One day, Kevin tells me what he overhears, that Violeta is saving up her money—her own weekly allowance, plus the five bucks she got fair and square from when Michaela G. bet her that she couldn't lift thirty pounds—to buy a Create-a-Chimera from the claw machine because there's a "fairy woods horse head" on top.

Fairy woods.

My horn—somewhere miles away on another girl's custom blue-raspberry-bubblegum llamacorn—remembered what real magic is.

The Claw, when it comes down at last, is not as cold as I feared.

My head remembers pain, but like every other memory, it is frozen, seen through a layer of ice or claw machine or terrarium or rose gold-rimmed glasses. No, the lasers and biogel are far worse. They wake up nerves that don't just *remember* pain, our ancestors *invented* it—a newly multi-celled, primordial blob figuring out how to communicate, *We are being eaten,* to itself.

I blink furiously in the bright basement lab, wanting to bounce and stretch my legs out. Legs? Yes, I have four again, two front and two back. They feel… off balance. I look down at thin, delicate forelegs—orange-brown reeds that bend back at the knee. They end in slappy webbed feet, and I plop-plop them a few times. But they shake with the effort of holding up a head and torso heavier than they were built for.

To help give them a rest, my back legs collapse with a *thump.* In these, I feel muscle, made to climb and amble and tumble. Fat and fluff, made to lounge and squish. Peering back, I can see them, black and fluffy, with squishy paw pads. Claws made for climbing bamboo rather than aggression.

My breathing is… wrong. Too shallow and too fast. Lungs too

small to gallop for miles. Back and belly too dry to properly breathe with those lungs. Need water.

Machines beep, lights and metal whirl around me and I slip in and out of… this. Cold splash. Gasping awake. Breathing better, but now wet and cold.

I look back at my shiny green torso—close to my head's shade of chartreuse, but *just different enough* to be visually jarring—now developing a nice layer of mucus. I feel my amphibian heart flutter as I realize I'm now part frog—just like Kevin.

All the way to the back—nothing? No, *someone's* back there. An experimental *fwip-fwip-fwip*—ah ha! Swishy, fly-swatting bundle of coarse hairs at the end. Bendy, gray, and tricksy, with a mind of its own enough to hold onto a palm frond fan or a friend's trunk.

I—we?—am pushed out onto a little conveyor belt, through a curtain of stiffened plastic film flaps, *pfft*, and into Violeta's waiting arms.

Violeta figures out—after another wheezing, blacking out scare or two—that my torso needs to be kept moist in order for me to breathe properly. She remembers reading about how frogs breathe through both their nasal airways and by converting oxygen through their skin. At the emergency vet, Violeta takes the spray bottle and nods solemnly as they discuss diet.

"At least he's made up of only herbivores, mainly," the doctor says. "After he gets settled, you can try a smoothie of mealworms and applesauce for his frog tummy and see how that goes, but I'd stick to the Veggie Mash pellets at first."

Violeta eagerly takes the neat folder full of information printed out by the just-as-excited vet tech, and they brainstorm names together—*Jimothy Higgins. Emerald Nightshade. Boopsy Cupcake. Dave.* Her father signs the bill with a gulp.

To the pet store next for food, squeaky toys, and a new pink spray bottle that Violeta can carabiner onto the belt loop of her jeans.

She says I won't need a bed of my own. "He can sleep in my bed. I promise I'll keep it clean. You're already teaching me how to do laundry, remember?"

Her father tries to draw the line at a paddling pool. "If you save up, you'll have enough by summer, and we won't need it until it gets hot anyway. Until then you've got the squirt bottle… which will drip onto the carpet in your room… So I can either figure out a way to put down a tarp that won't spill over onto the…" He rubs his fists into his eyes like Kevin. "Yeah, let's get the paddling pool to keep in your room until it gets warm enough to do it outside."

"Yeah!" Violeta yells with a hop.

"But we'll have to find another place for your keyboard setup. Wait, hold on—the bathroom. We'll just put it in the bathroom next to the litter pad. Wait, no, there's not enough room in the bathroom for both. I mean, I guess we could smush the paddling pool into the tub, but…" He mumbles something into his palm. "I'm so tired I forgot that bathtubs exist. No paddling pool until summer."

"Awww."

Violeta is the hit of her friend group. *"He's so cute. I'm so jealous!" "Oh, I'm one million percent sure his head came from a unicorn. He's just too magical to be from a regular horse." "Watch how he bounces his butt if you give him scritches on his panda legs!"*

Together they settle on the name Sir Verdelite Amalgam, Knightly Steed of the Fern Fairy Court—Verdy for short.

But beyond her colorful circle, Violeta is mocked.

She lengthens upward like a cobra, inches close to a face, and declares, "Never speak to me or my beautiful son again."

Violeta introduces me to the horses at the barn where she spends time. She gets free riding lessons in exchange for helping out, mucking out stalls while learning about how manure turns into compost, what the different brushes do, and how to train the gentle giants to pick up their feet so you can clean out their hooves.

I ended up being about as big as a large miniature horse or a small pony—"which are *not* the same thing," she explains.

I'm closest in height to Madeline the goat, but she wants nothing to do with me, clever enough to be suspicious of my fabricated freakishness.

Instead, a rust-brown horse called Gingersnap Crackerjack takes an immediate liking to me and says she wants to be my friend. She is not Kevin, and I don't know if Violeta is allowed to bring me back for a visit so I can see him again. But I want very much to get to know Ginger and be known by her.

With Violeta's patient curiosity and fierce devotion, I learn how to use my awkward stitched-together body.

Nullicorn head, frog body, goose legs, panda legs, and elephant tail all learn how to communicate with each other, to share what instinctual knowledge they each hold, and somehow work together. I/we learn how to run and swim again, to flush out the too-abundant adrenaline and cortisol. The vet says I might have up to a decade in me, if we're lucky.

Violeta becomes my world, and I gravitate around as her moon.

In summer, we pick blackberries from the overgrown alley. She gathers clover growing through the concrete and weaves it into a flower crown that we take turns wearing, then she lets me eat it. She buys the paddling pool, and every afternoon I splash and roll around, reveling in the glory of water and sun and Violeta's laughter.

win big at the body shop

Laura K. Burge

BY LAURA K. BURGE

The people working at The Body Shop didn't seem to expect actual customers, which was either a really good or really bad sign. When I pushed open the crusty glass door in the depressing strip mall off the interstate, a short teen boy with a septum piercing was hunched over the counter, staring at a jigsaw puzzle.

"You want next door," he said without raising his eyes.

I resisted the urge to lean forward and tug at that ridiculous piercing. I cleared my throat to get his attention, but it didn't go *super* well considering my congestion, so it turned into more of a hack-phlegm-cough-swallow-blush.

Sure enough, he looked up.

"Is this where I can buy new sinuses?"

He narrowed his eyes, looked behind me, then smirked. He hit a button beneath the counter, and for a moment, I thought he was calling the cops. But the door locked with a loud click, and the *shushing* I heard turned out to be the semi-functional vinyl blinds closing over the windows.

I'm not sure that made me feel any better. But I did look over my shoulder to see if there was still an exit—just in case.

"Come with me," he said and tipped his sparkly top hat. Had he been hiding that beneath the counter?

I opened my mouth to ask, and I could feel the searing sarcasm burning behind my lips, but I clamped my mouth shut.

Not now. Not again. Not when I was so close.

This was what I wanted.

I had been saving up my money for years, hunting all the online forums, going to sketchy antique stores and random arcades and greasy spoon diners, following whispers of a promise.

I was so ready. I was ready to be done with chronic sinus infections and never-ending runny noses and being sick and embarrassing myself in offices and stores, and *now*, I was so close. I had a dream of stockpiling my mound of tissue boxes and nose sprays and decongestants and having a big bonfire to celebrate never needing them again. I was ready. I couldn't mess it up this time.

I would finally be able to breathe easy.

The towering teen boy with the sparkly hat opened the stained EMPLOYEES ONLY door at the back, next to the obviously-never-before-cleaned bathroom.

Why were we hiding in a tiny closet?

He gestured for me to squeeze in next to him, but I bumped against the giant pile of toilet paper and they came tumbling toward my face. My arms flapped out to protect myself against the toilet paper—flock of paper—*flock of birds* attacking me, but I tripped on a rock and fell onto the mulch of the forest floor.

Where had those birds come from?

They didn't normally fly this low—in this oak tree grove… where I'd always been…

There was something I hadn't noticed, wasn't there?

Oh, of course. The shaded rocky outcrops were filling up with the audience, all moving at a strange pace and taking their seats. I squinted to see their faces, failed, then realized a huge crowd— wow, there were so many of them—had already arrived. Ready for the show.

Silly me. Obviously, I was here for that: the giant claw machine, between two oaks, looming in front of me.

The forums had not prepared me for this.

The towering, gorgeous man in the sparkly top hat gestured toward the huge machine. An excited jittering jeer roiled through the shadowed crowd. I couldn't see them—I never could—but I felt knowing eyes on me. They were hungry for something. The claw machine loomed above us; the claw itself obscured by the moonlight.

The machine, however, was perfectly visible and full of human body parts.

"Here before you is The Body Shop Machine! You have three tries to get what you most desire and one try to keep what you cherish the most."

"Huh?"

An image of falling toilet paper jarred me.

"For the first try—"

"Wait, what did that last part mean?"

"I—just—let me finish this, okay?" His eye twitched when he said it, and there was a momentary shimmer of green skin and a terrible smell. Then he was back, tall and beautiful and wise.

I nodded, trying to keep my stinging words behind my tongue—this is what I wanted. This is what I wanted.

"For the first turn, you must search for what you want to replace. If you fail, you have two more tries. For the second turn, you must do the same. For the third turn, you are free to change your mind and grab whatever catches your fancy. But you *must* try."

"Yes, thank you, that's why I'm here!" My sharp words had started to leak through. They usually did—and got me into trouble.

My mom was always mocking the guy in the apartment next to us for having a septum piercing—why was I thinking of this now?—but I guess I wasn't supposed to say it to his face. That was the third time we'd had to move that year.

A horrible disgusting burp wafted in front of me, and I choked, but the woman in her glittery top hat was just standing there perfectly composed, her long beautiful hair shining in the claw machine's sharp light.

"Yeah, sorry. Go ahead." I scratched at my nose in confusion and ignored my heartbeat urging me to get the fuck out.

This is what I wanted.

"On the fourth try, it's the machine's turn."

"I'm sorry, what?"

"Well surely you didn't think there was no cost to this, did you? Not in this economy."

"Yeah, of course, I brought this." I pulled out the wad of dollar bills and held it out to her, hoping she didn't notice it was practically a damp puddle.

"What use would we have for money?" she asked, fiddling with the long puzzle pendant between her breasts.

When I tore my gaze away from the perfectly rounded... puzzle piece, I realized that the audience was laughing at me.

"What do you want?" I asked her, staring at how the faces on her floor-length gown were shimmering, on and off, mocking me.

I felt smaller than ever.

But this was what I wanted. What I wanted.

"This isn't mass production here, darling. We need to maintain our supply. When you have your prize—if you get a prize—then it's the machine's turn to try. You cannot leave the theatre, but you can move, and the machine will only keep the first piece it catches."

I wanted to keep asking questions until the questions themselves were able to restart all of this—make it simple and joyful, and let me have this future I had dreamt of since I was five and beset by sinus infection after sinus infection and timidly standing up in class every five minutes to get a tissue while all the other kids looked on and mocked me.

I tried to get better I really really did but I never never never could—

My heart beat loudly in my chest.

—be the perfect child, perfect daughter, perfect student, who would never get her mother evicted from their apartment because medical bills meant there was nothing left for rent and—

"It's time."

It was hard to see through the spotlight of the sun shining down on me through the trees in this open-air theatre. The magnificent oaks stretched their long limbs, trying to see beyond the wooden risers to the show and the giant claw machine. The audience members, covered in robes and clothes and too many limbs and not enough limbs became hazy. I always performed here. Why get stage fright now?

Music started, the claw started spinning, and the joystick glowed with a benevolent light. It was giving me a chance to make things right. A timer, lit in bright lights and streaming above the giant machine, poised itself in midair.

I grabbed the joystick. I started to move it, but it jerked too far to the right, and my arcade instincts kicked in.

That's right, these things were tricky. I spotted what I wanted, nestled between a chin—ooh, that was a nice chin—and a thin and shapely thigh.

The claw glinted strangely in the wobbly lights as I moved it over the small plastic orb labelled SINUSES.

I pressed the big red button.

The claw plunged into view—how had I not noticed that before? The large metal claw was covered in a human hand. It had been put on clumsily, too, and perhaps some time ago. It was old and worn out, the skin peeling away and metal sticking through where it shouldn't. They really could have done a better job.

Not that they should have at all. Whose hand had that been?

FIRST TRY

SO CLOSE

KEEP GOING.

Cheering voices from the nosebleed seats buoyed my flagging nerves as the metal claw—human fingers—metal—grasped the orb, wearing away more of the skin. Soon it'll be all metal. That had better not ruin my chances.

It pulled up, the orb in its grasp.

"Fuck yes! I did it!"

I turned my head and laughed at the green-tinted man with a too-tight jacket and sparkly top hat.

I stared at the chute, waiting for my prize—finally!—but the orb wobbled on the edge of the chute, and rolled right back into the machine.

Laughter rang around the theater.

"No! That doesn't count! It was going in!"

His grin was too smarmy for me to handle—too beautiful, too —and I turned back to the machine.

"Okay, yes, two more tries!" My adrenaline was up. I could *do this*. I had to.

I slammed my hand on the button to get started. I shouted at the machine. I watched the claw's palm flake onto a bright red organ that must have been a kidney. But nothing was getting in my way.

"Yes… yes… oh, COME ON! I pushed to the right! Right, right, right! No, not another penis! No, come on, it's right fucking there!"

The claw plunged toward my prize, but just missed and hit the edge of a foot. I didn't even want a whole foot! Just those tiny little sinuses. As the claw retracted and the big lights flashed above, I yelled out again.

"Okay, okay, okay! I've got this now. I've got it."

That's okay, I was good at this. I just had to have a strategy. Besides, third time's the charm, right?

ONE LAST CHANCE shouted out an arcade voice. I could hear my mom getting impatient by the front door—getting late, school night, blah blah blah—but I really wanted this! Maybe I could win this prize and prove myself. No amount of "I'm counting to three" or classmates telling me I'd never win would dissuade me.

I pressed down and maneuvered.

I had to get it. This was what I wanted.

I avoided that hand, pushed the claw just a bit—no, no, just a bit!—to the side, waited for it to swing past the orb of long eyelashes, and then plunged it down. The sinuses orb was leaning against the eyelashes orb, but I got it! I got it!

I kept my eyes on the claw now, grey flesh and smeared rusting metal be damned, and whispered at it—*come on come on come on you can do it.*

A ding rang overhead.

The orb dropped neatly into the chute.

"HOLY SHIT, I DID IT!"

My mom would have been so happy for me.

Of course, the claw started up and came right for me.

The sound of the pinballs—birdsong—ping of pinball machines almost drowned out the grating metal of the claw, extracting itself from the machine's insides.

The claw machine, set between the pool table, foosball table, and the ATM, sprayed sparks onto the stained carpet. It probably hadn't been flammable in decades.

I clutched that orb close to my chest and dove for the pool table, getting an instant rug burn from the carpet and landing with my head smack against the chewed gum wads.

The orb bounced out of my hands—no!—and started to roll into the open.

Just as the claw came roaring toward me, I was able to snatch it and crawl under the foosball table. I held on with all my might, but the plastic orb popped like a bubble.

The squishy, wet, slimy pulsing organ melted into my hands.

I sneezed. It was mighty.

I took a deep breath and—OH CRAP! I could take a deep breath! Is this what everyone else always felt?

I had fresh sinuses!

I let out a whoop—

Which turned into a cry.

I'd been grabbed from behind.

Sharp stabbing pain. Rusty metal skewers reaching through my back and out of my chest. Rotting fingers stripped away from the metal, and I reached out my own hand, in awe, to meet the last remaining fingertip of whoever it had been.

The claw closed perfectly in a way I'd never seen a claw machine manage, and then it pulled backward.

"You're free to go," the short teen boy said from behind his counter, his eyes once again glued to his jigsaw puzzle and rubbing at the septum piercing.

Frantically, I checked myself. All seemed intact. There was no blood, no pain, no ragged holes in me. I took a deep breath—

"What did you do?" I wheezed.

"We have your lung. Don't worry, only the one. You're free to leave whenever you want."

Shaking, I started to turn, my body taking orders from this ridiculous boy for some reason.

"Unless—"

I stopped like a marionette on a string.

"—you want to play again."

When I looked back at him, her eyes glistened with possibilities, the low-cut dress showing off that puzzle pendant. The door beside the bathroom had opened without a sound, and the oak grove stood, serene with diffuse sunlight, and invited me back to the claw machine, its fresh new lung proudly displayed on top of the pile inside.

This was what I wanted. What I wanted.

"Can I get my lung back?"

"You can play for anything. Three turns for you, and one turn for the machine. You can play as many times as you want."

Well. Fuck. I walked back through the door, determined to get my own back. I'd know better this time. I'd dodge better this time. I would get my—

"Holy shit, are those perfectly toned arms?"

I barely heard the closet door shut behind me as I went to get a better look.

"Yes, they are. And you're welcome to take one or both or more. As much as you want."

The sunlight shifted in the open-air theatre, illuminating a disturbing hodgepodge of a body—one body? two? it was hard to tell—stepping forward from the wooden risers. It rolled forward on stumps to stand in front of the machine.

"When it's your turn again, of course."

I looked out on the sea of hopeful mangled half-formed faces.

This was what I wanted.

"Go ahead and take a seat while you wait."

the makeover

Summer Olsson

1.

Claire and Hawi were sitting at the bar where they met every Friday after work, splitting a bottle of Tempranillo, when Hawi turned to face Claire, took a deep breath, and said something ridiculous.

"I'm getting a new body."

Claire snorted, aspirated wine, and coughed for a solid minute before she could speak.

"I'm not kidding," Hawi said. "Haven't you heard of the show Claw Machine Makeover?"

Claire had not. Apparently, it was a gigantic hit, but it was on Apple Omni. She had Google All and couldn't afford both.

"There's a really big version of those old claw machine games, like from arcades a long time ago," Hawi explained. "Have you ever seen one of those?"

"Yeah, a bunch of stuffed animals, a sloppy claw that never held onto one long enough to pull it out. I thought they were always a big scam to take advantage of kids, who didn't know any better."

"Okay, right," Hawi said. "But in the claw game on the show, there are these big egg-shaped containers, and there are bodies inside."

That sounded to Claire like the opening of a horror movie, but she kept the thought to herself.

Hawi was so clearly excited about this, and she'd had a series of disappointments this year.

"When you're a contestant, you use a controller to drive a giant claw around, and try to scoop up the body you want. If you get the egg into the drop chute, it's yours."

"What do you do if you get it?" Claire asked.

"It's your new body," Hawi stressed. "They change you. They reconcile your outside with your inside."

It sounded like a slogan. Hawi tried to describe some new technologies in elective surgery, involving something called telomeres, that Claire couldn't exactly follow. Apparently, cosmetic surgery had evolved so far that the entire outside of a person was malleable, removable, even replaceable. The way Hawi explained it, they took your brain, your consciousness, your blood, maybe your spinal cord and nerves and stuff, and shifted the whole lot over to another package.

"It's like taking a sandwich out of one bag, and putting it into a different one," she said.

"Woman, you are not a sandwich," Claire said, almost laughing.

"That might be a bad analogy," Hawi admitted. "It was on the paperwork I got after I signed the contract. There were a bunch of 'helpful ways to explain your choice to your loved ones'. They're mostly silly. Do I really have to explain to you?"

Hawi was already selected, slated to be a contestant on the show. A little stitch of envy formed in Claire's chest. The concept was ridiculous, grotesque. And yet …

"How can that be safe?" Claire asked. "How will it feel to be someone else?"

"I won't be someone else," Hawi insisted, ignoring the safety question. "I'll still be me. I just won't hate my body."

She gestured at the right side of her face, which was splotched with vitiligo. She flapped her hand over her lap, where, Claire knew, Hawi thought her thighs were ruined by varicose veins.

The servbot rolled over, and the screen asked if they wanted to order anything else. Below the ordering box, an ad was playing. A smooth, pearly-skinned woman in a bikini ran along a white beach, her long blonde hair shimmering behind her. *Razehers*, the ad proclaimed, *for a hairless her*.

When Claire looked up, Hawi had tears in her eyes.

"Just be happy for me, okay? This is a lifeline."

"I'm happy for you," Claire said. "I support you, no matter what."

As she squeezed Hawi in a tight hug, Claire felt sad, because Hawi didn't love herself as she was. Claire also felt empathy, because she didn't believe that anyone really did.

That night, after her six-step glass skin routine, Claire shrugged off her robe and stood naked in front of the mirror. With both hands, she squeezed the flesh of her belly and pulled it up, trying to flatten it into her abdomen. This was the second part of her routine. She considered what she would look like if she lost forty pounds. She stood up straighter, lifted her boobs, one stupidly bigger than the other, into a better position, and imagined she could just wake up that way. After a few minutes of fantasizing, she put on her pajamas and got into bed.

Her boyfriend, Scott, was snoring softly. It crossed her mind to wake him up, but she hesitated, unsure if he would be angry or not. After several minutes of staring at his back, she rolled over and tried to sleep.

A few weeks went by, during which Claire knew Hawi was prepping and filming the show. They texted a few times, but couldn't meet up. Claw Machine Makeover wasn't live, and a tight non-disclosure agreement prevented anyone from talking about their experiences until after their episode aired. On the day Claire knew Hawi's shoot was happening, she received a message that read *Don't worry, I'm fine!*

It was five weeks before they saw each other. Hawi had asked Claire to meet for wine at their usual spot, and, after they agreed on logistics, sent the cryptic message, *I'll wear a blue hat.*

The moment before Claire stepped into the bar, it occurred to her why. Her friend of ten years had a new body. She would be a stranger.

No, she would only look like one.

Scanning the room, Claire saw a woman in a wide brimmed, blue felt hat, and realized it wasn't necessary. The woman's appearance was different, but still familiar. She both was, and wasn't, Hawi.

"Spoiler alert," Hawi said, gesturing to herself. "I won."

They laughed, and it felt almost normal.

"You look incredible," Claire said, sliding into the booth. "But I knew it was you, too."

"I know!" Hawi squealed. "Isn't that strange? Even my mom said I look like me, but not."

The Hawi that Claire had always known, besides having patchy melanin on her face, also had slightly smaller eyes and a lower forehead. Her cheekbones had not been as pronounced, and her skin, always dark brown, had not always had such a golden tone. But she had been beautiful before. Now it was a little, Claire thought, like Hawi's face had been pulled off, re-stretched over a new bone structure, and repainted. She shook her head to clear the grotesque thought.

"Tell me everything," she said.

Hawi said filming the show had been fun, and silly, with a studio audience that was rowdy, loud, and totally supportive. There were three contestants on each episode, but they weren't competing against each other. They encouraged each other, and the vibe was like a sorority or something. When Hawi succeeded in nabbing her prize, everyone hugged and cried.

After the filming, Hawi said, the CMM team took her right to a hotel, where she ordered room service, rested, and signed documents.

"There were a lot of forms," she said. "I felt like I was buying a house. There was an incredible therapist that I met with, who talked about expectations. But I knew I was going to love this, you know?" She flared her hand down her body like she was showing a car.

Early the next morning, she had been given an IV, taken right into surgery, woken up, and now was sitting there. The whole procedure was quick and painless.

It was just that easy.

They hugged when they stood up to leave. Claire noticed that

Hawi's body felt thinner and tighter in her arms. Hawi put her hands on Claire's shoulders and squeezed.

"I'm happy I…"

Claire nodded encouragingly.

"I'm happy I made…" She paused briefly. "My inside has been reconciled with my outside."

Later, when Claire told Scott about Hawi's new body, she expected they might discuss it from a critical angle. There were so many ethical and philosophical aspects they might have dissected.

"Huh," he said. "It worked?"

"She looks great."

He went to the fridge and took out a beer.

"Cool."

"Maybe I should apply to the show," Claire said, surprising herself.

"Sure," Scott shrugged. "If that would make you happy."

It was like he'd thrown the beer can at her face, she was so stunned. She had expected a little protest from him, at least as a formality. Now that the idea was out, it was real, and the barrier she thought would be there hadn't materialized. Now the idea demanded to be considered.

That night, after brushing her teeth, Claire cried for ten minutes in the bathroom with the sink running, and then quietly opened her laptop and filled out the online application for contestants.

2.

The stage lights were blazing hot, and Claire was sweating. She hadn't been prepared for that. They were also so bright she couldn't see most of the studio audience. She could hear them though, cheering and clapping. When the host asked her a question, she smiled out, into the brightness, hoping she didn't look deranged. Before the taping started, when the light was still normal, an efficient woman had walked the three contestants through the studio. They would enter through the curtain onto the stage. They would sit in the chairs. When it was each of their turns, they would ascend the metal staircase to the catwalk above the giant container, where the controls were.

That's where Claire was now, one hand on a joystick, the other on an oversized button. Looking down, she could see a three-pronged claw, seven feet long, dangling over a glass tank the size of her living room. The prizes were exactly like Hawi had described: big, clear eggs. Inside, posed identically, were what looked, almost, like mannequins. Their eyes were open, because color mattered of course, and they were naked.

The next step in your amazing new transformation, the host was saying, and the crowd cheered. Claire's hands trembled. *When the buzzer sounds, the claw machine will be active.*

The lights shifted, revealing the first two rows of the audience, and Claire caught sight of Hawi. Relief jolted through her; she hadn't known her friend was there. Hawi looked up at her, and they locked eyes. The crowd shrieked, and Claire felt a bead of sweat roll over her temple. Her stomach roiled. She stared at Hawi, looking for a sign.

Am I making a mistake? Is it worth it?

Hawi didn't yell anything up at the catwalk or mouth anything to Claire. She only smiled serenely.

Okay then.

The buzzer blared, and the crane with the claw began to lower into the tank. The crowd noise surged. Claire used the joystick to maneuver the pincher left, right, forward, back, while she frantically scanned the bodies. It felt the same as looking through ads in a magazine, scrolling social media, longing desperately after the models, not to be with them, but to be like them. Only this time, the feeling was tinged with elation instead of despair. Claire saw the lithe, milk-skinned, androgyne with black hair and a sharp jawline and knew it was supposed to be hers. *Her.* She zigzagged the joystick and slammed the button, lowering the claw. It caught the perfect body in a lax grip and slowly rose.

Half the time the claw dropped the prize before it made it to the chute. The contestant before Claire had gotten nothing. She

     The Makeover

could still lose. She squeezed the joystick fiercely, keeping it pulled in the right direction, even though she knew it wasn't doing anything. The claw's progress was ineluctable. Just before it arrived over the funnel, the claw released its grip and the egg plummeted.

The crowd gasped and Claire's heart shot into her mouth.

In a fortuitous moment of physics, the egg struck the side of the chute and bounced inside. The beautiful body was hers. *Her.*

The aftermath was blurred by adrenaline and euphoria. There was a luxe hotel room, a lukewarm entree under a silver cloche, and a stack of forms an inch thick, just like Hawi had described. Then there were the drugs administered to Claire before, during, and after the procedure. Loose, syrupy images were all she could recall.

The first moment of clarity was like waking up after a groggy dream. Claire found herself standing naked in front of a full length mirror. At least she thought it was herself. Sleek ebony hair spilled over delicate shoulders. Cheekbones jutted regally. The breasts were perfect, there was no belly fat to speak of. Putting a hand on her face confirmed it was her, but then a wave of dissonance hit that made her nauseated. As she studied the reflection, Claire could see that it was the body she had always wanted, but she was horrified to realize she still felt the same as she always had. She didn't like the person in the mirror. The thighs, her thighs, were weirdly straight all the way down, like telephone poles. Her feet were big, with gnarly toes. Her ass was puckered with cellulite.

A woman in a white uniform opened the door without knocking and told Claire it was time to see the doctor. She helped Claire into a thick white robe and led her down a hallway to a sumptuous office. The doctor was a gray haired man wearing an unbuttoned lab coat over a crisp shirt and tie.

"There's our beauty," he said, putting his palms out. "Have a seat."

Claire didn't really want to, but she sat.

"How are you feeling?"

She wanted to tell him that she felt awful—nauseated, angry, confused.

"I feel fine," she said instead, running a hand through her shiny hair. "Thank you."

"That's good," the doctor said. "It's important for you to know that the first few days will be an adjustment period. That's normal."

Claire wanted to tell him she had made a mistake, and ask that the procedure be reversed—surely it could be reversed, just put her in her old body like it was a new body. But she was silent.

"We want all of our success stories," the doctor continued, "to be exemplary representations of what we can do. We strive to create harmony inside and out. You will notice changes, not only to your appearance. You might think of it as the reconciliation of your inside with your outside."

Who is we? Claire wondered. *Why am I just sitting here smiling at this idiot?*

"It was in the contract," he said. "Pages seventy two and seventy three specifically. You are welcome to review the contract on your own time. The point is, you will find that self-mastery is much easier now. Any challenging opinions or complicated thoughts going forth will remain inert."

His big white smile didn't carry to his eyes.

What the fuck are you talking about? Claire's brain yelled, but her mouth opened and calmly said, "I see. Thank you."

"We gave you what you wanted," the doctor said. "And we made it easier for you to support our ability to help other women achieve the same goals."

Claire stood up.

No, she thought to stand up but her ass remained firmly in the chair. Where was Scott? Where was Hawi? Images flashed in Claire's mind. Hawi, squeezing her shoulders, maybe too hard? *My inside has been reconciled with my outside.* Hawi smiling up at her from the crowd. She hadn't been able to warn Claire.

"Do you have any questions?" the doctor asked her. "Do you have any quibbles?"

     The Makeover

He asked her as one might ask a child, only humoring her, knowing the answer mattered not at all.

Claire wanted to scream, to thrash against the chair, to leap over the desk and use her thumbs to push his eyes out. But she just smiled serenely.

purchase required

Wes Mitchell

BY WES MITCHELL

Slightly oversized and very overpriced cookie in hand, Connor strolled through the ever-mixing perfumes of the clothing stores, thinking about the new girl at school. Maybe she'd give him a chance. Every other girl in this god-forsaken town had already given him the "let's just be friends" speech. So she'd probably follow suit too.

His parents called him a "latch-key kid". Apparently, they both were alone a lot when they were his age. Lots of frozen pizza rolls and friends over when they weren't supposed to be. But after their eyes dazzled telling this long, overly done tale of adventure, they'd straighten up and say something about how great it was that he wasn't like them. *Wasn't like them.* Wish they'd heard themselves. That's explained a lot since then, though.

Most of his old friends moved away years ago, and the kids who switched spots with them weren't his type of people. That was fine. Now, Connor mostly kept to himself. That probably didn't help him with girls either.

He'd had a few hours to kill before heading home today, which gave him the opportunity to explore. And where better to explore, during the spring heat wave that popped out of nowhere, than an All-American Mall?

People-watching was by far the most entertaining distraction at the mall. Best of all, it was free. No purchase necessary to observe some of the stranger aspects of human behavior—social and anti. Some life skills can be learned just by watching people argue over prices that are clearly marked, scream at customer service for a refund, or by watching the other watchers.

From preppy polos to bell bottoms, full faces of makeup, and the classic overslept bedheads, everyone was mingling here today. The variety of styles was impressive. In a drive-through town, you get used to the same boots, jeans, and patterned flannels.

But in the mall, everyone's got their style. And most are unabashedly themselves in the confines of the cool concrete walls.

It's as if getting blasted with cool air as they enter takes away people's inhibitions. A coupon-clipping mom suddenly is charging everything with a beaming expression full of joy. Children running around as if the entire structure is a free jungle gym —other people included. Fathers actually trying on pants. Some even let others look at them in several options.

It's wild. He wouldn't seek this experience out if there was anything better to do right now.

As he walked by a particularly small, sugared-up kid doing their best to climb up a mannequin on the other side of a clothing store's display window, he got a great whiff of pretzel. Maybe he should have gotten one of those instead of the cookie. And now the food court was all the way over there. Damn.

Second only to people watching were the games. But the tiny section shrunk every year. Even the carousel was taken out before he was old enough to ride by himself—yet another missed opportunity.

Now, it was reduced to a fell pinball and other such machines.

Connor saw they had replaced a few of the older, broken-down thieves that took your change without any payoff. About time.

The new claw machine was almost cool. Some weird career-related theme. Firefighters, nurses, construction workers in plastic balls. People of all ages, races, and even heights. They were all so detailed, with little pieces that made look authenticate. Tiny cross necklaces, different style watches, and one even had an umbrella. Not one looked similar, like the painted models made in some cheap factory.

The prizes were actually decent for how much it cost to play. One or two could fit on a shelf, at least. There were a few collectables at about the same height.

He just needed seventy-five cents. He had more than that left over from the cookie. Perfect. His pants pockets had plenty of wrappers and stuff he'd since forgotten about. Right.

He tossed the change in the front pocket instead. He shook his hoodie. Two coins slid out without issue, but the third got stuck.

He impatiently yanked it out and threw all three into the slot as quickly as his hands would allow. The satisfying "chink" of the third quarter landing into the machine lit up the control buttons. Pretty good dopamine rush.

What should he go for?

At first, it was the doctor in the front left corner. But after noticing both the mechanic in the back right and the barista a few inches over to their left, he lined up his shot.

The claw descended into the pit, with Connor's stomach joining it. And despite his best efforts, he couldn't keep a calm heart rate. Over-eager, as usual.

It wouldn't pull anything up, he knew the scam. But maybe, if it was lined up just perfectly, he could get just enough grip, he could get lucky. Maybe the claw would just—

Nope. The moment it started coming up, it was obviously a failed attempt.

Shocking, he lost.

Normally, Connor would move along to the next section of the mall before turning home. It was about that time anyway. But something made him put another three quarters in. It wasn't like he'd gambled his snack money away. This was fine. He could lose a dollar and some change for the thrill of... nothing. He already had it in hand, anyway. Why not?

The claw descended again, and the same feelings seized him. But like the retreating tide, not to the same levels as before. Muted.

But this time, the claw almost caught the ball he aimed for! It even lifted up in the claw to be dropped as the machine rattled, changing from vertical to horizontal movement. Of course.

One more time. It was his last few quarters anyway, let's just get it over with.

He didn't even bother changing the position, just smacked the button. Connor walked away then, because as his Dad's favorite silly song said, "Cool guys don't look at explosions". Or, apparently, watch their claw machine failures.

After a few steps, he turned back to look anyway, because who needs to be cool, just in time to see that—IT ACTUALLY CAUGHT SOMETHING!

Oh shit.

Calmly, but with rushed breath, he speed-walked back to the machine. Opening the flap, he pulled out a tiny clear ball with a small key inside.

Weird, that's not what he lined up. It must have moved around after the 2nd try. Oh well. At least it was something, and he won it.

He opened the tiny plastic ball and dropped the key into his hand. Just a simple silver key, nothing special. What a weird prize, considering everything else inside the machine.

Connor looked around for a spot to use the key on the machine. Nothing on top, but on the side there was a sizable door he didn't remember seeing earlier. This must be how they refill the thing, and they accidentally put the key in as a prize.

Hilarious.

Since he didn't get the one he wanted, he would now—plus a few others. The key slid in and popped the door open without a hitch. It was surprisingly dark for such a small space and way bigger than the outside of the machine looked. Sticking his hand into air, he reached an entire arm in. Just empty space. How big was this thing?

Connor stuck his head into the machine to get a good look at what choices he had available. But that didn't help the darkness, it only overwhelmed his senses.

Reaching farther in didn't help either. The thing was a damned cave!

Once his hips had slid through the entrance, enough was enough.

It was weird and started to freak him out. Stupid figures were not worth this much effort.

Right then, a hand lifted his legs, and in one motion, threw him in—whole.

Rudy was tired, and her mom was taking too long to pick out a purse. She'd heard "you'll understand how important it is to get it right, sweetie" more times than she could count. And counting was so a few grades ago. So when she asked for some change for one of the nearby game machines to keep her busy, it was tossed out of the soon-to-be-old purse without a thought.

The shiny, new claw machine immediately became her target. There were so many people inside that came with all sorts of accessories she could add to her growing collection. She was missing a few, so this was a golden opportunity to expand her make-believe story options.

With a strictly business mindset, she mentally cataloged her options. The new characters and possible storylines were worth pausing for, to make sure she got the right fit.

The policeman, firewoman, and nurse were already big players in her story—no need to replace them. The construction worker would be a great addition, but Rudy was concerned he wouldn't bring the longevity needed for hours-long play sessions. So, she went for something new and unique that would really impress her friends the next time they came over.

There he was: a boy in a green hoodie and glasses. Kinda cute too.This might be a boy she'd want to wink at, like her teacher does to her mom. But only if he was nice and shared. If he was mean, he'd be restricted to Play Jail. And nobody liked Play Jail.

Rudy made sure of that.

She lined up the claw and got to work.

pilot program

Mark Teppo

Monday

Two men, wearing dark brown overalls, bring the machine in on a heavy-duty hand truck. The wheels squeak, which is why Tami— always hyper-aware of every sound in the office pod, especially repetitive squeaky sounds—is the one who braces them about its arrival.

"What is it?" she asks, as one of the two technicians positions the box against the wall in the break room. "Some kind of vending machine?"

"Suppose so," the technician says.

The second technician unstraps the box and starts to strip off the plastic wrap. Tami—almost as nosy as she is hyper-sensitive to new sounds—gets in the way as the pair shove and shimmy the machine against the wall.

"Doesn't look like a vending machine," she decides.

The upper half of the machine is a glass case, and a metal stick sticks out of a panel on the front of the machine. When it is plugged in, a string of lights sparkles along the top edge of the box and a discordantly atonal jingle fuzzes out of a hidden speaker. Also on the front panel are a slot and an electronic pad, presumably for accepting payment, and below the stick, there is a hard plastic flap, allowing to the insides of the machine.

The actual contents of the machine are a mystery, as the glass portion is obscured by dark curtains.

"Is it going to make that noise all the time?" Tami asks.

"Couldn't say," the technician says. He pulls a folded piece of paper out of his pocket. He offers it, along with a pen, to Tami. "I need you to sign for it."

"Oh, I'm not authorized to sign for anything." Tami takes a step back, putting up her hands in mock surrender.

"What is it?" Bill has entered the break room.

You can always count on Bill: always ten minutes early, usually stays a half hour longer than socially acceptable, and if you aren't on your guard, likely to stand way too close—and between you and the exit. More so when he's had a few, which is pretty much a given.

"I need someone to sign for it," the technician says.

Bill, being the man in the room, shrugs and doodles a scrawl on the invoice. Tami notices that he doesn't even look at the invoice.

Their job complete, the technicians depart with their hand truck and plastic wrap.

Bill wanders over, mostly—Tami suspects—as an opportunity to invade her personal space. "New vending machine?"

"You signed for it," Tami says.

The display on the electronic pad lights up, and Tami uses its activation as an excuse to put some space between her and Bill. In a digitally retro font, the display reads: *This EMMC has been provided by CoCoKaChing! Commercial Enterprises.* The lights along the top sparkle and flash, and after a moment, the box farts out its terrible jingle again, and having announced itself, it retracts the curtains.

Inside the glass case are a jumble of cardboard shapes. Squares, spheres, cylinders, a few rhomboids, and even something that looks like a giant tic-tac-toe piece. Dangling above the shapes is a metal claw on a motorized track.

The display panel changes. *$1*, it says. *No change given.* A tiny icon of a claw blinks below the words.

"You have a dollar?" Tami asks, even though she knows Bill's answer.

Bill makes a show of checking for his wallet. "Left it at my desk," he says.

Tami stares at him, thinking a number of thoughts—some of which aren't very generous about Bill. These aren't new thoughts. Most of the female staff of the company have had these thoughts at one time or another.

"Maybe you could go fetch it," she says, trying to be nice.

Bill hesitates, and she knows he's not thinking about his wallet —which she knows is most certainly empty; Bill never has any cash. No, he's thinking about who he can bum a buck from. Gerry, maybe. Or Don, or Leonard. One of the gang will spot him. They always do.

"Yeah," he says. "I'll get it."

As soon as he is gone, Tami goes over to the cupboard over the coffee maker and raids the plastic jar labeled "Coffee Fund." There is $8.74 in it, mostly small change, but there are two bills. Both are really worn—one has been torn in half and taped back together—and she expects the machine to spit one or both of them back out. But the machine isn't as fussy as she is, and it readily slurps up the first bill she offers.

The claw icon on the display grows until it fills the screen. Words flash over the icon: *Make a selection.*

Tami once had a boyfriend with a light touch, and during the six months or so where she managed to overlook his addiction to games of chance, they had some fun at the arcades and county farms. He showed her how to wiggle and jiggle these types of machines (usually while standing way, way too close, but in his case, she didn't mind). She surveys the jumble of shapes, looking for something with a distinct edge. Something that wasn't half-buried. Nothing too round. She grasps the control rod on the machine, and when she moves it, the claw adroitly shadows her. She wiggles and jiggles it, and confident she's got it positioned correctly, she presses the button on the top of the stick.

The machine goes *ding!* The lights sparkle and cycle. The claw descends. Its tines begin to close around the shape she's selected. Tami holds her breath. The tines close. The claw rises. Caught in its grasp is one of the rhomboids.

The claw trundles over to the chute in the corner of the box. It drops the cardboard shape, and when the plastic flap unlocks, Tami retrieves her prize.

"Whadcha win?"

Tami spooks. "For crying out loud," she snaps as she spins around.

She expects Bill to be standing right there, but it's Frank, the quiet guy in Sales. He rarely speaks above a whisper, which makes him impossible to hear in any gathering of more than three people. Tami knows he likes cats and that he's got a thing for Ruth-Anne in Accounting, but she hasn't told anyone about this but Claire, who can keep her mouth shut.

"It's a box." She shows it to Frank, but finds herself loath to let him touch it—no way in hell is she going to give it to him.

"What's in it?" Frank asks.

"I just got it," she says, indicating the new machine behind her.

"What's that?" Frank asks. He eyes the box suspiciously, as if it suddenly appeared—which, if he hadn't been paying attention (which is quite likely) it might as well have.

"Ho ho! How'd you get a prize?" Bill is back, and not only does he have a few bills in his fist, but he's brought the gang: Gerry, Don, and Leonard—and oh look, here comes Sheila, Rhona, Ruth-Anne and, well, just about everyone, frankly.

"Are you going to open it?" Frank asks.

The box has no markings and no flap or top or discernible seam. Tami squeezes and twists, and the box pops open. Inside is a folded piece of paper.

"Is it a fortune?" Frank asks.

"Well, read it already!" Bill crows.

Tami glares at him, the guy who signs invoices without reading the fine print. "In a minute," she says. She peers at the inside of the box, trying to find some sort of marking. All she finds is really small print that reads: *Services and securities provided by CoCoKaChing! Commercial Enterprises. Underwritten by your employer, who values your contributions highly.*

Bill groans—loudly—at her reticence, and reading the vibe in the room, Tami grabs the piece of paper. Tucking the box under her arm—she's still not interested in giving it to Frank, or anyone else for that matter—she unfolds the paper. It's—surprisingly—on the company letterhead, and she starts to read.

It takes her a minute, which is fifty-eight seconds longer than everyone's patience.

"Where'd she get that?" someone asks.

"Out of the new vending machine," Bill says.

The crowd presses in, staring into the container filled with cardboard shapes.

"Do you pick one?"

"You have to grab it, I think."

"Like at the arcade."

"Does it cost anything?"

"A dollar." Bill is waving the bills he managed to scrounge from Gerry or Don or—it doesn't matter.

"I've been let go," Tami says.

No one hears her. Except Frank, who is a pretty good listener —well, when you have his attention.

Tami raises her voice. "I've been let go," she says again. This time, everyone hears her.

"Yeah," she says, waving the sheet of paper at the group. "That's what it says. Even has our CEO's signature on it. 'Thank you for your contributions, but your services are no longer fucking needed.'"

Someone—probably Ruth Anne—gasps audibly at Tami's language, and, yes, at another time, she would contritely put a quarter in the swear jar Ruth Anne keeps at her desk. But right now? Well, she's pretty fucking pissed.

"A dollar," she says. "After fourteen fu—"

There's more writing on the backside of the page. Tami doesn't know how she missed it before, but there it is. Bold letters at the top of the page. "Severance package."

Tami reads the fine print.

"Is—is this for real?" Sheila asks.

"Yeah," Tami says. Her grip tightens on the paper. "Sure as shit. It's fucking real."

Ruth-Anne has big eyes and looks like she's about to start

crying. Tami is struck by a sudden pang of embarrassment for cursing so freely in front of the other woman. She mentally promises she'll be better.

"Fuck this place," she says, and she leaves.

Okay, she'll start tomorrow.

Tuesday

"Do you think they're all like that?" Bill has a hungry look in his eye. That sort of look a gambler gets when they're down more than a few month's worth of mortgage payments. When they've stopped looking at all the unread messages on their phones. When they've switched off the ringer because that incessant noise is ruining their concentration. All they need is one hand—one good hand—and then everything will be all right. Everything will be better.

"No," Gerry says.

Bill glares at Gerry, who—as far as Bill is concerned, though Bill doesn't spend a lot of time thinking and rethinking about others—is a bit of a downer. Certainly not someone you want as your wingman when you're rolling dice at the craps table. Nor when you're working on the cuter of a pair of blondes, and the thing holding the fun up is what to do about her friend and, well, you ain't getting anywhere with Gerry at your side, you know?

"I heard she got a year and a half," Bill says. "Kept her benefits too."

"I don't think that's likely."

"Why not?"

A lot of the reason Gerry is a downer is because he doesn't understand how to have fun. He lacks—Bill tries to think of the word—whatever. Something. Bill has it. Bill knows he has it. A lot of ladies know he has it. A lot.

"Are you going to…?" Gerry gestures at the machine.

Bill steps out of the way and waves a hand at the machine. "Be my guest."

Gerry has a mass of bills in his hand, and Bill hovers, eager to see Gerry's reaction when he sees the display on the machine.

$12. *No change given.*

"What the fuck?"

Bill smirks without realizing he's done so. "That's what I said," he says. "What the actual fuck?"

Gerry's face scrunches up and gets pink near his ears. "I bought a muffin," he says. "And coffee." He waves the mass of one dollar bills at Bill. "I got change, so I could…"

"I know," Bill says. "Me too." Which is a lie, but Gerry—and this is the dependable thing about Gerry—Gerry doesn't call him on his bullshit.

Bill meant to get some bills, but getting small bills isn't just a matter of visiting an ATM—which only dispense twenties, by the way, and yeah, he wasn't going to visit eighteen shitty little convenience stores after that, buying a pack of gum or a bag of chips or a fucking muffin in order to get small bills. Sure, he could have gone to Topley's and gotten a bunch of ones—they definitely would have changed some twenties for him, but—even to Bill— that felt a bit rude. If you bother to go, you should stick around for a song or two, and before you know it, you've stuffed forty bucks worth of singles into some girl's g-string, and now she wants to give you a lap dance, and that's going to cost you way more than forty bucks. So, no. He didn't get change at Topley's.

Gerry starts feeding bills into the machine. "I've got enough for one try," he says.

When he's given the machine twelve singles, it *dings!* with delight and the screen tells him to make a selection.

"You should go for that square," Bill offers.

"I don't want the square," Gerry says. He wiggles and jiggles the stick, moving the claw toward a cylinder that is protruding from the jumble of cardboard shapes.

"That one?" Bill shakes his head. "You're not going to get that one. It's—"

"I'm going to get it."

"No, you won't. Look at it. It's not even free. You're just going—"

"I'm going to get it."

Bill shrugs. "Okay, but it's a bad choice, man. A bad—"

Gerry turns, and Bill is surprised by the sharp light in the other man's eyes. "It's my money," Gerry says, and for a second, Bill sees that Gerry isn't talking about the twelve dollars he put in the machine. He's talking about all those times Bill has come to him. Six bucks for a beer here. Twelve for that sandwich last week. Those three drinks last month. Gerry never says anything, but oh, yes indeed, he's keeping track.

Bill puts up his hands and steps back. "Yeah, sure," he says. "You do... whatever."

"Thank you," Gerry says with conviction. He returns his attention to the claw, and his dismissal of Bill is a hard slap. Like a door being slammed. Bill—if he was a thinker, which, for better or worse, he wasn't—might have learned something about himself in that moment, but the moment passes as Gerry pushes the button. The claw descends, and grabs... not the cylinder, but the triangle next to it.

The tines close. The claw lifts. The triangle dangles. The claw drops it in the chute.

Gerry retrieves his prize. His hands shake a little as he twists it open. Inside is a small device with a button on one end and an opening on the other. Gerry frowns as he peers at the fine print. There are two words: "Insert" and "Press."

"Insert where?" Bill asks.

"Maybe up your ass," Gerry offers.

"Swear jar," Ruth-Anne says.

Neither man had noticed her arrival. Gerry flushes at having been caught using language inappropriate for the office.

"You won something," Ruth-Anne says.

"I did." Gerry shows her the device.

"What is it?"

Gerry shrugs.

She repeats her question to Bill, who has even less of a clue than Gerry. "You're supposed to insert it," he says.

He doesn't say it like *that*, but he does have a reputation after all, which he's suddenly very consciously aware of when Ruth-Anne blushes, which makes things even more awkward because now he knows what she's thinking, and she knows that he knows, and *oh my god!*, he's never even thought about her that way. And if there's one thing Bill knows, you never—ever—tell a woman that you've never thought of them *that* way, especially a co-worker. Well, if you're following HR guidelines, you shouldn't be thinking about your co-worker at all—*ever*.

"Here," Gerry says, holding the device out to Bill.

"What?"

"You do it."

"Do what?"

"Put it up your nose," Gerry says. "Or, I don't know. Somewhere else."

"Why?" Bill asks. "You won it."

"Yeah, and I want to give it to you."

"Why?" Bill asks again, and Gerry doesn't look away.

Gerry looks him straight in the eye, and Bill sees exactly how deep the ledger is between them.

"Fine," he says. He grabs the device from Gerry. He orients it and raises it to his face. He places the open end into his nose and winks at Ruth-Anne—because this is what Bill does, after all; this is who he is. He presses the button.

The device goes *click!*

Bill screams. It's not quite the sort of howl you make when your team scores a last second winning goal in their sportsball arena, nor is it the sort of noise you make when you put your hand in a dark place and something with sharp teeth bites down. It is definitely the sort of noise frowned upon in the workplace, which means it is the kind of noise that—after surviving the mini-stroke such a noise causes—you are likely to say, "Oh, ha ha! You are such an attention-seeking moron."

Bill removes the device from his nose. "The look on your

faces," he crows. He wipes at his nose and leaves the break room, tossing the spent device in the trash on his way out.

Wednesday

Due to the nature of the sub-contract of the sub-contract with the original service company, Errol—whose employment with the third- (or fourth-, frankly) removed service is strictly week-to-week, cash in hand every Friday—does his rounds between two and three in the morning. Which he doesn't mind, really. He can listen to whatever he wants to on his portable Bluetooth speaker; he doesn't have to talk to anyone; and when he has to clean up some dude's mess in one of the executive toilets, he can say all the things he's *not* been saying out loud for weeks, and no one will hear him. And so, yeah, this morning is one of those mornings because someone stabbed themselves with a fountain pen or cut themselves with the paper cutter. He's not sure how. That machine has, like, eighteen safety guards on it. But *somehow*, someone did *something*, because there's a fuckton of blood-crusted paper towels shoved in the trash can in the men's room.

As he's wheeling his cart toward the elevator, still a bit unnerved about the mess in the bathroom, he hears a weird melody. It's almost like that sample in that song he's been grooving to this week. The one about snatching and grabbing—anyway, he hears this riff, and it's definitely out of place in an office environment like this, and curious, he wanders over to the break room, where he finds the machine.

It's all lit up. The lights are twinkling and sparkling. And there's a message on the little display pad on the front. *Milestone achieved. Free play.*

Errol looks around. There's no one here. Just him. He looks up at the camera in the corner of the break room. He's pretty sure the security dude is napping. It's after 3:00 A.M. He'd be napping if he had that dude's job.

Errol nudges the stick on the machine. The claw shudders and jiggles. He grabs the stick, moves it, and when the claw is positioned, he presses the button.

The machine *dings!* The claw drops. The tines close around an ovoid shape. The claw lifts. The tines strain. The cardboard shape doesn't come free.

Errol shrugs. So much for that. Like every other chance he's had over the years. Yeah, sure, you can play. But he never really wins, does he?

The display blinks, but the words don't change.

Errol stares at the display. He's thinking too hard about this, surely, but… fuck it, why not?

He maneuvers the claw again. Sure, he should try for something easier. Something like that box in the corner, which is resting right on top, but no—and this is a thing that his girlfriend Shanice says about him all the time—once he makes up his mind about something, there's no changing it. Just like when he had that offer to work at the sportsball arena, but he didn't like the vibe the recruiter was giving him.

Or that time—

Errol goes for the egg again. He has a better angle this time, and the tines hold for a few seconds. But not long enough to get the egg over to the chute.

The machine makes a slightly sad noise, and Errol gives it the finger. As if that will make things better.

The display changes. *$20. Payroll deduction available.*

Errol laughs. "Yeah, right. Payroll deduction, my ass."

He does, however, have a couple of twenties in his wallet.

"One time," he tells himself as he feeds a bill into the slot.

A few seconds later: "Okay, two times."

He gets it on the third try. When he opens it, he finds a watch. And not just any watch, but what looks like a really fancy watch. Errol's not a watch guy, but Shanice? Well, fancy things make Shanice happy, and when Shanice is happy, Errol is happy. And so he slips the watch into his pocket, thinking, "This is going to be a really nice surprise."

However, Shanice—who, yes, certainly does love fancy things and is always up for the *good* kind of surprises—knows there's no way in hell a man like Errol, who empties the trash cans at the big corporate offices and who gets paid *in cash* on a weekly basis, can afford a Rolex Cosmograph. Clearly, he's stealing shit from those corporate high-rises, and she doesn't want to be a party to any of that sort of nonsense, and so, after *ooh-ing!* and *aah-ing!* and promising to give him the best blowjob of his life *later,* she ghosts him as soon as he goes to bed—at eight in the morning. Which has been one of the dumbest things she's ever put up with in a relationship. God knows why she's bothered these last six months.

She keeps the watch, however. She's not a fool—and it is, after all, a Rolex Cosmograph.

Thursday

Leonard is sitting in Bill's cubicle, chasing some paperwork on an important licensing deal Bill had been working on. Management had sent Leonard an email, requesting that he watchdog Bill's workload while Bill was out of office. Why was Bill out of the office? The email didn't say. Leonard knew better than to ask that question in his reply. He merely read and acknowledged the email and wandered over to his co-worker's desk and tried to make sense of the scattered stacks of folders.

This isn't a surprise to anyone, but Bill wasn't very good with paperwork.

Anyway, Leonard is sitting there, fussing and looking and not really finding anything useful, and he hears Rhona and Sheila gabbing away in the next cubicle over.

"You just swipe your badge?"

"Yeah, you swipe and play. That's it?"

"That's it?"

"Just swipe."

"Isn't that…? I mean, what sort of deduction?"

"I don't know. Does it matter? I mean, come on, Sheila. Forty-two weeks."

"Is that how much Tami got?"

"That's what I heard?"

"That's… that's almost a year."

"I know. And so, yeah, they can deduct a couple hundred or so, right?"

"I… I guess. Sure."

"I heard Abby won some steak knives."

One of them laughs. Rhona, perhaps? Leonard isn't sure.

"That's a consolation prize, if there is one."

"I know, right?"

"Irving got a gift card to the steakhouse."

"Really? How much?"

"A hundred bucks or something."

"No, how much did he spend in the machine to win that?"

"Oh, I don't know. Probably at least that much."

In the break room, the machine *dings!* Someone starts shouting. Rhona and Sheila leave the cubicle to find out what's going on. Someone has won a trip to Alaska. A trip for one.

Leonard never finds the deal paperwork.

Bill doesn't come back to the office, either.

Friday

Frank had spent the week watching everyone else throw themselves at the new vending machine, and, well, he had been to Vegas a few times. He knew how these things worked. They were rigged, of course. The house always wins, but they do have to pay out now and again in order to get the suckers to think they have a chance. And Frank… Frank wasn't a sucker. He was careful.

Sure, the first time he had sat down at a blackjack table, he had lost six thousand dollars. Six grand! Twice what he had allotted for his trip. All gone and then some. In the first hour! He barely

left his room the rest of the time he was there, so absolutely morti-
fied at his loss of control.

The next time—and yes, he knew he shouldn't have gone back,
but he wasn't going to let this moment of weakness define him.
He was going to do better, and so, the next time, he remained in
control, and it took him thirty-six hours to lose all the money he
brought.

And then he won a grand in a slot machine at the airport as he
was leaving, which complicated the weekend's math, but that
wasn't the point. He had been steadfast. He hadn't embarrassed
himself.

And so, as the week went on, Frank resisted the lure of the
vending machine in the break room—especially when it started
taking payroll deductions. *You're going into debt!* He wanted to
shout at Rhona and Sheila as they giggled and swiped their
keycards on the machine. *You're going to be working for free for how
many months?*

They wouldn't have listened. They would have given him
that look, that pursed lips look that made them look like they
were constipated fish. And they were friends with Ruth-Anne.
Not friend friends, but, you know, Friday afternoon cocktail hour
friends. And they would say something, and Ruth-Anne
would—

Frank didn't need it.

Except—and this was what kept him flailing about in his bed
last night, all sweaty, slick, and nervous—what if he did win? The
machine wasn't like the slots. It wasn't like the blackjack table. It
was, ostensibly, a game of skill. You could find the right angle on
the right shape. You could win. You really could.

And so, when he finally gave up on sleep, he showered,
shaved, and put on one of his nicer suits. He wore the tie Ruth-
Anne liked—the one she had commented on during the holiday
party last year. He eschewed taking the train and drove in, getting
to work an hour before everyone else. If he was going to play the
machine, he didn't want everyone hovering. Watching him.
Waiting for him to fail.

No, he was going to let the machine deduct—how much? He didn't even know. Did the machine tell you? He wasn't sure.

It didn't matter. He was going to play.

It's nice and quiet in the office when Frank arrives, and he doesn't stop at his desk, afraid that if he does, he'll lose his nerve altogether. No, it's best to do it first, he thinks as he heads right to the break room, the sort of focused confidence that usually turns heads.

The machine is waiting for him. The string of lights along the top are winking slowly. When he touches the claw machine lever, the lights inside the box brighten, and somewhere deep inside the box, a circuit connects and the machine plays its little jingle.

Frank tenses. The song is annoying. And so loud! He looks around, afraid he isn't alone. That the stupid jingle will summon people. Like Rhona. Or Sheila. No, no. He can't have that. Frank waffles, thinking that maybe this is a stupid idea. Maybe he should go to his desk and get to work. Maybe he'll leave an hour early today. He's got his car. He could go do something…

"Do it," he whispers. "Just fucking do it."

Again, a furtive glance. No one else is here. No one heard him. He doesn't owe a quarter if no one heard him.

He presses his badge against the machine's panel. It beeps, happily sucking away part of his paycheck. The display reads: *Make a selection.*

Frank licks his lips and carefully studies the landscape within the box. There's the rectangle that Don has been working on all week. He pulled it free Wednesday afternoon, but he could never manage to grab it again. And that triangle next to the chute. It looks like it'll come right out, but Frank isn't so sure. And the spheres? Forget those. No one has gotten a sphere yet. The claw can't even reach all the way around one.

No, it's the 'X.' Right up against the glass. Frank knows he can get it. The angle is good. It's not tangled with any other object. One swipe with the claw and it'll be his.

Frank's hands are sweaty. He wipes them on his pants. He is struggling to breathe, and for an instant, he thinks his tie is choking him, but it's not. It's a nice tie. Ruth-Anne likes it. It's not the tie.

Frank wipes his hands again. *Go for the 'X,'* he thinks.

He works the lever. When the claw has stopped swaying—because it always sways when you move it—he presses the button to make it descend. The machine goes *ding!* Frank closes his eyes. He can't watch. He starts counting. *One. Two. Three.* It takes the machine about fifteen seconds to complete its cycle. He knows, because he's been watching it all week. *Eight. Nine. Ten.* Did he hear it click? That noise it makes when the tines close after dropping—no, no, he's not going to look. *Thirteen. Fourteen. Fifteen.*

Frank opens his eyes.

The 'X' is gone.

His knees shaking, Frank crouches and looks through the plastic flap. There's something in there. Frank reaches in and pulls out his prize.

He tears the box open, and inside he finds…

Well, not a watch. Not a plastic fern, like the one Leonard won yesterday. It's just a piece of paper. Like what Tami won. How many months of severance? The number kept growing, frankly, and according to Claire, Tami has already booked a very long vacation to Aruba or someplace.

But that's not what Frank has.

His prize is a printout of an email.

To: CEO@ . . .
From: Sales@CoCoKaChing!
Subject: EMMC configuration

Congratulations on participating in a pilot program with CoCoKaChing! Commercial Enterprises's new Employee Motivation & Management Console. Each EMMC has a comprehensive package of features that may be customized to best suit your workplace environment.

Whether you are seeking to incentivize, motivate, or to reduce head-count, the CoCoKaChing! Commercial Enterprises's EMMC provides an experience that will galvanize your staff without the untidy awkward-ness of direct C-level interaction.

Please choose from the following configuration options.

Product Selection Success Rate: [x] < 1%

- First Reward: [x]

- Milestone Rewards: [x]

- Milestone Selections: [x] Budget Recovery [x] Workforce Reduction

Incentive / Motivation Selection Rate: [x] 5%

- Incentive Pool Allotment (based on corporate income, previous year reported): [x] .02%

- Incentive Monetization Ratio: [x] 1200 / 1

Headcount Reduction Rate: [x] 75%

- Mortality Stage Index: [x] 9

NOTE: Changing this setting requires approval by the company's Board of Directors. CoCoKaChing! Commercial Enterprises requires proper compliance and liability documentation on file before any changes will be allowed to the MSI.

refresh

Pia Baur

<u>reFresh</u>

By Pia Baur

A few months after I started my dream job, the nightmares returned. I used to wet the bed as a child, waking up screaming sometimes, imagining that my father's dead hands were wrapped around my neck or my mother's neck, then my Grandma Deedee would hobble into the room, tell me that I was safe, and we'd sit in the kitchen and drink hot chocolate while my sheets and pajamas tumbled in the dryer.

It was Deedee who inspired me to focus on neurology and specialize in memory research. She knew that she was at high-risk of developing early-onset Alzheimer's, and when the medical company myCap Innovations first began offering what they called memory-preservation Capsules, she signed up right away. *Like a back-up drive for your brain* is how they initially described it.

The first Capsules weren't fancy. You had to climb inside a machine that looked like an MRI scanner and lie patiently for hours while they uploaded everything onto an egg-shaped device.

Of course it didn't solve everything that comes with Alzheimer's, like the eventual loss of motor skills, but as long as you faithfully backed it up, you could retrieve whatever was starting to get hazy as your mind regressed. The process was called *reFresh*.

It allowed Deedee to keep living as the person I'd always known.

Nathan Meager took on the role of CEO of myCap Innovations, and he promised he would push the capabilities of memory-preservation Capsules.

He announced his vision of a technology that could do more than just help us remember—it would erase what we *didn't* want to remember. An unwanted experience could be wiped. Something as horrific as the source of PTSD could be wiped away, but so could something arguably more frivolous, like a painful end to a love affair.

It was a procedure myCap would be working to perfect, but big corporations were already utilizing the basic technology. Capitalism always steps in.

A mandatory reFresh could be issued by a company under terms of employment to prevent corporate espionage. This was entering shaky legal ground. Should an entity be allowed to *force* an individual to erase a memory? Who did the memory *really* belong to?

The courts would battle this one out for a long time. But while they did, myCap Innovations acted quickly. They were eager to move forward with their ideas and wanted someone to spearhead a big project for a year.

Nathan Meager reached out to me personally. I was shocked because I'd pointedly argued against corporate initiatives to erase the memories of their employees.

I alienated many of my colleagues when an abstract of mine was misconstrued as being anti-science. I wasn't an outcast, but the paper had isolated me from the people in my field. My research funds were depleted, and my work came to a near-standstill.

The first cheesy thought I had when I met Nathan Meager was anything but. He didn't have an imposing build, but his presence was arresting, even in a room that held just the two of us. His face was all sharp corners and angular features, lacking any softness in his cheeks or forehead.

He straightened his tie and folded his hands on his desk, looking very much like an attentive student, as though he was the one being interviewed.

"Dr. Breashears, you're one of the most knowledgeable neurologists in researching how we humans manipulate our own memory."

I paused. "My interest in memory is to preserve what's important and find a treatment for degradation of memory, not about creating a product for the masses and selling it to them."

He waved that aside. "I didn't ask you here to defend yourself. I was hoping you'd humor me with a thought experiment."

I met his gaze.

"What's the number one reason for wrongful convictions?"

"Faulty eyewitness testimony," I said immediately.

He nodded. "That's something you could help prevent by working with us." He unclasped his hands and gave me a pointed look.

I didn't answer.

He switched gears. "But memory can be an encumbrance too." He relaxed in his chair. "What do you know about PTSD?"

I was now sure he had researched my past as thoroughly as I had tried to look at his. "Some people would want to separate from their traumatic memories, and there's a good chance they *could* be erased, but the body remembers trauma even if you attempt to excise the memory itself."

"But it can help treat trauma. Isn't that worth something?"

"So, essentially, you want me to figure out how to target specific memories? That's already being done."

"In limited ways. I'm talking about beyond refining that ability, I'm talking about harvesting and preserving a very *specific* memory in a separate capsule."

I stiffened at the word "harvest."

"I understand your personal stake in this. We all have loved ones we'd like to hold onto for as long as possible." He cast a quick glance at me before continuing. "What if that technology could benefit humanity as a whole?" His gaze shifted upwards, as if he was telling me about a distant prophetic dream. "On a scale much larger than treating PTSD and dementia or preventing wrongful convictions?" He sat up and leaned forward. "*True* empathy. You could make people real empaths with open access to memories. Allow others to feel what someone else felt at that precise moment."

"I don't want to package your memory product for the masses," I repeated, just as I had when Meager had first called me in to meet with him.

He shook his head and sat up again in his upright, student-like posture. "This isn't a product to be sold—we don't want to profit from harvesting people's memories. This is about helping people. It'd be just like a medical research experiment, and you would be in charge of the lab."

I could sense a big asterisk somewhere in what he'd just said, even though I wasn't quite sure what it pointed to.

"Consider our thought experiment. Think of what you can do for your own research passions after running this project for myCap," he said, his pupils still growing larger.

"You would help me with my own research?"

Meager nodded earnestly. "You're brilliant. You'll reach break-throughs in your dementia research, and myCap Innovations will help you get there."

He held his hand out across his desk. I stood up and shook it.

Setting up a Capsule had become simpler since Deedee's time. For an upload and a reFresh, clients went to a myCap Innovations Laboratory where there was a treatment chair and a helmet-like contraption that connected to the Capsule.

For a reFresh, a specialty appointment was made and a myCap technician would examine the most recent myCap upload, make a neurological map, erase what was requested, usually workplace memories per employment contracts, and then return the modi-fied upload back to the client.

I knew that I, too, would have to undergo this type of reFresh procedure after my employment ended.

I understood that at least part of my job would be perfecting the harvesting of memories and making sure that the reFresh procedures were as smooth and undetectable as possible. Clients shouldn't be able to sense a gaping hole where the undesirable traumatic memory had once been, like the pain from a phantom limb. In essence, my job was to improve the reFresh procedure itself.

I told Meager about the difficulty in erasing significant memories or entire periods of time, that there would be inevitable difficulties.

I reached back for an analogy that I'd used with acquaintances not in my field. Imagine that an explicit memory stored in your brain is like an object placed in a field. Like any object, it casts a shadow. And you can remove it from the field, but unlike a regular object where its shadow also disappears, this shadow does not disappear completely.

I anticipated that the main problem would be related to sensory memories, which can be difficult to access and extract completely. Olfactory memories, for instance, are buried so deeply and are easiest for its owner to recognize but the most difficult to recall. Quite possibly, random sensory input might make a client's brain try to look for a memory that was no longer there.

But that didn't happen to me after my own reFresh.

For me, I started having nightmares again.

Not the kind of night terrors I'd had as a child, but I would feel something like fear in my sleep and the same image came to me again and again: a vintage arcade game. A claw machine. At one point, almost omnipresent, found in malls, arcades, the county fair, and always filled with prizes—the kind you could win with a token and a little skill.

My time at myCap ended up flying by.

Nathan Meager said it would be a "hardcore" immersive year, after which, I would get the radical reFresh procedure, erasing my entire year working for myCap.

With an entire year gone, it took me a moment to regain my footing as I moved to a new city. San Francisco is often the cool gray city of love. I embraced it immediately, and as fall arrived and the fog lifted, I felt like it was opening itself up to me, embracing me back.

I decided on a rigid routine where I started my mornings early, going to the bakery on Jackson Street where I bought coffee and a bagel on my way to work. I had secured the new director position at the Neurology Research Center, funded by myCap Innovations, part of San Francisco Medical School.

I dipped back into my past and got former colleagues to join my team. I paid off my med school loans and bought a small but beautiful apartment near Fisherman's Wharf with waterfront views.

I felt happier than I had in a very, very long time. Of course, I couldn't remember if I'd been happy during my year at myCap, but I had the distinct sense that it had been a stressful year. "Hardcore", just like I'd been told.

I'd been warned about the weirdos in San Francisco, but I only had one odd encounter as I was settling into my new life. I was accosted by a strange woman just as I finished eating my lunch in the courtyard of my lab at a picnic bench. My head down and putting things away, I thought I heard someone call my name.

When I looked up, she screamed an expletive at me and shouted about myCap. I was so shocked I barely picked up what she was saying. Then, she threw a bucket of unknown liquid at me and ran away.

Had I heard her right? Had she actually said, "myCap"? How would she have known that I worked there or who I was?

I looked at my things, wondering if maybe I had something with the company logo on it. I wondered if she might be an old coworker from myCap. But with my memory wiped, I had no way of knowing.

The only thing I'd mentally noted was that upon examination, my lanyard had an extra key that I couldn't ever remember carrying before—and it hadn't been noted after my employment ended.

Part of my contract included a mandatory health check-up with a myCap doctor for the next five years. I understood that, while

 reFresh

they said this was part of the generous health insurance package, it was also a way for them to make sure the reFresh procedure had worked and that there were no after-effects.

"Lucy Breashears?" The medical assistant called me into the office.

I often corrected people and added that my title was actually "doctor." But in this case, I decided not to. I knew that if I did, I would stand out, and I intuitively understood from the moment I woke up to my new life in San Francisco—post-myCap—that it would be bad for me to stand out.

"So you worked for myCap on a temporary basis and agreed to have your time there erased in a reFresh procedure?"

I nodded.

"Any strange side effects or symptoms recently?" she asked. I found the way she had said "myCap" odd, almost disdainful, as if she disliked her own employment there.

She studied my face carefully, and my hand found its way into my pocket, fingering the jagged edge of the mystery key and thinking about the arcade game in my dreams. My nightmares had expanded beyond the claw machine and had become increasingly more disturbing, but I was reluctant to disclose this to anyone, least of all my former employer.

She clocked the hesitation on my face, leaned in, and spoke more quietly. "Are you looking for information on what was erased while you were working there?"

She handed me a pamphlet entitled, *myCap Cares*, which she pulled from her inside coat pocket.

I bowed my head towards her, and she continued, "A number of ex-employees are getting together to find out what was actually erased. A 24-hour chunk of time, gone."

24 hours? I had been there 365 times longer than that.

But again, I had the feeling that it would be unwise to make myself stand out and tell her that I'd been there much longer than that.

She pointed to the pamphlet.

"There's a contact card tucked inside. You should get in touch with her."

Back in my apartment, I pulled out the contact card. The name read Sylvia Vye. A reporter sniffing around. Potentially trying to break a big story. Exposing a corporate scandal. It felt like a trope. Had I been tricked by myCap? Were there others like me? People who had been offered great opportunities by myCap without realizing what the real tradeoff was?

Sylvia gave me specific instructions to follow before she would meet. I was to go to the underground Embarcadero BART station and stand by the second bench situated by the south stairs, sit for ten minutes while flipping innocuously through the myCap pamphlet given to me by the doctor, then get up, and walk across the platform and exit via the north stairs.

After that, she called me to meet in the Tenderloin at a dilapidated café called the Art Bistro.

"I had to confirm your identity," she said. "The cameras on the platform captured you doing exactly what we instructed you to do and confirmed your physical appearance. It's really you, Lucy Breashears."

"Dr. Breashears," I said, despite myself.

Sylvia studied me for a moment as I said this. I thought of the network she must have in order to have gotten access to BART's surveillance footage. This was real.

She was tall and slim, with long hair that fell around her face, nearly hiding her profile. I was initially startled by her face, because at first glance, I thought she had no lips. Eventually, I saw that she wore a large quantity of lipstick that matched her exact skin tone.

"The lipstick makes it harder to read lips. If I'm captured on camera or someone is tracking me," she said. "But I know the places that don't have cameras. This is one of them."

"What's going on?"

She studied me. "Were you hired by myCap for a 24-hour special project?"

I considered whether or not I should tell her the truth. After a minute, I decided that she would likely reveal more if I told her the truth. "A special project at one of their labs. But it was a year long."

"You weren't a two-four employee?"

"What's that?"

"Two-fours are what we're calling the employees who came to myCap Lab for twenty-four hours and agreed to have their memories of working there erased." I could sense that she wasn't quite sure whether to keep talking. I remained silent, and she drained her mug, then continued, "You weren't a lab tech?"

I shook my head. "I was in charge of a lab."

She caught herself quickly, but I could tell she was excited. "You might be the key here," she said.

"In what sense?" The word *key* embedded itself in my ear, and I thought again about the unidentified key on my chain.

"We're trying to find all the two-fours who came to myCap. They were all told that the job was product testing and focus groups at a lab—the one I think you were in charge of. Something was happening there, but the victims have no memories. But you —*you* might have crossed paths with the victims."

"I'm like them, I don't remember my time there." I took my first sip of coffee. "I don't remember last year at all."

Sylvia leaned in. "We have to get those memories back. We have to figure out what you were doing that year."

"What makes you so suspicious that myCap was doing something nefarious?"

She stared at me. I noticed she had almost colorless gray eyes lined with heavy kohl. It made her look as if the pigment in her eyes had flowed out through the corners of her eyes.

"An entire year of your life has been stolen," she said simply.

Hearing it phrased that way gave me pause. Had myCap really stolen an entire year of my life? I'd agreed to it. It wasn't *stolen*. It was donated. I can only guess what my facial expression was.

"How much money did they give you for that whole year?" She didn't give me time to answer. "I'll tell you what the two-fours got. $30,000." She paused for emphasis. "Lending their minds and bodies for 24 hours. Wouldn't you want to know what you allowed a company to do to you for a day in exchange for $30,000?"

I bit my lip.

"You see what I'm getting at." She took a sip from her drink. "How much were you paid for your work with them? Not $30,000 every day?"

"My role must've been simple. Just a supervisor," I said, shaking my head. "If I even *had* a role," I added quickly. "Maybe I was something like a janitor."

"You think myCap hired you—a *doctor*—for a janitorial job?" She eyed me suspiciously. "We *have* to find out what's on your original Capsule, before you' reFreshed, what myCap wiped after you stopped working for them."

"How do we do that?"

"I have a network I've been building for a long time." She looked at me. "But you're key in all of this."

There was that word again. I examined my lanyard again. It was a very distinctive key that did not look like it belonged to a door. A very clear number was stamped on it. I wracked my brain. Had I rented a mailbox?

When I went to bed that night, I had another nightmare. There was more unsettling imagery, but this time, my mystery key made an appearance. I used it to unlock the claw machine.

I started meeting with Sylvia regularly. Sometimes, I wasn't sure who I was really dealing with. She changed her appearance frequently and always wore her strange lipstick.

We met as though I was an informant, a whistleblower, but

really it felt like the opposite. I was telling her what felt like ordinary facts, and she was attempting to interpret them into something whistleblowing-worthy.

She told me she had been building a lab. "We've managed to hack into the myCap cloud," she explained. "Eventually, I think we can find at least the chunk of data they took. It's probably encrypted, but we'd at least have it."

I hadn't experienced any odd triggers from sensory input as I'd suspected might happen with others who'd had a reFresh procedure, so all I could really tell her were the nightmares I'd been having, which had since expanded beyond the uncanny feeling associated with imagery of the claw machine.

Once, I'd been watching a shape I couldn't identify trapped inside a plastic bag, frantically trying to get out. Another time I was tied to a bed, and someone had stacked teacups on my legs. More than once, I was in some kind of water, feeling like I was drowning.

"Your expertise is memory," she would mumble absentmindedly. "None of your nightmares feel like memories? They don't feel familiar?"

I always shook my head.

After a few more meetings, I reluctantly told her, "I was diagnosed with PTSD in my teens. I still have plenty of bad memories from that, but I can't imagine that I would have that sheer number of additional traumatic experiences that I've been dreaming about."

Eventually she finally announced, "I think we've accessed your original Capsule, with the erased data before your reFresh."

"Did you look at any of the memories on there?"

"Not yet. It's time for you to come to our lab and meet Lars, the wunderkind. He predates Nathan Meager."

The lab was a garage. The very cliché of what you would think of when picturing a hackers' garage filled with computer geniuses.

"Lars, our missing piece is here," Sylvia said by way of greet-ing, as she ushered me in.

Lars looked as if he hadn't been outside in years, a bit like a droopy houseplant. But when he saw me, his face became ener-gized. "I know all about you," he said. "You were doing for myCap what I'm trying to do right now—take apart and piece together memories."

"Harvesting memories?" I asked.

"From other people. But I've been trying to focus on finding something linked to myCap, but it's hard."

"What have you found?"

"I would need a super computer to decrypt everything completely, but I've been able to access snippets of your erased memories based on temporal location. We can view them on my screen. Obviously, we can't experience some of the other sensory experiences stored on the Capsule—we won't be able to smell anything, and some of the audio might seem garbled or odd."

I nodded.

"You've experienced or viewed memories from a Capsule before?"

Sylvia spoke for me. "Dr. Breashears's job was to do the harvesting and modifying for the two-fours. So yes, and then some."

Lars beckoned to us to sit by him and watch his screen.

I saw that he had tried to sort the jumbled data from my Capsule into discrete, singular memories—difficult, and some-thing that I know I could've done better though I didn't have his ability to hack into a stranger's Capsule on the corporate. In a way, I realized, Lars and I had done similar work: isolating and deciphering memories.

The first visuals were in a dark room. There was a vintage claw machine, just like the one I'd been dreaming about. This one was filled with what looked like golfballs.

Sylvia and I stepped closer to the screen. Some vague outline of a person had just successfully claimed one of the golfballs.

"What are those?"

"They look like the capsules that myCap uses—but these are spherical, not egg-shaped."

Then, all three of us saw the myCap logo on the golfballs in the claw machine.

"That's the claw machine you talked about?"

"Yes," I said. My breath stopped for a fraction of a second. You could dream erased memories?

The screen went black.

Then lit up again.

In the next one, there was an urgent, hectic motion; someone was running. There were strange echoes that sounded like screams and the frantic breathing enveloped everything.

Sylvia looked at me. "Do you think this is one of your memories? Does this *feel* like it belongs to you?"

I shook my head, though I knew there was something familiar about it, even though I understood that it wasn't mine. Had I dreamt it?

The image changed. I recognized another dream.

Someone was being pulled by their hair, legs kicking. A sound as if trying to scream, but muffled. Duct taped? Had I ever been kidnapped and duct taped?

There was jarring movement on the screen, and I realized we were experiencing another memory entirely. The image was turning as if a camera had been dropped and was rolling over several times. It was so disorienting that I had trouble recognizing what was happening, until I saw a steering wheel and blood streaked across glass. Had I ever been in a car wreck?

Lars and Sylvia seemed to be thinking the same thing, because they both looked at me.

"I've never been in anything but a fender bender when I was a teenager," I said. I thought I should tell them that they had hacked the wrong Capsule as we watched, but I could feel my trust in the whole situation waning.

We went through several more. They were all abrupt, short files that made it hard to determine context. I had the distinct sense that they were not my memories.

Then, another image, but even though this was the most blurry of them, I recognized it the way I hadn't recognized the others. It was me adding the mystery key to my key ring and as I let myself sink into the memory, suddenly I understood what it was.

Sylvia called me while I was on the road back to San Francisco. The Capsule I'd retrieved from Deedee's safe deposit box was sitting securely inside my bag in the seat next to me. The key for it was back on my lanyard.

She told me that Lars and others from the underground were making progress decrypting my memories, but it seemed myCap had taken even more protective measures than they were known to.

I told her to keep me updated and then we hung up.

I didn't tell her that I had realized I'd made a backup Capsule for myself, and that I'd just retrieved it.

Back in my apartment, I entered my office.

I didn't have the same myCap equipment to view and reFresh memories, but I had a rudimentary setup with a screen and a plug for a Capsule, similar to, but less sophisticated than, the technology in Lars's garage.

From the closet in my office, I grabbed the helmet-like device and sat down to put it on, plugged in, and prepared to dive into my original Capsule.

I had an innate feeling that letting myself remember would make the nightmares stop. Not just the dreams of the claw machine, but also the nightmares that had plagued me as a child, that had once been quelled by Deedee's presence.

The first memory I reentered had me standing in a deserted arcade draped with the myCap Innovations logo. The games were all lit up and flashing impatiently, waiting for players while Nathan Meager gave me a tour. He held several game tokens in his hand.

"I thought you deserved to see what your hard work has led to so far." He grinned at me.

I expressed nothing.

"Did you know that CEOs are over ten times more likely to suffer from psychopathy than the general population?"

"Suffer? I don't think I've seen you suffer the entire time I've known you," I, Lucy Breashears from the memory, said.

Meager chuckled. "What would you charge for this claw machine?"

"I don't know anything about profit margins."

He shook his head. "No, you still don't understand. It wasn't about the money. That part was never a lie—there's no monetary profit here." He looked up at me. "I mean, getting to see PTSD up close—humanity at its lowest, and its most base and unforgivable, the stuff that makes people have nightmares. What would you charge for that?"

"For a real nightmare? Trauma is priceless."

"Spoken like a true capitalist, but I'm about to demonstrate that you can," he said, and winked. He took one of the tokens in his hand and inserted it into the slot of the claw machine. "You want to see how this works?"

"Someone's personal hell is another person's playground?"

"That's the idea," he said, and expertly began moving the two levers to control the claw.

"Do you know which memory is in which Capsule?" I asked.

"That would take the fun out of it," he said. He managed to snatch up one of the Capsules. It seemed impossibly difficult when the Capsule had no angles or squeezable elements that would make it easy for the claw to snatch it. He picked the Capsule out of the prize drawer. "Should we look at it together?"

He opened the booth and beckoned me inside. When he closed the door, he explained, "This is one of the experiential chambers. Maybe I can get you to work on this, but it seems like it's a different skillset. We'll get it down eventually, but we want to make it more immersive—so that the sensory memories come to life as well. That's why I was pushing so hard about making the memory as complete as possible."

He plugged in the Capsule then sat back in an armchair. There was only one.

The screen turned on. Just a flicker, but I could read the words. *Arbeit Macht Frei.*

Then: humans. Were they alive or dead? I wasn't sure. The olfactory memory was present too. Human waste. Putrefaction. The images were a bit jumpy, moving around, but I could tell we were in the same place.

I looked at Nathan, whose eyes were fixed on the screen. I could tell his mouth was open by the light that reflected from his teeth.

I found myself breaking away from the memory, stepping back slightly, and reaching for the doorknob, but my hand seemed to pass through it as if it wasn't there. Why couldn't I leave?

Then I realized it was because I was inside the memory my Capsule stored. This was the memory as it had happened to Lucy Breashears from last year, not the Dr. Lucy Breashears, who had retrieved the secret backup Capsule from Deedee's safe deposit box. I couldn't change what I was watching because it had already happened. I was both grounded in reality and trapped inside the Capsule memory.

Nathan insisted we both play the claw machine game again, and then we experienced two more memories that he told me were exceptional and had been extremely difficult to get. One was from 1978 in the mortuary in Guyana at Jonestown. The other was a newer one from 1999 in Columbine, Colorado.

When we emerged from the memory chamber, Nathan's lips were turning inward, like he was suppressing a smile.

"Now you know where the bad memories I've been asking you to harvest go."

"Are these just for you?"

"Of course not. I thought you understood that by now. It's for anyone willing to lay down a lot of money for the chance to experience *true* empathy."

"True empathy," I repeated.

"Feel what that individual was feeling. Have you ever experienced anything more thrilling than that?" There was a wild look on his face that he attempted to gain control of before he looked at me again, much more reigned in, but his face was still made of sharp and unforgiving lines. "You see now why it's better that you don't remember any of this?"

"I'm doing this to help treat PTSD, just like you told me when you first hired me," I heard myself say.

"What about your own PTSD? For your memories, I'd pay more than $30,000." His pupils widened as he looked at me. "A child witnessing her parents' murder-suicide? Sole survivor of a family annihilation attempt? That's a good one. There are people who'd want that memory, and you wouldn't have to live with it anymore. You could be just a regular orphan. A rich one. And with your dream job."

"How much would they pay for it?"

He looked up at the ceiling again, as he often did, just like during our first meeting, as if he was receiving a prophetic sign. "I think we could easily get $250,000 for each turn to play the claw machine."

I didn't know whether to say yes. Just as I'd told myCap before, once a shadow is cast inside the mind, it can't be fully excised. The body remembers even if the mind does not. Was I the kind of person who would monetize trauma?

I decided then that I would need to make a secret backup Capsule and put it somewhere safe and leave a clue for myself in a form so innocuous that myCap wouldn't think of wiping it during my reFresh at the end of my employment. A figurative key. Or a literal one.

I woke up feeling rejuvenated.

For the first time since meeting Sylvia and Lars, I had experienced what felt like dreamless sleep. No claw machine or any of the harvested memories it held inside the special spherical Capsules, nor any nightmares of my father's hands.

I felt more clearheaded and vigorous than usual. I showered and got dressed and went to my usual coffee shop. The cream cheese on my bagel tasted fresher and tangier than usual, and my coffee was the perfect temperature—strong and robust.

As I hurried across the sidewalks of downtown, everything felt *newer* somehow, and I wondered if it was because accessing my erased memories had allowed me to jump back in time a little, to before San Francisco was my home.

I greeted my employees, some of whom used to be classmates, sat in my sunny office to do some work, then decided to eat my lunch in the courtyard, at exactly the same bench where the strange woman had assaulted me with her bucket.

The feel of the power I had felt delicious, knowing that it was due to knowledge I now had that Sylvia Vye and her underground whistleblowers wanted, and what Nathan Meager and myCap had wanted to prevent me from holding onto. But I had my memories. I knew.

Sylvia wanted to be the heroic journalist, and she wanted to cast me as the whistleblower.

I called Sylvia from my desk, and we made plans to meet at the Art Bistro.

I made sure to put on nude lipstick before I left my office, and I rehearsed what I would say to her. *Sylvia, I can't help the movement anymore. Not directly. But I can point the way. If you want, you can fall down the rabbit hole. All you need is $250,000.*

bad news

Elle Mitchell

BY ELLE MITCHELL

The first time it happened, I was in an abandoned house at the end of a street high on a hill—the most stereotypical place to see a ghost. There she was, though. Or rather, there her story was.

I saw everything through her eyes. She was washing the dishes, singing with the radio. Her husband joined her to dry them, humming quietly along. They swayed side by side for a while, keeping the rhythm of the music.

After drying the last plate, her husband stepped back from the counter and pulled her to him, sudsy hands and all. They laughed and kissed and started to dance. She was thinking about how lucky she was, how happy she was to be a new wife, how they could do dishes like this forever, how wrong her dad had been about them. *Of course they'd last.*

When her heart gave out, she was only an arm's length away from him. He spun her out, but she didn't make it back.

Inconsolable, I was. For days, maybe weeks; I'm not sure. It all got blurry for a while as I waited for more spirits to tell me about their deaths. Dark alleys no longer just held wolves. Swimming in any water felt like a risk.

I retreated.

It took a while for me to realize that it doesn't work like that. Avoiding areas wouldn't keep me safe. Avoiding *objects* would. Which objects acted like invitations were impossible to guess. Nothing seemed off limits.

Washing my hands in a craft store bathroom gave a young boy an opportunity to slip into my skin and show me his mother driving him to the store and promising to buy him something to paint.

They were in the ceramics section when she needed to pee. He sat on the edge of the slippery counter playing with the faucet as she hummed in the bathroom. He turned it on and off, like music for his mother.

The young boy fell off just as she opened the stall door. He'd been thinking about how he'd like to put glitter on the trunk of the elephant.

The older I got, the more I saw. The dead's thoughts were mine, their memories as well. I smelled what they smelled. I was wherever they were, *whenever* they were, lost in their life.

Some deaths were so dark I worried I'd never sleep again. I spent countless hours thinking, worrying, researching. *Could I help these people? Tell someone who their killer was? Find their bodies?* But I knew some of their cases were solved. The souls just wanted to be heard one last time.

So I tried not to touch *anything*.

No matter where I went, no one talked to me if I didn't touch their objects. Most people thought I was a germaphobe. There was no harm in that.

I could walk by a graveyard, and no one would stroll out and demand I watch their last moments. I could walk on streets I knew were stolen land, and no Indigenous person would come to share their tales. I did my best to let the dead rest.

I thought I was safe.

Then I got Multiple Sclerosis. Early. *Very* early.

Managing one thing, caught by another.

The MS was a catalyst of sorts. A clarity came with it. Not in body—far from that. In mind. I'm able to get a sense now. Some objects practically scream at me, beg me to touch them. I hate being unable to avoid those. It's like watching my disembodied arm reach out and touch a burner.

At Wendell's Bowling, less than a month into my acceptance of color blindness, a lost soul has found her way in. I'm taken aback.

So much for knowing what to avoid.

I was trying to picture the colors of this claw machine that looks broken—but is still flashing and begging me to feed it.

Was the machine once blue or purple? Were the lights and knobs and accents red or pink or orange?

My defenses were down, and she snuck in like a windstorm. I felt her, and now, I'm seeing through her eyes.

She wears me like a skin, comfortably settling in my damaged nerves. I know her name as if it's mine—*Dina*. We are running late —only by five minutes. Still, *Dina* is rushing behind the shoe rental counter, happy that no one is waiting.

I force myself to keep my distance, knowing how easily I can get lost.

The world is awash with color I thought I lost forever.

Pins crash against pins, high-fives and a *woo-hoo* from a tall well-dressed woman come shortly after. It's another day, another strike. Dina notes that Wendell is not on the floor, so he won't notice her lateness.

The balls of her feet already hurt. The flats she's wearing now don't make up for the stilettos she wears on Saturdays and Sundays.

Jack rushes in front of Dina, shifting her thoughts.

"Nope. If I told you once, I told you a thousand times—no darting in and out of the shoe rental area. Don't care that it's a throughway to the arcade."

His hands fly behind his back, and his head drops. "Yes ma'am. Sorry, Aun—sorry. Yes, *Dina*. I know better. It's just—"

"Just *nothing*. Don't care. Now get. Your daddy sees you running around here like that, and he's liable to smack you something fierce and ban you from being here after school at all," Dina warns.

She hates that her brother would lay a hand on her nephew, but what can she do? Love Jack and be around as much as possible, that's all.

Jack's speed slows to a walk as he heads towards the modest arcade area.

Three women come up to get shoes—size 7, 8, and 8 1/2. They're chatting about the 502 killer being caught and how truckers are bad news.

Dina can't tell them they've got it wrong, but she wants to. *Yes*, the truck driver named Xander Freedmen was bad news, but they aren't all. Dina comes from a line of truckers, and so far, there hasn't been a bad apple in the bunch.

Her brother is the first to break the mold and do something different. If anything, *he's* the bad apple. But still, Dina wouldn't call him *bad news*.

Maybe it's just a certain kind of person that's bad news. The look in their eyes gives it away, not what they do for work. They can drive trucks or teach history at a community college.

And it doesn't start then. Three boys who were bred to be just the kind of bad news that would keep these women glued to the TV walk in, making the point to no one but herself. They make a beeline to the arcade. Not for the games, but for Jack. They've come in before, but usually, they just glare or snark about missing a split. They've got different intentions in their dark eyes today.

"Jack!" Dina shouts. "I need some help over here."

The pinnacle of the triangle has a moment of fleeting disappointment across his pug-like face. Doesn't stop him from punching Jack in the side as they pass each other. Jack wraps his arm around himself as the boy says something.

Jack's eyes go wide.

Oh, how Dina would slug that kid in the mouth if it was legal to hurt a kid. She's seen him sneak into the Pussycat Room before, seen the way he watches her from the corner booth, tucked away in the darkness. Just one crook of the finger, and Dina could get him alone.

Physical strength means nothing when fear kicks in, though. Losing the upper hand is all too easy then, she thinks, remembering his eyes flashing like the apex predator he so wants to be— like his daddy.

"FLORENCE!"

My mother is all but screaming in my ear, tearing Dina from me as I step back from the machine, hands reaching to cover my ears.

     Bad News

I turn towards her, blinking away the vivid memory and color. "Yes?"

"You go deaf as well as color blind?" she asks, trying to make a joke of what I haven't adjusted to yet.

My whole family has been trying that all week. *It's been almost a month, Flor.* As if it takes no time at all to adjust to a world where most colors have been filtered and others have faded like a worn towel.

It feels especially painful now, in this moment.

"Sure, let's go with that." I'm still with Dina, back only a year and a half ago when the 502 killer was caught, wondering what happened to her and why I hadn't heard about it. The predator boy did something to her, surely. I don't want to see it, but I have to know. "What do you need?"

"Grabbing a snack. Do you want anything?"

A pretzel. "No," I say, for fear of being bothered again. "Thank you, though."

"Did you eat breakfast before we came?" Mom asks. She's blonde, but telling her that she's gray and watching thin lines grow deep brings me great pleasure. "Because the doctor said—"

"Okay, okay," I relent. "A pretzel."

As she saunters away, I place my hands back on the claw machine. Maybe the memory is short, maybe I can see the rest of Dina's life before Mom returns with the reheated salt-covered bread. Maybe I'll regret this. Maybe I already know what happens next.

Dina's dark thoughts are fading as the carpet becomes green with pink and white and yellow triangles again.

Jack lets his arms hang by his side, turns his look of terror into a strained smile, and leans against the counter. "You rang?"

"Just needed you over here with me for a bit, is all."

Dina hands him one shoe absentmindedly. What can she say? That she wants to keep him safe from the monster-in-the-making? Of course not.

"What's this for?" Jack asks.

She shrugs. "Don't know. Just do something with it."

Confusion floods his face, but he starts to look for a cubby with a missing shoe.

Dina switches three other pairs while he's distracted. "I think Samantha mixed up a few pairs last night too. Could you go through them and check? Just 7, 7 1/2, 9, and 12 were rented, so it shouldn't take too long."

The hyenas cackle, and Jack's head swivels towards the arcade where Pug Face is playing the shooting game and cheering every time a digital deer dies. His joy makes Dina's skin crawl. He will be an awful man one day.

Skinny Neck is laughing in the racing car chair. He doesn't know it, but if he isn't careful, he'll fall out. The bolts holding the chair to the platform are loose. Dina's not sure if it's even on The List. The clogged toilet, chipped sink, butter machine that sticks, soda fountain that needs a new line, and broken bumper in Lane 4 will come before it, even if it was.

Pimples' crotch is pressed up against the thinner-than-normal claw machine. He pulls a dollar from his pocket and shoves it in. Dina doesn't bother watching, because no one wins.

It's an old machine. Wendell bought it broken—cracked glass, teal paint chipping off all over the place, wrong color replacement button—from a man who'd altered it already. The edges of the claw are like a torn fingernail, sharp and slightly jagged, not smooth and flat like most. The guy said he shaved them like that because he won more often that way, never mind that it tore the plushies.

Wendell *fixed it up* just enough to make it move again, but the claw won't go all the way down. To top it off, he broke the lock as he was working on it, so it doesn't even fully shut at the top.

Once, Dina found a kid trying to climb in to get a stuffed dolphin. It was a mess—crying, screaming, accusations, threats of a lawyer. She said they should get rid of the machine then.

"When you're done, I want them all resprayed," Dina says, recognizing the fear that their innocuous actions—the kids just being here—has caused her. "Sorry, looks like you'll be here a while."

Jack turns to catch her eyes over his shoulder. "Thanks, Aunt Dina." He pauses, realizing he called her Aunt at work again. But no one is near, so he says nothing.

Time flies for once, which is nice. Her ankles ache, her feet burn, but the clock says it's nearly time to leave.

The boys left in silence, the women left after shouting that they had a lot of fun, the two couples who were on a double date that ended terribly left separately, the family who needed the good bumpers left with the youngest wailing about not wanting to leave, and the bowling league practicing for next Tuesday's tournament left in a cluster of laughing bodies. Only Dina, Jack, and Wendell are in the building.

Wendell is *doing the books*. Though he has an accountant, he still tallies things every night—from the cups and popcorn buckets sold to guesstimations of how many sprays of the disinfectant Dina and Jack may have used. He and his wife don't get along well, so he just *avoids*.

Jack and Dina are scooping up the trash and wiping down the plastic seats and laminate tables.

"Going to take care of the ladies' room. Holler if you need me," Dina calls to Jack.

She's wiping down the second mirror when she hears a crash. It's not the familiar disturbance of a bowling ball smashing to the floor or a chair tipping over and a loose metal leg breaking off. It's not a table being tipped over with food on it. It's not even the butter machine crashing to the floor—a surprisingly common occurrence.

She calls out to Jack, asking if he's alright.

He doesn't answer.

"Jack?" she calls again. "What happened?" Another pause. Still nothing. "This isn't funny. It's been a long day, in a string of long weeks. What's going on? Don't make me come out there."

Dina pushes the bathroom door open, and a voice rings out over the quiet lo-fi. "Whoa! You didn't say…"

A hard nudge jostles me, and I don't know where my nephew is; that didn't sound like him.

I mean—*Dina's* nephew. Jack. Can't get us confused. I've been doing well, won't start slipping now.

"Got your pretzel," my brother says with a grin. "Still trying to win something? You know those are rigged, right?"

"I do, yes." I sound out of breath. No, *Dina's* out of breath. I'm standing still, doing nothing, here with my brother.

He pushes my hair away from my face, his tone changing a little. "You okay, sis?"

I nod, turn to him, smile. An older brother taking a moment deserves my attention—no matter how much Dina wants to tell me her story or how much I need to know it. "I'm just sad that things aren't… right. This machine isn't what it should be."

Hudson nods solemnly. "Shoulda known. Sorry. This place must be impossible. Want to leave?"

"No, no. I'll be okay. Just having a moment. It's good to get out. And I'm determined to master this claw machine." I smile, though we both know it's hollow.

He leans and hugs me. "*Shit.*" Muttering to himself, he pulls his arm away from me in a wide, sweeping move and shakes his hand. "Just spilled my drink. No big. Hope you get the prize," he says.

I kiss him on the cheek before he rushes away. "Thanks," I say to his back.

Reaching for the claw machine, I steel myself, thinking *this must be it.*

But that wasn't her nephew, it wasn't her brother either.

Skinny Neck? His voice is nasally and high-pitched—a combo not easily mistaken.

"Help!" Jack's voice is clear as day.

Another male voice tells Jack to shut up, *it's not that bad.*

Dina remembers the first time she heard Jack call for help. He was stuck in a slide. Really, he was just scared and holding himself halfway down. His poor shoulders were sore for weeks from catching himself mid-slide.

She wants to rush in, but hesitates. Was it just two of them, or was the whole trio here?

     Bad News

Without her purse, she doesn't have pepper spray or her work keys that have the kitty with sharp pointy ears and eye finger holes. Many times, Dina has stabbed herself when just trying to unlock the supply cabinet.

They're just kids.

Skinny Neck's height, his weight, his aggression all play out in her head like a movie reel. So like the man in the parking lot after work, can she risk it? Should she?

A feeling of being stupid and overdramatic mixes with fear and old trauma as she drops low to the ground and sneaks out of the bathroom, wishing the door didn't open out towards the main area—but that was her idea.

She'll just grab her cell from her purse under the counter and call the cops. They'll come get the delinquents for breaking and entering.

The cops? Why aren't there better options?

Crawling toward the shoe rental area is harder on her than she thought. Forty-three isn't an age when one should be on their hands and knees on a cement floor—no age is good for that, really.

When she gets there, her purse is not in the cubby reserved for employees. *Fuck.*

Dina's mind swirls with thoughts of where she put it. Was it in the car? Did Jack move it from the top of the counter and put it elsewhere?

A *yelp* from the arcade area tells her this isn't a time to wander, to retrace steps. She's still crawling—just in case. She feels stupid, but his eyes, his dad, that one time at the bar.

Wendell's office has a landline. Dina makes her way there so quickly, she fears she's leaving a skin trail on the carpet.

The door is wide open. Wendell is not there.

She reaches for the phone, pulling the tan monstrosity from its cradle. There's a sense she's in a different time, trapped in the 70s with most of the furniture and lead paint that still coats the walls.

Holding the receiver to her ear gifts silence.

She smashes the clear plastic prongs that should give her a dial tone over and over. *Have they cut the phone line?*

"Attention: Wanda, Lane 3 is now open. Please come to the counter to get your shoes." Over the intercom, the croaky voice has all the enthusiasm of a child having leftover casserole for the third day in a row.

I steady my heart. I shouldn't let Dina tell me the rest of her story. I'm doing this to myself. I could stop at any time. But it's like a movie.

Ripping at the pretzel that my right hand has all but smashed back into dough, I nod to myself. It's clear that Dina needs me to be. No other souls have shared so much.

So I'm here, Dina. I'm here with you.

The button meant to make the claw drop is warm from my sweaty hand. The sensation melts to my palm clenching around a drawer pull—Wendell's top desk drawer.

Dina's stomach drops as she gropes around. *Am I doing this?*

Her fingertips touch the metal of the handgun that sits there. She's never agreed with this—it being so easily accessible. Today, she's grateful for her brother's poor decisions, bad takes, gross views. Today, she's glad she's safe.

Just to scare them, she assures herself.

Tucking the gun in her waistband, she goes back crawling towards Jack's plea for help. Each time her knee touches the floor, it's like a bowling ball careening onto the lane from a bad throw and stripping the paint from the wood. It throbs and sears and aches. Not important now.

Nearing the arcade, she hears the sounds of the games being played, laughter, someone mumbling.

"Shut up, Jack," Pug Face says. Dina still can't see anything as he snaps, "If you hadn't talked to Penny, this wouldn't be happening."

"My dad will stop you," Jack's voice still sounds muffled, even as Dina grows nearer. "You'll be really sorry then."

She tucks herself behind a fake ficus in a large green pot.

It's not the best hiding place, but most of the lights are off, so hopefully, she's not too noticeable. It's better than nothing.

Scanning the area, she sees him.

No.

Jack is in the claw machine. Pug Face is sitting on top, playing with the broken lock.

"Just tell us what she said," Skinny Neck says. "It can all be over."

Pug Face's expression darkens. Dina knows what that look means—he has the power.

Who does Skinny Neck think he is?

Pimples slides a dollar into the claw machine. "Think you can get me that panda? I paid for it."

The claw whirrs a little, waiting for instructions.

"Tell us," Pug Face says. "Tell us or Johnny Boy here will make you regret it."

Johnny Boy must be Pimples, as he holds his hands up when Pug Face calls him out. "What? This was your idea. I just wanted the stupid panda. I told you Penny doesn't like him. He's just a kid. What are you, like, nine or ten?"

Small for thirteen, actually. Jack says nothing. The teens are sixteen, seventeen. If Penny is their age, the likelihood she is interested in Jack is more than slim. But that doesn't account for Jack's interests—or lack thereof.

"You'll do what I say, or I'll tell about your secret rendezvous." *What a word for a kid like that to use.*

Johnny Boy put his hand on the joystick obediently. "There's nothing to tell."

Tears flow freely from Jack's eyes now.

Skinny Neck isn't close enough to Pug Face and Johnny Boy that Dina could control them all at once. *Scare them.* She means only to *scare them*—not control—with the gun. Dina had no intention of pulling any trigger. Her dad always said not to pull out a weapon if you aren't prepared to use it. It's why she doesn't own one.

Still, they need to be closer together.

Johnny Boy shifts the joystick, and the claw begins to move right.

Jack shouts, "What the fuck?"

"I'm sorry, but no one can know. You understand, right?" Johny Boy says, as the claw glides along the track. "I just need another year. She won't lose her job in another year."

Pug Face barks a laugh. "Don't be sorry. This asshole is trying to steal Penny."

"I'm not! I *told you.* I saw she was working on math homework, so I made a calculus joke I saw on TV, and she laughed. That's it. I don't like her." Jack's eyes are facing up towards the claw.

Jack is in a comedy phase, trying out every joke he has on everyone, desperate to get his timing right.

After a moment of the joystick's stillness, the claw falls down. With little room in the small machine, Jack can't move much. As he's shifting, a point on the jagged claw nicks his hand.

"Ow. Guys, stop! You had a good laugh. One for the books, a good story to drink to one day, I get it."

Kids don't talk like we used to, Dina thinks.

"You will get in serious trouble if I get hurt, you know. My dad and aunt are here," Jack says.

"Your dad is on his way home to see about the man your mom is fucking. He flies off the handle really easily," Skinny Neck says, laughing and reaching up for a fist bump from Pug Face. "And your aunt already ran away. We saw the bathroom door open and close. It's just us, buddy."

The claw drops down again. This time, it closes over a toy but doesn't have the grip. It comes back up empty.

Johnny Boy slides in another dollar. "Please, just tell him," he says, moving the claw once more.

"Again!" Skinny Neck says, slapping Johnny Boy on the back.

This is it—they are clustered together now.

But Johnny Boy is not slow. Before Dina can do or say anything, he's hitting the center button on the claw machine. He does it so quickly that Jack can't move out of the way.

It lands on Jack's shoulder. Barely registering it, he doesn't try to move it off of himself. And then it's closing. He screams as the metal claw bites into his shoulder and moves back up, tearing his shirt and leaving angry red drag marks in its wake.

Then, four things happen at once.

Pug Face plugs his ears dramatically. "It can't be that bad. It's not like it has a decent grip or anything."

Johnny Boy's eyes are wide as he slides in another dollar, whispering, "This is my last dollar… I'm so sorry."

Jack tries to dodge the shifting claw in his confined space.

And Dina stands up. "Don't fucking move, or I'll blow all three of your puny little heads off."

She didn't want to do it, hated holding the damned gun in the first place—nonetheless pulling it on teenagers. She wanted them to leave, to get bored. But Skinny Neck won't stop, no matter Jack's answer. And there is no way in hell she'll let this go on. She should have already stopped it.

A shame spiral threatens to overwhelm her.

"Hey." A young voice cracks through the last moments of Dina's life. "Are you going to play that, or—?"

I can't shake what's happening. I slide a dollar in and reach for the joystick, sickened that I'm mirroring Johnny Boy's actions in this moment.

"I'm playing," I croak out.

Dina snatches me back as she sees Jack out of the corner of her eye. Shock has painted his face a mottled white and pink.

Johnny Boy's hands fly to the air faster than Skinny Neck's, but not by much.

Pug Face looks trapped and angry, baring his teeth. "Is this his aunt? I thought you said she left, you piece of shit!"

"Get off the fucking claw machine." Dina's voice is as calm as it was the day she pulled a gun on Harold and told him that if he ever laid a hand on her again, she'd start with his dick. It was the only other time she pointed a gun at someone—his gun, in poetic karma. Then, too, it was only meant to scare.

Pug Face jumps down, his expression matching Dina's insides: shame, shame, shame. *At being caught?*

The claw follows suit, doing what it was made to do. It falls onto Jack, who still hasn't moved—too stunned to see Dina.

Her eyes are trained on the boys until he shouts. The boys use the momentary distraction to make a run for it.

She spins towards them as they run past her.

A gun goes off.

Dina didn't pull the trigger. Still, she drops the weapon—safety still on—quicker than she let go of the cookie sheet burning her uncovered fingers last week.

It's Wendell.

He's blocking the exit with a gun in his hand. A gun with him, a gun on the floor, a gun behind in his desk drawer.

So many guns. Three too many.

Pug Face has collapsed onto his side.

Skinny Neck is on his knees, burying his forehead into the ugly carpet covering the cement. He's muttering something.

Johnny Boy stands still, hands raised like when he was *just wanting a panda.*

"Get Jack out of there and go. I'll handle this," Wendell instructs Dina. His thinning hair is matted to his sweaty forehead.

Dina rushes to the claw machine and sees Jack in the corner, eyes huge.

"I'm so sorry, Mr. Jack's Dad! I didn't want to do any of this," Skinny Neck says. "They made m—" His words are cut short with a click and a bang.

When Dina turns to see Skinny Neck, the dim lighting gives the illusion he's still just kneeling.

Dina turns her attention back to Jack. Pushing the broken lid off takes more strength than Dina expected, but she has to hurry. Once it's moved enough that Jack can get out, she runs back to the scene where Wendell is still pointing a gun at Johnny Boy.

"Jack out?"

"He's getting there," Dina says, slowly moving towards Johnny Boy, leaving Jack to climb out on his own.

"You okay, son?" Wendell calls. "Dina, I said to help him out. I meant *all the way*. You take him to the ER, and I'll clean up this mess." He waves his gun towards the two dead boys and Johnny Boy, who may be holding his breath, slowly killing himself so a bullet won't. "You want to go free, boy?" he asks the teen.

Johnny Boy nods slowly.

Wendell's brow furrows. Dina knows she's been wrong about him. He is bad news—always has been. She's pulled the punches he never has when she talks about him, looking for the good.

As he moves his finger back to the trigger, Dina rushes in front of Johnny Boy.

I gasp back to my watered down world. That was Dina's last act.

The kid who wanted to play the claw machine is standing beside me, still watching me with interest. I pay them no mind.

Instead, I turn to look at the space where the boys and Dina were shot. There are no blood stains, but the carpet is a little darker, the pattern of triangles is slightly different. New manufacturer, perhaps.

I step back, unable to see anything but Jack's face behind the plexiglass, Pug Face's legs dangling from the top, and Johnny Boy in control of the joystick. Though this happened more than a year ago, it feels like the police should be on their way here now.

My hands are shaking. *No more claw machine for me today.*

"All yours," I say to the kid.

the witches of the neon carousel

Erik Grove

Ian and Miles became best friends over a lunch room tray of tater tots the first week of 7th grade—not that Ian had much to do with it.

"You're new," Miles said when he sat across from Ian without warning or invitation. He wore a shabby hand-me-down ski coat with frayed lift tickets dangling from one sleeve. Acne and grease glistened across his forehead, cheeks, and down his neck. He took three of Ian's tater tots and dipped the first in Ian's ketchup. "We have pre-algebra 3rd period. Mr. Fox. He's a real capital A asshole sometimes. Ranch is better by the way. What'd you get for the homework?"

Before he could answer, Miles pulled Ian's worksheet from his backpack and took the rest of his tater tots.

"You're good at this. A real brainiac," Miles told him. "Want to stay over Friday night? There's an arcade around the corner with those big old video game cabinets and *terrible* microwave pepperoni pizza."

Ian never said yes, but still spent every non-holiday weekend for the rest of middle school eating *terrible* microwave pepperoni pizza, playing Tekken, and sleeping in a mummy bag that smelled like old milk on the floor of Miles's bedroom. Ian rarely needed to say anything for himself when he was with Miles.

"Ian only ever plays Heihachi," Miles would tell people. "He knows all the moves." (Ian didn't.) Or, "Ian and I like root beer," (he didn't particularly) or, "Ian is probably going to do basketball freshman year. He's tall."

Bit by bit, Miles defined an all-new version of Ian, and Ian went along for the ride. Miles's Ian was more interesting than Ian's Ian anyway—better at math, video games he'd never played, and, eventually, talking to the girls that started hanging out at the same arcade.

There were three of them, all black haired with different colored striped long nails that reminded Ian of candy corn.

They never played any of the games but sat in the small dining area of the arcade snack counter by the soda machine. All the money losing machines whirred and flashed colors on the other side of a half wall behind them.

Miles called them money losing machines because for a quarter all you got was a chance to pilot a rickety crane to pick up a little plastic egg full of some kind of trash or maybe make an avalanche of pocket change fall down if you timed your drop right. It didn't take long and hardly anybody ever won. Only suckers played them, Miles said, and always dragged Ian to the fighting games or racers.

"I don't recognize them from school," Ian said when they first noticed the girls. "Maybe they go to South or Roosevelt?"

Miles chewed on the straw sticking out of his root beer. "Maybe," he said. "You should go talk to them."

Ian stuffed his hands into his pockets. He rubbed a couple of quarters together. "Why don't *you* talk to them?"

"You don't get nervous." Miles took the lid off his drink cup and shook ice out. He broke the cubes between his teeth and gulped them down. "Go *on*."

Ian didn't know if he got nervous or not because he'd never talked to three girls he'd never met at an arcade before. "What do I say?"

Miles punched Ian's shoulder. "You know."

So, Ian tossed his empty root beer into the trash and went into the dining area. The girls saw him coming and laughed and tapped their candy corn nails. Were they sisters? They could be sisters, all dressed in black and in matching lip gloss that looked to Ian, for lack of a better vocabulary, plum.

"Hi," Ian said. "I'm Ian. That's Miles."

They laughed a little more, then all said, "Hi," together, and Ian felt like he might throw up *terrible* pepperoni if he didn't leave immediately.

"Bye," he said.

"Bye," they said.

Miles gave him a thumbs up when he retreated to the Skee-Ball. "You made first contact," he said. "Next time you'll be prepared."

"Next time?"

Miles paid the machine and gave Ian a Skee-Ball. "Plan it out a little better. You've got this."

That night, neither of them could sleep. Ian kept hearing the clicking of nails, pinky rolling to ring finger, middle, and then index. A staccato rhythm. Clack-clack-clack-clack.

"What do you think their names are?" Miles wondered. "You need to ask their names. Which one did you like? I bet you liked the tall one. You always like tall girls."

Did he? Ian didn't know what kind of girls he liked. He never liked girls before. Those three with their black shoes crossed at the heels under the lopsided table, silver rings and studs in their ears, braided necklaces and charms at their wrists, a smell like the spice section of the supermarket—cinnamon or pepper or cloves. Those three staring, clack-clack-clack-clack, clack-clack-clack-clack.

"They were sitting down," Ian said. "I couldn't tell how tall they were?"

Miles shifted to the edge of his bed and stuck his head over the edge to look down at Ian. "You can tell," he said and nodded, certain the matter was settled.

Between classes and on the bus the next week, Miles gave the girls names and personalities. "Melissa is the funny one," he explained. "And I like funny, but not *too* funny. I don't want to laugh all the time, you know?" He chicken-winged Ian. "I think Ursula, right? Has to be Ursula. She has serious C cup potential."

Ian nodded or said, "yeah," but when he thought of them, the girls weren't three separate people and Miles's names slid off of them. They were a single unit, an indivisible whole, a coven or cabal maybe, their braided voices, eyes, and those nails, all part of a six-armed mythical beast.

"But I wouldn't want to hurt Penelope's feelings, you know?" Miles continued on. "She's sweet and all, I just wish I didn't have to choose."

"Which one is Penelope?"

"The funny one."

"I thought… never mind. Why do you have to choose? What are you *choosing*?"

Miles leaned close and whispered. "How many tits have you seen, Ian? Real life *tits*? Your mom's don't count."

"I've never seen my Mom's…" Ian shook his head. "You don't know them, though. You didn't even talk to them."

"I'm your wingman," Miles said. "You'll get first pick obviously, but if Ursula isn't interested… Well, we need to have rules of engagement, right?"

Ian looked out the bus window. He nodded. "Yeah," he said.

In the halls at school, Ian looked at his classmates differently. The girls in his year that he'd never noticed—why hadn't he noticed them? And the other boys—what were they noticing? Ian wasn't blind or clueless. He'd agreed with Miles that he had a crush on Stacy probably or Trina, the tallest girls, and he'd picked out details about them to answer Miles when he asked, "well, what do you like *like*?" and even blushed when he found himself alone with Trina in Mr. Ziegler's room. But he didn't see them the way Miles saw them, in C cups and skirt lengths.

"It's okay, Ian," Miles had said to him. "You're not a wolf. Not yet, at least. That's why they're not scared of you. But you'll get a taste soon enough."

But what if he never did? What if he wasn't a carnivore at all?

The next weekend, Ian and Miles were back at the arcade and after a round of air hockey (Ian won but Miles kicked the table, "it's broken," he said) and a couple dollars into one of the shooters the girls were back by the snack counter.

"You've got this," Miles assured Ian. "Names. And bra-sizes, if you can tell. Their shirts are kinda loose."

"I don't want to," Ian said.

"Of course you do," Miles said. "You're being stupid."

Ian nodded. "Yeah," he agreed. "Yeah."

This time they weren't rapping their nails on the table but spinning quarters.

"He's back," one said.

"He's brave," the next continued.

"Hi, Ian."

"Hi," Ian said.

"What do you want, Ian?" they all asked, the words bumping into each other out of their glossed lips. "What" and "want" hit him the hardest.

Ian felt heat rush to his cheeks. "What are your names?"

They exchanged looks that said something Ian couldn't decipher and laughed while the quarters spun in place.

"Is that *really* what you want to ask us?" they wanted to know.

It wasn't.

Miles went to the money losing machines trying to listen in. He plunked quarters down the slots and lost them all, one after another.

"If you would ask us your questions three," one said.

(Was she taller?)

"First, you must bring us a bauble worthy of we," the next.

(Was she the funny one?)

"There are rules to this game, you see."

Ian fidgeted uncomfortably in place. "I don't understand," he said.

"Poor Ian."

"Poor, poor Ian."

"Scared of your shadow, Ian?"

"I'm not… I'm not scared," he lied.

Cinnamon and pepper and cloves.

They slapped down the quarters in unison. "We know," they said and laughed. "We *know.*"

"Play the game," they said. "Play the game, and you'll know too. Games have rules, and the truth will change you."

Ian ran to the men's room and spat up *terrible* pepperoni in the stall.

"We know."

Clack-clack-clack-clack.

Those weren't fingernails. They were *claws*.

Ian felt as if he were paper thin and torn in too many places.

On the wall of the stall, rendered in permanent marker, a set of eyes above perfectly circular tits with stars for nipples stared Ian down. "Ursula," it read in Miles's hand writing beneath.

Ian washed up and met Miles outside the men's room.

"What happened?" Miles asked, grabbing him by his shoulders excitedly. "Did you choke?"

"I didn't... I didn't choke."

Ian wanted to make a fist. He wanted to throw it into Miles and walk home. But he didn't.

"They want us to win them something," Ian said. "From the machines. It's stupid."

Miles checked his pockets. "I'll get more quarters."

He hurried out of the bathroom, leaving Ian alone with his pale reflection.

What did the girls know? Was it about him, or was it about Miles? He bet they knew about everything. When he closed his eyes, he saw them, their knowing smiles, their indecipherable silent language.

If Ian was supposed to be a wolf, those three girls were hunters stalking him in the forest.

The girls weren't at their table when Ian returned to the arcade floor. But they left behind three quarters and the hint of them lingered. Plum and spice.

Ian picked up a coin from the table. It was warmer than he expected, as if it had been held tightly in a fist only moments before.

Miles broke a roll of quarters in the middle and gave one half to Ian. "Divide and conquer," he said and continued on to the money losing machines.

"Right behind you," Ian said, but Miles didn't seem to care.

Ian slid the girls' remaining quarters from the table into his palm and kept the three of them in a separate pocket.

He went left to the dining area and around to the claw machines and gum ball dispensers, those glass boxes filled with off-brand stuffed animals or cheap jewelry. Miles fed them quarter after quarter, jabbed and prodded at the controls and kicked the base.

"These fucking things," he said. "Are you going to try?"

Ian stepped to a claw machine and put in the coin. He moved the claw with the small joystick, directing it along the rails in hiccupping jolts.

"You're wasting your time," Miles coached. "There's no skill in it. Just chance. Take your shot, and move on to the next."

"I will," Ian said. "I will."

"What are you waiting for?"

Miles picked another machine in the row and left Ian to his fiddly work.

Ian got the claw where he wanted it to be finally and hit the red button to drop it. The claw descended, crashing into a chaotic pile of toys no one would ever want enough to buy but might spend dollars and an afternoon to win. The claw closed and came back up on a wire, carrying with it, to Ian's astonishment, a prize.

He waited for Miles to be looking the other way to check the machine's prize chute and pulled out a plush witch with a tapered black hat and a wicked grin.

When squeezed, the witch laughed and laughed and laughed.

Ian threw it in the trash and never told Miles what he'd won.

By the time the arcade closed, Miles and Ian had gone through eight dollars in quarters. Miles had nothing to show for it, and Ian hid all the prizes he won. A bouncing ball that looked like an eye, a pack of miniature cards, and several necklaces and sets of earrings; he split them between trash cans or slipped them between arcade cabinets.

"We'll come back," Miles said. "After school."

"I can't. I'm not allowed on school nights," Ian lied.

"We'll figure out a system." Miles knocked on the side of one of the claw machines. "Next weekend."

Ian moved through the next week on the edge of a razor. On one side was dread and on the other a numb denial. Ian found excuses to avoid Miles, but Miles was too self-absorbed to even notice.

When Mrs. Lee split the class into groups, Ian was so careful to dodge Miles, he didn't realize he'd ended up with Trina and Stacy.

"Are you two fighting?" Stacy asked him.

"What?" Ian asked.

"You and Miles," she said. "You two are *always* together."

Ian shook his head. "No, we're not," he said.

"Not fighting or not always together?"

"Whatever."

Trina spoke quieter. "He's a *creep*. I caught him trying to look down my shirt in English."

Ian nodded. "He's a real capital A asshole sometimes," he said.

Stacy covered a smile with her hand and traded a look with Trina Ian couldn't decipher.

Could all girls speak that way?

Trina took a tube from her backpack and pursed her lips before applying fresh gloss.

'What kind is that?" Ian asked her.

"Pink Midnight," Trina said and slid the gloss across the table. "Want to try some?"

It had happened so fast, hadn't it? The transition from learning fighting combos in Tekken to lip gloss colors. Ian felt that he had been invisible or frozen maybe before Miles saw him at school and picked him. He'd never been picked by anyone before, had never been told who he was or what he liked. Then the three girls, with their matching laughs, they'd seen deeper. And they knew.

Both Stacy and Trina laughed, and Ian slipped his hands into his pockets.

He hunched forward and quirked an awkward smile. "I think I'd like a darker shade," he said, and they laughed more.

When the weekend came, Ian went with Miles back to the arcade. It was inevitable, wasn't it? The simple inertia of who he was, who Miles was. Ian could play at independence for a few lunch periods but where else would he go? Who else would he be?

They were always together.

"The Neon Carousel," it said in bright lights out front. "All games twenty-five cents!"

"I figured it out," Miles told Ian in a quiet voice. "This week. I figured it out. Come on."

A knot formed in Ian's gut. He followed Miles inside expecting them to head right for the money losers, but instead Miles led them to a door marked, "STAFF." Miles knocked and grinned at Ian. "There's always a system."

An employee only a handful of years older than Ian and Miles opened the door. Ian had seen him around, emptying the cabinets and hanging Out of Order signs. He had a gold name tag pinned to a red vest that said his name was "Keith."

"Be cool," Keith said and nodded them inside.

"What are we doing, Miles?" Ian whispered.

Miles brushed off the question. "It's *cool*."

The staff room smelled like ramen noodles and BO. It wasn't very big but had a bathroom and what looked like a large closet leading off it.

Keith closed the door after them. "Well?"

Miles took out a twenty-dollar bill, and Keith nabbed it. He led them to the closet and pulled out a big clear trash bag full of stuffed animals and junk from the money losing machines.

"These things are worthless, you know," Keith said. "A lot of people throw them away or forget them. We recycle right out of the lost and found. Kids are idiots."

In the bag, Ian saw everything he'd tried to make disappear.

Miles dug through the bag and the plush witch laughed. Miles pushed past it.

"This is stupid Miles," Ian said. "What if they were joking?"

"Then *we're* joking too."

"My boss is going to bust my balls if I'm not back up front in a couple minutes," Keith told them. "So, hurry up. This isn't a shopping spree or nothing."

Miles plucked out a heart pendant on a chain. "Here we go. This is perfect."

Ian shrugged. "I guess."

Keith gave a thumbs up. "Real panty dropper." He pushed them out of the staff room before anyone got caught.

"Are they ever here when we're not?" Ian asked Keith.

"Who?"

"The girls," Ian said. "Three of them. They… they…"

He didn't know what to say. He didn't know how to say it.

"Kid," Keith said. "Leave the arcade and you'll find about a *billion* girls."

"Ian!" Miles called back to him. "Quit messing around. Let's *go*."

They snaked through the arcade back from the staff room, and the girls waited. Of course they waited.

Pinky rolling to ring finger, middle, and then index. Clack-clack-clack-clack.

"Ready?" Miles asked.

Ian shook his head. "No," he said. "I'm not a wolf. I'm *never* going to be a wolf."

"You're not funny, Ian."

Ian lowered his head. "You've got what you need. You go talk to them. Find out their names and cup sizes."

"This is for *you*," Miles insisted.

All the root beer, the 10 hit combos, the decisions Ian never made, all for him.

"I don't want it," Ian said. "I'm going home."

"You can't go home. It's like 20 *miles* away."

"Fine," Ian said. "I'll wait for you outside."

He left the arcade and sat with his back against the wall beneath the lights.

"Play the game, and you'll know too. Games have rules, and the truth will change you."

Miles came out of the arcade, and Ian thought maybe he'd choked, maybe he'd tossed the cheap locket and given up, and they'd call for a ride. But Miles's face was pale, and his eyes were dazed. The locket dangled from his slack grip.

Ian scrambled to his feet. "What happened?"

"I lied," Miles said.

Thick red ran down the locket chain and drip, drip, dripped onto the sidewalk. It stained the concrete between blobs of stomped in gum and old cigarette ash.

A long, slender line darkened on Miles's shirt, followed by another and another and two more. The five lines moved toward each other, forming what Ian at first thought was a kind of star but, no, not a star. It was the center of a claw.

Blood wet Miles's lips, a grisly gloss, and where his heart should be, a ragged hole wept. The locket dropped, and Miles crumpled after it.

"I lied."

The bright lights flickered, and the wind carried a vicious perfume.

narrowly, narrowly caught

Katherine Quevedo

<u>Narrowly, Narrowly Caught</u>

By Katherine Quevedo

"Every individual ... generally neither intends to promote the public interest, nor knows how much he is ... led by an invisible hand to promote an end which was no part of his intention."
—Adam Smith, *The Wealth of Nations*

Skill, luck, and inevitability don't always play nicely together. Mallory, for example, skillfully avoided the light rail tracks across town as much as possible. But as luck would have it, on the way to her five-year high school reunion, she couldn't avoid driving over the tracks—inevitability. First, a red light stopped her at the intersection right as the crossing gate started blinking and lowering and dinging its bell. She drummed the steering wheel and gritted her teeth as the train zoomed past. Just a little phobia, an irrational fear. Her mom, an economics professor, spoke about rationality a lot. When the coast was clear, Mallory passed through the intersection without issue.

She'd gotten her heart rate back under control by the time she arrived at the restaurant. She headed into the large private room, where reproductions of vintage light bulbs cast a dim yellow light over the venue. A banner welcoming the Class of 2000 hung on a red brick wall, with a balloon shaped like a five on each side. Exposed ductwork crisscrossed the ceiling in bold silver lines, completing the industrial chic vibe. A few people milled around clutching drinks and making awkward small talk. A certain heaviness hung over everything, although she couldn't pinpoint why. Maybe it was the music—right now, the Gorillaz song "Feel Good Inc." was wrapping up with its maniacal cackling. Then came a mashup of two songs, "Boulevard of Broken Dreams" by Green Day and "Wonderwall" by Oasis. It put her in a somber mood.

She walked over to a tablescape of photo collages on posterboards. Familiar faces grinned out at her. Her old friend Zaya, with that toss of her curls she always saved for the moment the camera snapped. Linus and Desdemona, inseparable as always, he with his bushy eyebrows, and she with her striking green eyes. Chauncey, so comfortable in his own skin. At their small school, with a graduating class of less than a hundred, you knew everyone at least a bit.

A hand on her shoulder made her jump. She spun to face an older version of Chauncey, same strong chin, same floppy hair, but much more hollowed out eyes. In fact, all of him looked scrawnier than she recalled, as if he'd gone through another growth spurt after high school but somehow hadn't gotten any taller.

"Hey," he said. "Long time, Mallory. Sorry about Zaya."

Mallory cocked her head. "Is she not coming? We kind of lost touch during college."

A disconcerted look passed over his features. "You don't know? I'd heard you fell out of contact after graduation, but I didn't realize how much. You probably don't know about… anyone, do you?"

His tone was more perplexed than rude, but she glowered at him nonetheless. He made her sound like some kind of hermit just because she didn't have a MySpace account. Plus, he was keeping her in suspense about whatever news he had about her former best friend. Even worse, this grown-up rendition of Chauncey had abandoned his carefree attitude. He looked too hounded by adult worries. She didn't want this impression of him to supplant the teenage one.

"So, about Zaya?" she said, gesturing for him to fill her in.

He gazed at the concrete floor. "She died last year."

Mallory gasped.

"She was horseback riding, and the horse she was on tumbled off a cliff."

The Edison bulbs around them flickered. Mallory's stomach flipped, as though she were the one who had plunged over an edge.

"She's not the only one," Chauncey continued. "Linus died the year before that in a freak accident. I heard a couple others from our class died, too. It's weird. Our class wasn't that big. It seems like an unusually high percentage." He hugged himself and ran his hands up and down his arms a couple times, as if he had a chill. "Anyway, sorry to bring up such bad news, and at a party no less. I just never thought the last time I'd see so many class-mates would be grad night, you know?"

Well, that explained the somber feeling here. Five years ago, grad night had started off so promising but had ended up unnerving her, too, in its own way. Mallory remembered the flut-tering in her stomach, the good kind, in the evening leading up to it.

A few hours before grad night, Mallory found her mom at the kitchen counter with her hair pulled up in a messy bun and a chunk of pork steaming from the crockpot, ready for the next step in becoming dinner. The room filled with its thick, savory scent. Mallory sat at the kitchen table while her mom grabbed a fork in each hand and tore at the meat. It gave way so easily; her mom always knew how to make it tender and moist. Shred, shred.

Mallory's stomach growled.

Her mom glanced over. "Excited for tonight?"

"Yeah." Her nonchalant tone didn't match her true eagerness. She could be entirely herself tonight, because soon she wouldn't be a part of any of her former classmates' lives except as an occa-sional memory (besides close friends like Zaya). She could put everything behind her except only the greatest memories from the past four years. And if everyone else did the same, then they'd all look their best in each other's eyes. It felt *freeing*.

"I heard a rumor that we're going to that '80s arcade."

Her mom paused. Then the shredding resumed. "The economics of arcades is so messed up."

Mallory braced herself for a lecture. "'Messed up,' is that a technical term?"

"Let me tell you, claw machines are the worst offenders. Did you know they can make it so the claw doesn't fully close except once in a while? Maybe after the machine has earned a certain amount of money? So you think it's all about talent and lining up the crane just right, but it's not. It's engineered to drop your prize before you want it to most of the time, and there's nothing you can do about it. It's a messed up feedback loop."

That sealed it. Tonight, Mallory would test her mother's rationality against the popular rhyme she'd learned as a kid:

If you watch when the claw makes a tight silver fist,
Narrowly, narrowly missed.
If when the claw closes, you snap your eyes shut,
Narrowly, narrowly caught.

The kids used to make fun of how "shut" and "caught" didn't quite rhyme. They'd shortened it to "Look and you lose; close your eyes, win a prize"—even though the first part didn't even rhyme. So, which would win out: a childhood superstition or one of the econ professor's insufferable lessons?

Her mom eyed her sitting there. "Any chance you could help out? You could mix the salad."

"I've got a lot on my mind right now, okay? You know I hate doing that stuff."

Her mom's frown made it clear she thought Mallory was being immature and selfish but refused to say so aloud. Well, why shouldn't Mallory be immature for one more night? Why not let this be about her, the graduate, the one with a milestone to celebrate?

Her mom cleaned bits of pulled pork off her hands, then moved to the glass salad bowl and poured French dressing over the contents. She grabbed a pair of silver tongs. "I can picture you and your classmates moving through that arcade, guided by the Invisible Hand."

"Oh no," Mallory groaned. "Is this that Adam Smith guy again?"

"The father of modern economics? Yep." As she spoke, the silver tongs flipped so deftly, drenching everything red. "All of you weaving around each other, spending your tokens based on your individual preferences and self-interest, making some kind of order out of chaos." Leaves of spring mix smashed against the inside of the glass bowl, sticky and torn. Toss, toss. "But arcades don't play fair, and the Invisible Hand breaks down in imperfect markets like that." She'd added too much French dressing, and way too many cherry tomatoes. "Of course, Adam Smith's theory was more about tariffs, but people latch onto the concept and try to make all kinds of extrapolations."

"Mom, I just graduated. I really don't need to be thinking about tariffs right now." Or ever, she thought. Every time her mom brought up the Invisible Hand, Mallory couldn't help but imagine something literal, a ghostly outline hovering above her like a puppet master. It gave her the creeps.

Right now, her mom's gifted, visible hands manipulated the ingredients before her into a greater whole. The seasonings had lost themselves into the meat long ago. A bottle of barbecue sauce sat on the counter awaiting its turn to contribute. The salad flipped in quiet obedience. Cherry tomatoes rolled around as the tongs snapped at them.

Mallory fancied picking one up and squishing it in her bare hand. Better than having to taste it. "Did you have to put tomatoes in there?"

"It's not always about what *you* want," her mom said. "We have to share. Adam Smith promoted self-interest, not selfishness. There's a difference. But I do apologize if I've lowered your level of utility for this salad." She chuckled. "Another econ thing."

Mallory rolled her eyes. Grad night couldn't come soon enough.

The school did indeed bus the class to the '80s-themed arcade that night.

The doors slid open to reveal old music videos playing on a bank of TV screens. Mallory followed Zaya inside while the band Heart rocked out to their song "Never," with netting hanging behind the musicians. To the left of the screens lay the prize area with checkerboard flooring, while the main gaming area's carpeting featured squiggly lines in clashing pastels. It felt like she'd stepped into a scene from the film *The Chipmunk Adventure* or straight into her Barbie Ice Cream Shoppe set. She half expected the workers to wear shoulder pads. The arcade's retro ambiance gave her a funny mix of delight from familiar things from her childhood and embarrassment from how dated every-thing felt after a decade or two. She and her classmates were entering adulthood, about to embark on the next phase of life. How strange to celebrate at a place that felt plucked right out of their grade school days.

Zaya snorted. "My cousins in SoCal got to go to Disneyland for their grad nights. It's so unfair." Apparently other grad nights let teens be kids, too, not just this one. Zaya jingled her cup of tokens. They'd each been given a bunch. "To the Claw Corner?"

That sounded good to Mallory. Her mom called those machines rigged, a waste of time and money, a rip-off. Well, she'd prove her wrong. They took a hard right to the section where you could earn prizes directly instead of accumulating tickets to redeem later. Yeah, her mom would hate this section.

Sandwiched between two other claw machines—one with rubber duckies and the other with chalky fruit candies—lay a cabinet she'd never seen before labeled UB4Me. It glistened and hummed with temptation as Mallory approached. The other vending games revealed their prizes too easily, in mounds of molded plastic or rainbow wrappers piled up like tiny landfills. But the UB4Me's tinted red eggs lay waiting in graceful billows, like suds begging to be popped. Just let the gangly metal claw get close enough. You couldn't see through them, and that made her want to snag one more than ever. Like squishing one of those cherry tomatoes, only this one held something good inside.

Mallory inserted a coin, and the claw machine activated its

countdown while Exposé's "Point of No Return" played in the background. As she maneuvered the joystick, she did her best to block out Zaya's frantic instructions from over her shoulder, guiding her toward the easiest eggs. Mallory wanted to really test this out. She aimed for a tougher-to-reach egg, recited the full rhyme in her head, and closed her eyes at the pivotal moment.

Sure enough, she snagged the prize on her first try! It tumbled safely into the chute while little prize bells dinged and red lights blinked across the top. The egg weighed next to nothing as she pulled it from the machine. The oval dome may as well have been a glass cloche protecting a rare artifact as she opened it.

"What'd you get?" Zaya asked. "Is that a sticker?"

Mallory pinched the prize between thumb and forefinger. "I think it's a temporary tattoo." Disappointment leaked out through her tone. She wrinkled her nose and wished for a split second that she'd kept her eyes open. At least then she could've tried for a different egg and not ended up with this—what was it?—segment of railroad tracks that she would definitely not transfer onto her skin, temporary or no.

"Wow," Zaya said, not bothering to hide her sarcasm. "You'd have been better off with that gross candy or a duck. Okay, my turn." She got a small figurine, also on her first try; apparently they'd found the one claw machine that wasn't rigged—or else the rhyme worked. "Aww, so cute!" she gushed.

It was. The little brown horse stood on spindly legs, with a wavy mane and forelock that made Mallory wish she could pet it. Each eye consisted of a twinkling black rhinestone. Zaya had gone for the most obvious egg, sticking out the most from the pile, and she'd gotten a much better prize. How could the UB4Me offer such unequal things? At least the duckies and candy were all roughly the same. Cheap and disposable, yes, but similar in value.

"Scoot over," Mallory said. "I'm going to try for something better." She popped in another coin, but the machine spit it back out.

"Weird. It obviously doesn't like you." Zaya fondled her precious horse. "Come on, let's go do air hockey."

"I'll be there in a minute." Mallory tried again and again, with different tokens. Each time, rejected. She jammed her tattoo into her pocket and stepped back from the machine with her arms crossed, while Gloria Estefan sang "Rhythm Is Gonna Get You" from the bank of TV screens.

Desdemona and Linus ambled up to try their luck at the UB4Me machine. Before they started, Linus made a big production of saying, "'Look and you lose; close your eyes, win a prize.' Remember?" He got an orange glow-in-the-dark ring in the shape of flames, and Desdemona got a temporary tattoo, this one of an old woman. *Narrowly, narrowly caught.*

Desdemona seemed as displeased with her prize as Mallory was with hers, while Linus busted up laughing.

"Can't wait to see where you put that one," he wheezed, sliding his ring onto his pinky.

Desdemona declined to play again. When Linus tried it, it refused his coin. They both shrugged and moved on.

Mallory didn't. The more she gazed at the UB4Me machine and thought of that rhyme, the original version, the more her scalp prickled.

If you watch when the claw makes a tight silver fist,
Narrowly, narrowly missed.
If when the claw closes, you snap your eyes shut,
Narrowly, narrowly caught.

The night didn't feel so freeing anymore. A horrible taste filled her mouth, like burning wires. *It obviously doesn't like you,* Zaya had said. The letters above the UB4Me's display case flickered.

A hand on her shoulder made her jump.

Chauncey laughed as she spun to face him. "Don't know my own strength," he said. "Zaya wanted me to tell you she already got her fill of air hockey and moved on to Skee-Ball."

"Okay. Are—are you going to try that new machine?" Her voice quivered as she said it. She jabbed a thumb toward the UB4Me.

"Nah, those things are rigged."

"Yeah." She forced a laugh. "Seriously." Her tone must've sounded so fake, he backed away and headed for the pinball aisle. Up on the TV screens, Kim Wilde sang "You Keep Me Hangin' On" in front of a dark doorway with light radiating from behind the rectangle. Silhouetted hands appeared through the beams to grab at the singer.

Now, at the class reunion, Chauncey had once again backed away. Mallory didn't bother looking for him in the growing crowd. She stood near an entire posterboard dedicated to grad night. She scrutinized the photos while Chevelle's "Vitamin R (Leading Us Along)" reverberated through the speakers. Maybe one of the photos showed more prizes from the UB4Me.

"I remember that night," Desdemona said over her shoulder.

Mallory faced her. This older Desdemona looked skinny and harrowed, like Chauncey, with similar janky movements, marionette-like.

"I can't stop thinking about it, ever since Linus. It couldn't be a coincidence, could it? The prize he got in that little egg. I remember you were kind of spooked by that machine. I laughed about it behind your back at the time, but I think you were onto something. Did you see the prize it gave me?"

Mallory nodded. Under other circumstances, her classmate's comments would've embarrassed and annoyed her. Hadn't Chauncey's statement about her falling out of touch irked her just a few moments ago? But with the new knowledge from tonight, and Desdemona's offhand delivery just now and the obvious underlying pain, it just saddened and unsettled her.

"How did Linus die?"

Desdemona's green eyes bore into her. "I think you know."

An image of a flame-shaped ring flashed in Mallory's mind.

Desdemona finally turned back to the posterboard. "After Linus, then with Zaya, I put two and two together. I've avoided visiting my grandma ever since. Or any old lady. Like if I pass one in the grocery store, I rush by as if she's going to stab me or something."

Just as Mallory had avoided trains all these years.

"But my grandma's health isn't doing so great. And my mom is heartbroken I won't go see her. It doesn't feel right." Desdemona gazed up at the ceiling for some reason. "I used to think it'd be worse to fear every possible danger than just one specific, highly likely one. But it isn't that simple. For all I know, maybe that old woman is me, and maybe I live to a ripe old age. I just need to go live my life, you know? No matter how long or short it is."

Mallory glanced up, too, and her gaze landed on the exposed ductwork. What had looked sleek and trendy when she'd arrived now looked out of place, like it could swoop down at any moment and snap at them like tongs, or like a claw. *Narrowly, narrowly missed.* She shivered. She needed to get out of here. When she looked back down, Desdemona had disappeared. All that remained of her was a younger, carefree version smiling next to Linus from the posterboard.

Mallory drove a different way home from the reunion, a circuitous, inconvenient route that didn't cross any tracks. She looked Linus up online, and sure enough, he'd died in a house fire near his college campus. Faulty electricity. A burning taste spread over her mouth and made her gag.

She found a forum thread from the week after his death that talked about the tragedy, other students decrying the state of housing in their area, the need for better codes and enforcement. One of the last comments, from a year later, listed some safety improvements they'd observed after the fallout. Mallory knew she should find some comfort in that outcome.

Instead, she lay awake in the moonlight, staring up at the large, unmoving fan. Its blades cast a wide shadow across the ceil-

     Narrowly, Narrowly Caught

ing, like the spread fingers of a hand. Or claw. Waiting. Waiting. She didn't want to snap her eyes shut.

Any class reunion would stir up old emotions—long-encapsulated memories hauled up and dropped down the chute of consciousness. But this was more. This was heavier. It had been barreling toward her for the past five years, ever since that night. Her relatively tight-knit class had scattered down varied tracks, with different career paths, different futures, and apparently different life expectancies. Different fates, one might say. Skill, luck, and inevitability all at play.

Maybe the UB4Me machine had doomed them all and manipulated them like some Invisible Hand. *It obviously doesn't like you,* Zaya had said. Or maybe it didn't matter; maybe the machine looked upon them indifferently. Or maybe considered itself generous—you before me—a harbinger offering up knowledge as the true prize. She wished she could discard that so-called "prize" like a piece of plastic. She didn't want to flinch each time she heard train crossing bells. She didn't want to live under the dangle of fear, irrational or no.

Desdemona was right. They needed to go live their lives.

She closed her eyes.

A while later, Mallory shivered while waiting for the light rail in the frigid blue dark of nighttime. The only other people on the raised platform were two parents admonishing their young girl to stay back from the yellow line. That seemed to tempt the girl to remain as close to the line as possible, like telling someone a game is rigged only for them to want to prove you wrong. The parents moved on to some animated argument between the two of them.

The warning bell of an approaching train sounded. Mallory's pulse picked up. Her dry mouth filled with that taste of electrical burn.

Out of the corner of her eye, she saw the girl slip over the platform edge and onto the tracks. The parents hadn't noticed yet, too invested in gesticulating and griping at each other. Only Mallory saw. She rushed to the yellow line and found the girl staring up at her, stunned. The train's growing headlight cast her in ever more defined detail: puffy coat zipped up to the neck, a little pompom on her stocking cap, a grimace of fear forming as she came out of her shock. Even with the train decelerating for its usual stop, it would come into the station massive and fast.

A push between Mallory's shoulder blades forced her down, down, down onto the track. No one had stood behind her, though —the parents were still off to the side. The Invisible Hand, perhaps, or maybe she jumped.

In some moments, everything converges and total clarity kicks in. The whoosh of metal. Bells dinging. Flashing lights. The burning reek of electricity. A countdown, mere seconds to choose between your life and that of a child who should really listen to her parents. Not right now, though, with all their screaming as they finally realized what was happening on the tracks. Seconds until a skull gets crushed like a red plastic egg.

Mallory heaved the little girl up onto the platform to safety, then turned to see the beam of the train's headlight bearing down on her, fanning out in all directions, as if from behind a doorway. It swallowed her vision. She hoped Desdemona visited her grandmother and lived to a ripe old age. *Narrowly, narrowly caught.*

Narrowly, Narrowly Caught

they died
alphabetically

THEY DIED ALPHABETICALLY

Oh, what a shame.

A IS FOR:

Agoniste Megid fell in a vat of semi-soft butter.

Alnaaze stumbled over a pebble and bounced down a hill towards a low tree branch; caught in an empty bird's nest and carried away to be dinner for a pterodactyl.

Angela Yuriko Smith dove into a frozen pool.

Angelique O'Rourke bitten once, a hundred years ago, and still not shy.

Anonymous smushed by a falling display of lotion facial tissues.

August Paterson spontaneously combusted on a park bench.

B IS FOR:

Beth Cook bitten by an amethyst bat and turned into a crystal cluster.

Brittany danced too long in haunted shoes.

C IS FOR:

Curtis Chen walked through the door that read "DEMONIC WORLD".

D IS FOR:

David drowned in a teaspoon of vanilla cake batter.

E IS FOR:

Eleanor Todd heated until molten, then inflated; cooled too quickly and cracked down the spine, now easy to shatter. Destined to be cullet for another time.

Elizabeth Mitchell buried alive in a coffin of daisies and leeches.

Elizabeth Williams gifted oneness with the universe by a jinn.

Ell Bradshaw caught in a field of ravenous sunflowers.

Erik Grove caught in his own bear trap and eaten by a mountain lion.

F IS FOR:

Fun no one had.

G IS FOR:

Gigi Little snapped in two by an inquisitive giant.

H IS FOR:

Happy birthdays gone south.

I IS FOR:

Iffy fish.

J IS FOR:

J.B. Kish juiced like an orange and drank for breakfast.

Julia Woolley cursed by an untrained Sprite.

K IS FOR:

Kasi followed the whispering voice into the haunted woods.

Katherine Quevedo dragged Below by the monster under her bed.

Kate Boyes exploded in the atmosphere and streaked across the sky in a brilliant display of shooting stars where the people of Earth wished for peace.

Keo squashed between idiots playing chicken.

L IS FOR:

Larina garroted with barbed wire during a youth ballet depicting Sweeney Todd's life while wearing a red satin dress; accused of bad manners for not standing for the ovation.

Laura Burge sucked into a portal of stardust and goo.

M IS FOR:

Madrox stepped into a mirror world of monsters.

Marriane Xenos listened to crows and tried to fly.

N IS FOR:

Nick Dikas pumped with helium and popped by a tree branch.

O IS FOR:

Ophelia Keene tumbled in the dryer on delicate.

P IS FOR:

Pendleton Martin devoured by a starved Goliath Tigerfish.

Pia Baur drowned playing bumper boats with a passing ship.

Pyndan Wülffe flattened by a werewolf with no spatial awareness.

Q IS FOR:

Queens with no heads.

R IS FOR:

Richard Leis aged for three months and thinly skinned; served chilled on sourdough toast with olive oil, balsamic vinegar, Parmesan, arugula, and a crack of fresh black pepper. Wine accompaniment: Cabernet Sauvignon.

S IS FOR:

Sarah Walker who saw the beginning of the universe.

Shyla who investigated a fairy mound.

Skye tripped and suffocated in the plushie aisle.

Simone Cooper lured to the Bermuda Triangle by a siren.

Steve Pattee crushed like a junked car.

Summer Olsson who never rematerialized.

T IS FOR:

Teppo who was eaten by a goat.

U IS FOR:

Underworlds filled with beasties.

V IS FOR:

Valerie Geary tried witchcraft in high school.

W IS FOR:

Wes Mitchell fuelless and lost in space close to a black hole.

Will Errickson folded like paper and thrown out the window.

X IS FOR:

Xylophones—always xylophones.

Y IS FOR:

Your death or mine?

Z IS FOR:

Zoo stampedes lead by the youngest child on a field trip.

acknowledgments

There are so many people to thank—over 100, to be inexact. I want to thank everyone who backed the Kickstarter, everyone who shared the link or told a friend about it or mentioned it in passing to a person at the bus stop. Your help in bringing this project into fruition means more than I can express. Being able to pay the hardworking authors who wrote this book was all I really wanted, and you made that happen!

I cannot tell you how much it means to me that sixteen authors wanted to share their stories with me, that an author would write an introduction to an anthology I put together, that such brilliant people I admire would entrust me with their words.

Angela, Angelique, Beth, Curtis, Erik, John, Katherine, Laura, Marianne, Mark, Pia, Sarah, Simone, Summer, Valerie, Wes, and Will, you are all incredible. I thank you all so much. I hope you love this book as much as I do. I'm so proud to call you *my authors*. I have claimed you, like prizes I've won (hope that's alright). But I feel I did win out, having you all bring your creativity to an oddball theme like this one. You also all inspired me and gave me the confidence to do it, rather than talk about it and let it sit, getting dusty on the shelf.

Thank you, Jen, my darling sister, for bringing me this theme (unknowingly). I truly wouldn't have done this without you getting my wheels turning. You're always an inspiration.

A huge thank you to Bubee for his patience whenever I lost track of time and edited until my eyes went blurry. A huger thank you for his taking care of me for the following days when my body didn't work because I pushed too hard. And the hugest thank you for bringing me a delightful story. It would have been terribly awkward had I needed to tell him I couldn't publish it.

Okay, obviously the taking care of me was more important than the story, but it didn't have the same punch at the end.

And, as always, if I missed you, I'm sorry.

If you and I have ever come in contact with one another, if I have ever seen a photo you've taken or street art you painted, if you have ever walked past me or held the door for me, you are probably owed a thank you.

So, thank you, strangers, acquaintances, friends, exes. I'd have fewer stories without you.

CLAW MACHINE

an anthology of speculative and dark fiction

www.ingramcontent.com/pod-product-compliance
Lightning Source LLC
Chambersburg PA
CBHW061754190726
48289CB00007B/1951